After a successful career as the CEO of two companies, William C. Johnson helped a private equity company pursue and acquire companies in the retail, distribution, and consumer sectors. Although occasionally working part-time, playing golf, and traveling, Mr. Johnson found time to write *Just an Ordinary Guy*, his first novel. He lives in Rancho Santa Fe, California, with his wife, Fran, and visits his two adult children, their spouses, and his five grandchildren, as often as he can.

William C. Johnson

JUST AN ORDINARY GUY

AUSTIN MACAULEY PUBLISHERS™

LONDON • CAMBRIDGE • NEW YORK • SHARJAH

Ordering Information:
Quantity sales: special discounts are available on quantity purchases by corporations, associations, and others. For details, contact the publisher at the address below.

Publisher's Cataloging-in-Publication data
Johnson, William C.
Just an Ordinary Guy

ISBN 9781647509767 (Paperback)
ISBN 9781647509774 (Hardback)
ISBN 9781647509781 (ePub e-book)

Library of Congress Control Number: 2020913271

www.austinmacauley.com/us

First Published (2020)
Austin Macauley Publishers LLC
40 Wall Street, 28th Floor
New York, NY 10005
USA

mail-usa@austinmacauley.com
+1 (646) 5125767

I want to thank Van and Jeanne Hoisington who were the first to read *Just an Ordinary Guy* and encouraged me to turn what was originally a short story into a novel.

Thanks to Dick and Clara Kennedy who gave me the glowing reviews I needed to put energy into getting the finished book published.

To my daughter, A. J. Czerwinski, for her early editing of the manuscript, and her husband, Mike, for convincing me to change the name of my main character from Ramon to Rico.

Also to my son, Scott Johnson, a published writer in his own right, for understanding and supporting my effort, and his wife, Erin, for supporting Scott.

And lastly, I want to thank Fran Johnson, my wife of over fifty-seven years, for listening to me read unfinished and unpolished chapters to her ad nauseam, late into the night, and for offering just the right balance of encouragement and helpful criticism.

Prologue

Rico hears nothing. No alarms. No shouts. No gunshots. And he begins to believe his plan might actually work. He's hidden in the trees. The lights from the safe house that has been his prison for two days now, flicker through the branches.

Rico's hosts are not visible but he knows they are there somewhere, busy with the things that normally occupy them after dinner. Soon, they will settle in for a few hours of mind-numbing inactivity, probably dozing in front of the TV set, or checking emails, before going off to bed. With luck, it will be hours before anybody discovers that Rico is gone.

He takes one last look back, then, stumbles down the barely-visible path toward the small boat he saw earlier.

Rico is about to take matters into his own hands.

Chapter 1

By most standards, Rico Lopez is a successful man. But he didn't start out that way.

He grew up in a modest barrio in the heart of Mexico City and, at twenty, his parents decided to move Rico to Los Angeles. They needed to get him away from the corrosive influence of Santiago "Santa" Sanchez, a charismatic neighborhood gang leader who taught Rico how to fight, steal, and sell drugs, all skills under appreciated by normal people in the real world.

Rico moved in with his uncle and thrived in his new home. Although he became a U.S. citizen as soon as he could, he remained proud of his Mexican heritage. Still, he credits his adopted country for much of the success he enjoyed later in life.

Now in his early fifties, Rico owns an apartment building, an office building, and four warehouses; all in the Hispanic section of Los Angeles. The cash flow is steady and the work relatively stress-free. Still, given the debt he has built up over the years, Rico is hardly wealthy.

Like many men in California, Rico has been married twice; once to Teresa, his childhood sweetheart, and again to Rita, an attractive woman who married him for his money and left when she'd burned through most of it. Lesson learned. Since then, Rico hasn't dated much, partially to avoid another failed relationship, but also because, most women don't find him all that attractive.

Relatively short, with a build that could charitably be called non-athletic, Rico has a longish, somewhat weathered, brown face and a small mustache that peeks out from beneath his aquiline nose. Rico's best feature is an ever-present and engaging smile which makes him look friendly but a touch dim-witted as well; which can be off-putting to some.

Still, his modest exterior hides a deceptively active mind and an impish sense of humor, both of which tend to sneak up on people over time.

His normality may not have served Rico well romantically but it has proven to be a big asset in business. His clients immediately like him for exactly the same reason most women don't. He appears dependable, honest, and forthright. Boring, perhaps, but a perfectly ordinary guy that clients feel they can trust with their business.

Of course, most of Rico's clients are Hispanic and it helps that he shares their heritage and value systems. But it goes beyond that. Rico genuinely cares about his clients in a way most of his competitors don't. He's interested in their profession, yes, but also in their backgrounds, their families, their personal goals, and lots of other information that his competitors tend to overlook. Over time, Rico has learned that he's in the people business every bit as much as the property management business. And he's good at it.

Above all, despite being born in Mexico, Rico knows that his success would never have been possible anywhere but in America and, for that reason alone, he is a patriot; a fact that will play a role in all that's about to happen.

Given his nonexistent social life, Rico spends most evenings at home, working, and tonight is no exception. He's in his second-floor office, cleaning up some paperwork, when his cell phone rings, startling him a little. It's rare for Rico to get a phone call this late at night.

"Mr. Lopez?" the voice on the other end of the line asks.

"Yes," Rico replies.

"Are you alone?"

The question is surprising. Rico is always alone this time of night, as anybody close to him already knows. Rico considers just hanging up but his curiosity gets the best of him.

"Yes," he answers.

"I have an opportunity for you to make a lot of money," the caller says. "I am a real estate lawyer working on a transaction that's going south, fast. My client is experiencing a cash shortage and he's looking for someone to take him out of the deal."

"Okay," Rico says cautiously.

The voice continues, "We did a little research and your name came up. If you're interested, though, you'll need to move fast. The closing is mid-morning tomorrow, and, if we don't get it done by then, the sellers will probably take the property off the market and reprice it. Can we meet?"

Despite having what some would consider a snooze job, Rico Lopez fancies himself a risk-taker. In fact, some of his best deals have been opportunistic like this, and, as a sole proprietor, he's in a perfect position to move fast should the deal warrant it.

Rico replies, "Where do you want to meet?"

"Actually, at your home. I'm only fifteen minutes away. And, Mr. Lopez, if you'll give me just a few minutes of your time, I should be able to convince you, one way or the other, and be out of your hair quickly. What do you say?"

The fact that the guy is so close and so persistent is a little disconcerting but, as Rico knows well, every good real estate deal has a short shelf life and what can it hurt to listen?

"Okay. See you shortly."

A few minutes later, the doorbell rings. When Rico turns on the light, and opens the door, he's startled by the size of the man standing there. The lawyer stands, at least, six feet four inches tall, black-haired with mustache to match, sturdily-built, and blessed with movie star looks. In his left hand, is a cheap, worn, leather briefcase, quite unlike those lawyers normally carry. In fact, upon closer inspection, the guy doesn't look like a lawyer at all.

Rico feels even more uncomfortable but, as is often the case, his greed kicks in and he invites the man in anyway.

"I'm Mike Andress," the guy says, extending his hand, "with Andress and Porter. We represent a number of the major REIT's in the area. Perhaps you've heard of us?"

Rico hasn't, but that's hardly surprising. He's too small-time, and too cheap, to deal with any of the major firms anyway. However, this guy does have a certain presence, like somebody who's somebody and, as his friends know, Rico likes to hang with important people.

Once they are both seated at Rico's dining room table, Mr. Andress pulls out an official-looking letter and presents it with a bit of a flourish. It isn't at all what Rico is expecting. Instead of a law firm's name across the top, it reads *U. S. Drug Enforcement Agency.*

Looking closer, Rico can see that the letter is actually introducing the man sitting across from him who, when Rico looks up, is showing him a badge as well.

Oh, oh, Rico thinks.

The guy's name is, indeed, Mike Andress but, as he explains, he's not a real estate lawyer at all. He's a narc agent, and not just any agent. He's the director of the DEA office here in Los Angeles. Now, both his physical appearance and serious demeanor make sense. But why Mr. Andress is here, in Rico's house, does not.

The last drug Rico used was a joint over thirty years ago, and the statute of limitations on that must have run out decades ago. Same with his brief gang dalliance. What could a drug agent possibly want with him now?

After gathering his thoughts, Rico decides that an ordinary citizen would respond with outrage. So, putting on his most indignant look, he bellows, "What the hell's going on here?"

"Nothing yet," Mike replies calmly. "But we think something is about to, and you can help us with it. You speak Spanish, right?"

"Yes, of course," Rico answers. "I grew up in Mexico City. But, then, I'm guessing you already know that."

No answer. Mike doesn't seem much for chit-chat. Especially if it involves giving out information he would rather keep to himself. His face speaks volumes though, and what it says is Rico would be shocked by what Mike knows about him.

Finally, after a too-long pause, Mr. Andress says, "Rico, I'm here to ask you to do me, or perhaps I should say, your country, a big favor. We have information that a representative of Miguel Espinoza, the infamous head of the Calexico drug ring, will be coming to Chula Vista tomorrow to discuss the purchase of a warehouse. The owner tipped us off to the meeting but he's too scared to meet with the guy. So, we would like you to take his place. It will only take a few hours of your time."

"Why shouldn't I be scared as well?"

"Well, I've been told that you don't mind taking risks and this one is really quite small. It's just a business meeting, like hundreds you've done before."

Rico is still skeptical.

Mike continues, "But, above all, this is a chance to repay Uncle Sam for the life you've been blessed to live."

That seems to resonate a little more, so Mike continues, "Our standard rate for this kind of work is $250 per day. In your case, however, we'll pay for lunch on the way down and, if the operation is successful, a nice dinner on the way back; but I say again, this isn't about what you get out of it. Your country needs you."

"Why does it have to be me?"

"You have the look, the experience, and you speak the language," Mike says. "But, most importantly, you have the anonymity and the moxie. You are very believable as a small business owner. Because you are one."

"I'll take that as a compliment."

"Just to be totally above board," Mike continues, "a lady friend of mine recommended you. She says you're courageous, smart, and nothing like what you look like."

"Which is?" Rico asks.

"Perfectly ordinary," Mike replies with a grin.

"Again, thanks. OK, Let's say I do it," Rico seems to budge a bit. "What's my downside?"

"Not much," Mike replies, "You'll only be there about an hour. We've hired a real estate lawyer to do the talking. And we'll have dozens of agents close by. You just need to look the part which, of course, you do."

"Will I be armed?"

"Of course not. Believe me, the most dangerous part of the whole thing will be your drive down to Chula Vista. You never know what crazies you may run into on the freeway these days."

Chapter 2

It turns out Mike is wrong. The drive south is not dangerous at all. In fact, it is downright pleasant.

First, the scenery is spectacular, ocean on one side, villa-dotted hills on the other.

Second, after clearing the normal Orange County congestion, Rico drives by a number of charming beachfront communities like San Juan Capistrano, Laguna Beach, Dana Point; all quaint and picturesque, tucked in between the hills and the beach.

At one point, Rico notices the controversial, and now-shuttered, San Onofre nuclear plant, incongruously sitting between the freeway and the sea, with its two large concrete cones blocking a spectacular view.

Next, Rico drives right through the heart of Camp Pendleton, its miles of beachfront property now being used only to train troops for deployment to the Middle East. Surprisingly close to the highway are a couple of large troop-carrying helicopters, hovering just above the sand dunes, and depositing dozens of tan, desert-camouflage-clad soldiers out onto the beach, where they crouch and run, in a zig-zag pattern, toward the sea.

How strange, Rico thinks, that these supposedly top-secret desert training exercises are being held on some of the most expensive land in America and in plain sight of one of the busiest freeways in California.

Further down the coast, Rico drives by the San Diego suburb towns of Oceanside, Encinitas, Del Mar, and La Jolla, each with its own funky personality. The only thing common to all of them is the horde of surfers dotting the ocean just off their beaches.

Rico notices that the drivers are less aggressive the further south he drives. Maybe it's because the traffic has eased but it could also be that people are just not as stressed in San Diego as they are in LA. Life seems easier the further south you go.

Until one reaches Mexico, of course. Rico fondly remembers how laid-back and relaxed his native country was before the drug wars. Maybe what he's doing today can help bring those idyllic days back.

But, first, before saving Mexico and helping America, he needs to find his exit. Fortunately, it isn't that hard, and the warehouse in Chula Vista is even easier. As a result, Rico arrives fifteen minutes early.

Once the car is turned off and keys deposited in his front pocket, he looks over at the warehouse and is shocked at how dirty and run-down it is. He would never own a warehouse that looks like that, much less offer it up for sale. Still, the price seems right, and that's probably what attracted the Mexican drug lord in the first place. *How attractive does a building have to be, anyway, to just hide drugs in it?* Rico thinks.

He decides to take one last look at the paperwork. After a quick review, he concludes that everything is in order. It promises to be a very simple transaction but Mike has been smart to enlist the help of a real estate lawyer anyway. As Rico can see from the paperwork, the lawyer's name is Javier Montez, and Rico's alias for the day will be Santiago Ramos.

There's a light tap on Rico's side window, startling him a little. Peering in is a serious-looking Hispanic man dressed in a dark-colored coat and tie, obviously the lawyer. Rico rolls down the window, introduces himself, and shakes Mr. Montez's hand.

Javier explains that everything has been fully negotiated and the conversation should be brief and in English. If it slips into Spanish, the lawyer says, he'll nudge them back into English. Javier also asks Rico to let him do the talking and only answer questions when directly addressed. No concessions should be made without the lawyer's approval.

Javier goes on to explain that Espinoza may have asked for this meeting only so his guys can intimidate the owner. By way of reassurance, Javier tells Rico that federal agents are only a hand signal away. If something goes bad, don't risk arguing with them. Just raise your hand and walk away. Agents will be there immediately. Rico isn't comforted by Javier's assurances.

As the two men are talking, a beat-up, old, blue Ford makes its way, noisily across the warehouse parking lot, toward them. Inside are three surly-looking Mexicans, hardly the type that would be there just to buy a warehouse.

Rico begins to doubt his decision. There must be a better way to show his patriotism, one without so much risk.

When the car slows, one of the men jumps out and walks toward Rico and the lawyer. The other two thugs remain in the car, looking young, scared and angry, all at the same time; a dangerous combination. Their slumped-over posture suggests that they are holding guns down low, out of sight.

The man approaching looks a little older and more confident than the two boys in the car. But nobody would mistake him for a businessman, that's for sure. He doesn't appear to be carrying a piece, which is promising, and he's certainly not Espinoza, even more promising.

No cordial words of greeting are exchanged. Javier opens the discourse by introducing himself and, with only a slight nod of acknowledgement from the gang member, begins to carry the first part of the conversation. Square footage this. Monthly rentals that. All the time Espinoza's guy is looking at Rico, not Javier.

Finally, the thug speaks, "My boss wants to meet with you," he says, pointing a finger menacingly at Rico, "and only you."

The simple job Rico had signed up for the night before just got immeasurably more complicated. The last thing Rico wants is a face-to-face with a drug lord, especially one with a reputation like Espinoza's.

Still, Rico's mind starts spinning. Maybe he can wiggle out of the situation somehow. He's done it before, admittedly in far less stressful situations. Let's see. Set up a meeting date for next week. Then, call Mike and tell him to get another patsy, essentially wash his hands of the whole thing. Let the professionals handle it.

"And right now. He wants to see you right now," the drug dealer continues. "Get in the car with *mi amigos, por favor.*"

So much for wiggle room, Rico thinks, and he raises his hand to let Mike know he needs help. If the Feds are on their toes, they'll abort the operation and rush in to save him. But, no such luck. Rico is on his own.

He has no choice but to walk to the car, hand still waving in the air, escorted by one of the young gang members. Javier makes a valiant attempt to join Rico, but after a brief scuffle, he is pulled away, and Rico gets into the car.

Rico glances through the back window to see Javier shaking hands with the drug dealer, then walking back to his car to get in. A little puzzling, to say the least. The gang member comes back to the Ford and slides in beside Rico.

The Ford exits the parking lot as quickly as possible, its oversized tires kicking up dust and gravel, trying to gain traction.

Contrary to what he had been told, no agents appear or follow, and Rico finds himself all alone in the car with the three thugs. An unpleasant smell of sweat, mixed with stale Mexican food, permeates everything, and Rico begins to feel nauseous; not entirely because of the smell.

Where are they taking me? Rico wonders. *We are very close to Mexico. At this time of day, they could cross the border in less than an hour. Does Espinoza plan to meet me on the other side?*

Upon reflection, that seems unlikely. The gang members can't risk an inspection. It's more probable that they are on the way to some heavily-guarded complex near the border where he will be what? Interrogated? Tortured? He's read the stories about Miguel Espinoza and it's hard to imagine a good outcome at this point.

After a just few minutes of driving, however, they pull up to a small house in the Hispanic section of Chula Vista. The border is still miles away and, supposedly, so is Espinoza.

The house looks no different than the other houses around it; peeling paint, weeds, patches of bare dirt. Not much on the outside to suggest that a drug lord lives there. *Maybe that's the point,* Rico thinks. *Of course, it may not belong to Espinoza at all,* Rico surmises. *Maybe it's just a place the cartel uses to kill their enemies.* Not a very comforting thought.

There might even be a tunnel underneath the house, Rico imagines, *which they can use to dump his body in Mexico, never to be found again.* Rico conjures up an image of his body being carried through the dank, dark tunnel while men carrying packages of drugs pass by him the other way. *Just a normal day in the drug trade. Tit for tat, so to speak.*

Rico is so lost in his morbid thoughts that he doesn't even see a small figure coming out from the house and approaching his car.

"Good morning," the man says as he opens the car door. Rico is surprised by the feigned friendliness of the unimposing figure reaching out to shake his hand.

"I'm so pleased to meet you," the man goes on. "I hope I haven't inconvenienced you too much."

"No. Not at all," Rico responds, as if being accosted at a warehouse, dumped into a car alongside aggressive, smelly, young thugs, and being abducted against his will is something he enjoys doing.

"I'm Miguel Espinoza and I want to welcome you to my home, such as it is. Sorry about the drama but I just don't like to do business with people I don't know personally. Makes me uncomfortable."

As if anything could make Miguel uncomfortable, Rico thinks, *especially surrounded by heavily-armed men with itchy trigger fingers. Miguel should be the only one really comfortable at the moment.*

"Please come in," he says. "Have a seat."

The inside decor of the house complements the outside perfectly. It's sparsely furnished. One wooden table. Four upholstered chairs. A threadbare, sickly-green couch, with some kind of orange Afghan thrown across it. A couple of non-matching chairs finish off the look, more appropriate for a barrio in Tijuana than here in a suburb of San Diego.

Miguel is a genial man, with considerable charm. Not at all what Rico expected. A real gentleman, one might say, but something about the contrast between how friendly he is acting and his reputation for violence makes him even more menacing to Rico.

Still, showing more bravado than he feels, Rico looks Miguel in the eye, relaxes a little bit, and settles back into the couch pillows. He even crosses his legs, and his arms, as if to say, "Bring it on."

It is all for show, though. Inside, Rico is a mess, all sorts of thoughts swirling around in his head. *Why did I find property management so unfulfilling? I could be back at my desk now, staring at a pile of papers, with nothing in front of me but hours of tedious paperwork. Who knows what I'm facing now? I should never have listened to Mike.*

"So, tell me a little about yourself. How did you come to own a warehouse?" Miguel asks, interrupting Rico's thoughts.

"Four warehouses," Rico corrects him, then, realizes he is there as Santiago Ramos, not himself. Under pressure, he can't remember how many warehouses Santiago owns, or anything else about Santiago, for that matter. So, he just lets the comment ride, hoping his cover isn't blown right off the bat.

Miguel says nothing, and Rico continues, finally remembering and telling the story Mike has concocted for him. How his brother works at a bank and helped him get his first real estate loan. How he bought a small rental house, then another, then, an apartment house, a warehouse, and more warehouses. He's selling this warehouse now to get money to buy a small office building, which he thinks he can make more money from than the warehouse. The American dream, with a little Mexican twist.

The story sounds good to Rico as he hears it come out of his mouth but the drug lord looks skeptical. After listening for a few minutes longer, Miguel grows weary of the whole process, rises abruptly, and shows Rico to the door. After exchanging pleasantries, Miguel disappears back into the house. It's an anticlimactic but welcome ending to what had been, for a few brief moments, the most terrifying experience of Rico's life.

Once back at the warehouse, and reunited with Javier, who seems as shaken by the whole episode as he is, Rico starts to come to grips with what has just occurred. Miguel Espinoza has seen his face, sized him up, and made some decision. Whether the guy buys his story or not is yet to be determined. But Rico doubts that he has seen the last of Miguel.

17

Shortly thereafter, Mike pulls up and gets out of the car.

"Where were you?" Rico confronts Mike immediately, "I thought you were going to have men protecting me. I could have been killed."

"Sorry, Rico. They surprised us by leaving so quickly," Mike answers. "By the time we got our cars turned around and in position, you had already exited through an alley. Where did you go?"

"To meet Miguel Espinoza,"

"You're kidding. Here in the states?" Mike stammers.

"I think it was him. Not at all what I expected."

"I know. That's what everybody says. This complicates things quite a bit," Mike thinks aloud, "We need to move you out of harm's way right away."

Then, turning to one of the agents with him, he barks out some orders, "Call Caroline. Tell her she needs to pick up Mr. Lopez at the Hyatt Regency. Also, call Scott. Get him to round up all of our agents in the area. We will reconnoiter here in an hour. We gotta find this guy."

The agents turn to go and Mike remembers something else, "Oh, and call Immigration. We need all of the border crossings alerted to watch for Miguel and his cohorts. Be sure to warn them that he's likely to be violent."

Chapter 3

After Mike organizes his team, he turns toward Rico and says, "Okay, now, we have to get you out of here immediately. Get in your car and head north on the 5 until you reach La Jolla Village Drive. Take the exit to your right and there is a big hotel, the Hyatt Regency, on your immediate right. We'll meet you there."

No need to hear any more, he thinks. *If Mike is nervous, Rico should be, too.* So, he gets in his car, exits the lot, and, fortunately, reaches the freeway without incident. Finally, a few miles and a few minutes later, Rico begins to breathe a little easier. He's driving slower than normal and nobody else is driving at the same pace, a good sign. Hard to follow somebody going fifty on a freeway without being spotted.

Still, Rico can't really go much faster because his hands are shaking so much. Also, his heart is pounding, and he's sweating, and he's holding his breath. Cars whiz by as he tries to get his emotions and nerves under control.

Rico replays what just happened over and over, thinking of all of the things that could have gone wrong. It isn't often a guy faces somebody who, no matter how unimposing he may look, likes to kill people.

Then, a strange feeling comes over Rico. He begins to calm down, get his wits about him and not only feel alive, but incredibly alive; nerve ends tingling, heart jumping with excitement instead of fear. He can feel the adrenaline pumping. Something he hasn't felt in years, and exactly what he was looking for when he said yes to Mike.

Finally, after cruising at the speed limit for a few more miles, Rico exits and almost immediately sees the entrance into the hotel parking lot. He feels truly safe for the first time in hours, relieved, yes, but also exhilarated enough to want to share his recent experience with somebody, anybody. *The valet, perhaps,* he thinks*, or the doorman.*

Fortunately, Mike and his team pull into the hotel parking lot at the same time, preventing Rico from doing something stupid. They all go into the hotel together, find a corner table in the coffee shop, and Mike explains his concerns in more detail.

"I don't know why Miguel was here or why he wanted to meet with you but it is entirely out of character. He never comes to the U. S., never meets anybody outside his trusted circle, especially not over a penny-ante warehouse deal, and, frankly, the fact that he wanted to meet only with you is not a good thing either. I suspect he either saw through your story, or even worse, he may have believed you, and wanted something more than a warehouse out of you."

"The fact that you're not dead," Mike continues, "is the only good thing we have going for us right now."

Rico blanches a bit.

"We have to get you to a safe house, out of harm's way. But first, a few questions. When they drove you to Miguel, did they blindfold you?"

"No," Rico replies.

"Okay, then, can you give us directions to the house where he met you?" Mike asks.

"Not really. I wasn't familiar with the area and they took a pretty confusing route, but the house wasn't very far from the warehouse, I know that," Rico answers. Then he asks, "What do you mean safe house?"

"Please describe the car they used," Mike says, ignoring Rico's question.

"It was a beat-up old Ford sedan. Dark-colored. Blue, I think. About the safe house, I think I prefer to just go home and hide out there. I should be OK. Miguel doesn't even know who I am."

Mike doesn't respond because his mind has already moved on to other, more important matters. Over the phone, he tells one of his agents to organize the available team into two-man groups; then, to set up a perimeter search, moving in concentric circles out from the warehouse. Let him know if they find a house matching Rico's description.

Good luck with that one, Rico thinks. *All the houses are exactly alike.*

Mike then turns back to Rico and explains that this is a rare opportunity for the agency, and for him. He has never had Miguel in his own territory before and he sure doesn't want him to slip away.

Having said that, Mike abruptly stands up, shakes Rico's hand and says, "Thank you, Mr. Lopez. Incredible job. You'll be appropriately rewarded in due time. Now, I gotta go. Work to do."

Rico responds, "Thank you." But, upon reflection, other than staying alive, Rico isn't really sure what he did to warrant the accolades or why he should be thanking Mike. The agent turns to go, turning back briefly to say, "Caroline should be here any minute to take care of you."

20

"Who?" Rico asks. But Mike is already out the door.

So, Rico turns to Javier, who just shrugs his shoulders, saying, "Welcome to Mike's crazy world of policing. Just go with the flow. It'll work out better for you."

Rico isn't so sure. And going with the flow is just not his nature.

"The thing is," Javier explains, "Miguel has seen your face. His guys may be researching your background as we speak. There is a good chance they know where you live, already."

"But why would he care about me at all. I haven't done anything to him."

"Maybe he thinks you're somebody more important than the owner of a warehouse. Maybe Mike even put that word out," Javier replies.

"Why would he do that?"

"To flush Miguel out of his hideout in Calexico, perhaps. And, if that was his plan, it seems to have worked."

So, with those words of enlightenment, Javier bids Rico adieu and walks out of the hotel, leaving Rico wondering what to do next. If he's really being hunted by the bloodthirsty leader of a Mexican cartel, can he just get on with his life? Hardly.

Enter Caroline, a Scandinavian-looking, 40-something, with her blonde, hair in a bun, no makeup, trying to look ordinary, which, to Rico's eye, isn't really working. She walks right up to him, extends her hand, and grips his firmly.

"Hi, Mr. Lopez. I'm Caroline Pendley. We can talk later but, now, we need to move quickly. Follow me."

That's it. No how do you do or nice to meet you. She spins on her flat heels and marches briskly out, Rico in tow.

Once they are both in her car and on the road, she warms up a bit but, on balance, isn't all that helpful. She doesn't know why Rico was recruited. She doesn't know anything about his meeting. Or even who he met. All she knows is that Rico needs to get to the safe house as quickly as possible and she's damn well going to make that happen. Efficient to a fault.

She finally does explain, though, what a safe house is and where she is taking him. She is to drop him off at a secluded house, near Lake Arrowhead, with controlled access in and out.

Rico will be protected, not guarded, by three agents, and will be there only until Mike thinks the threat has gone away, which could be a few days or a few weeks.

"So, tell me about Mike," Rico asks.

"He runs the DEA Office in L. A."

"Good guy?"

"The best."

"So, what's he really like?" Rico asks, trying to get a little more insight.

"He thinks differently than most in our business. He isn't afraid to use techniques not in the manual. A field guy. Not a headquarters guy. Those of us who work for him respect that."

"Any concerns?"

"Why would I tell you?"

"Good point."

Rico asks to use his phone in order to call a couple of business associates.

"Okay," Caroline agrees. "Here. Use this," handing him her own cell phone, probably because it can't be traced.

Rico makes several calls to business associates while Caroline listens in; but, when she seems to lose interest, he calls his brother, Roberto, to check if the family cabin in the Lake Arrowhead area is occupied right now. A backup thought has begun to form in Rico's head.

The trip to Lake Arrowhead is long, but largely uneventful, which, given the day Rico has had, is a good thing. And the scenery, that was so breathtaking on the way down, doesn't interest him much anymore. He's hardly in the mood to reflect on anything around him.

Once they arrive at the safe house, Caroline makes sure Rico has what he needs. There are clothes, toiletries, and even snacks that somebody brought from his house in Manhattan Beach. Rico wonders how in the world they accomplished all of that in such short order. *Can this be the same organization that lost track of him a few hours back?*

Caroline checks out all of the accommodations carefully, meets with the agents that will be protecting him, and, then, leaves. As unsocial as she has been, Rico will miss her. The guys he'll be spending the next few days with are not nearly as attractive and don't promise to be as much fun either.

Sure, they are professional, courteous, and official; all qualities that should make Rico feel better. But he doesn't feel better, probably perhaps because they also are unfriendly, humorless, and seem much more interested in watching him than protecting him.

In fact, at one point, he overhears them talking about his background. They mention an incident long ago when he was picked up in Mexico City for smoking pot. *Why would these guys know that? And why would they care?*

Rico isn't sure that the so-called safe house is all that safe, and the alternate plan that has been kicking around in his head seems to be a better option than staying around here and trusting these goons.

So, on the second night, Rico waits until after dinner, then, slips out his back-bedroom window and disappears into the foliage around the cabin. The half-light makes his descent to the lake very difficult; but, finally, after falling down once or twice, skinning his knees in the process, Rico finds the rowboat he saw earlier.

Pushing off in the dark is no easy task; but he manages to do it without getting his clothes too wet. The oars are a bit unwieldy in such tight quarters. Still, he's able to use them to clear himself from the underbrush surrounding the lake, and feels safer, and freer, with each pull on the oars.

It's just light enough for Rico to make out the shoreline and, fortunately, he doesn't have to row far before the familiar landing, where his brother keeps his boat, comes into sight. The cabin itself is a considerable distance up the hill, back up in the woods. Unlike most of the houses around it, the cabin has no view at all, and is poorly-lit. That's why he and his brother could afford it.

When Rico finally finds the cabin and locates the key under the mat, he begins to breathe a little easier. At least, he won't share the cabin with people that make him as uncomfortable as he was at the safe house.

Rico turns the key in the lock, fumbles for the light switch, flips it on, and is startled by what he sees. There, sitting in the old leather chair facing the door, is the drug lord, Miguel Espinoza, smiling broadly as if he's happy to see Rico.

So much for being comfortable.

Rico is surprised, of course, but mostly scared. Miguel just sits there for a minute. Finally, he speaks, "Hello, Mr. Ramos. I'm glad you could make it. For a little while there, I wasn't so sure you would. What took you so long?"

"How do you know about this place?" Rico says.

Miguel ignores the question, "I have a proposition to make to you, and I don't have much time. I like your warehouse, and I'll buy it from you, but only if you work for me as my main cook in the U.S.," Miguel says. "I want you to set up a drug-production operation in your warehouse. I will provide you with the raw materials and pay you 30% of the gross," Miguel says, calmly. "What you clear is your own business, but you have to produce at least 1,000 kilos of quality product a week. That should allow you to clear about a million dollars per year."

"There must be some misunderstanding," Rico interrupts.

At that moment, a shot rings out, followed closely by two more. Both Miguel and Rico are startled by the noise; Rico more than Miguel. Then, several more shots, followed by an explosion of gunfire, some of the bullets kicking up splinters in the walls of the cabin.

23

Miguel pulls out a pistol and goes quickly to the window. It's totally dark and eerily quiet. Suddenly, he spins around and points the pistol directly at Rico.

"Mr. Ramos, you'll have to be my ticket out of here." He starts to cross the room toward Rico. But, suddenly, the front door slams open and Mike, followed by two of his agents, bursts into the cabin, semiautomatic weapons at the ready.

"Drop the gun," Mike demands. Miguel takes one more step toward Rico. Then, he thinks better of it and does what Mike asks.

Immediately, Miguel is thrown on the floor, face down, legs splayed. It is amazing how small and insignificant he seems there on the floor. Then, Miguel turns his head toward Rico and the evil that has driven the guy through the years is clearly visible on his malevolent face. "You traitor," he mouths. "You're as good as dead." Rico turns away quickly in an unsuccessful attempt to erase the discomfiting image from his memory.

Later, after Miguel has been carried away, literally, with two six-foot somethings on either side, each holding him up by the armpits, Rico turns to Mike and says, "I have some questions."

"Of course, you do," Mike responds. "But I don't have the answers. Or, to be more exact, I can't give you the answers you really want. Frankly, it's better that you not know."

"Why me?" Rico asks.

"Your ordinariness," Mike answers after a brief pause. "You have the real estate knowledge, of course. But, mostly, you have an innocence that can't be faked, not by any of my agents, or even a trained actor. We had to protect that innocence throughout the operation and I think we did."

"Did you know it would play out like this?"

"Of course not. We wouldn't have involved you if we had known. We expected you to be in and out, just like I said in the beginning. We were going to grab Miguel's lieutenant right after the meeting and squeeze him for information. You would have been long gone, with Miguel none the wiser. When the man himself showed up, it was a big bonus for us, of course; but not for you," Mike said. "So we had to change the plan."

Then Rico gets down to what he really wants to know, "How did you know about our family cabin?" Long pause. No answer. "How did Miguel know about the cabin?" Still no answer. "Did you tell Miguel I could cook drugs for him?" Silence. And finally, "Did you know that I would escape the safe house?"

Mike grins briefly, then answers, "Let me just say this. Nobody has ever left one of our safe houses before, without our knowledge and cooperation. And that record is still intact."

"Now. Enough of your questions," Mike says, cutting short the give and take. "I need to prepare you for what happens next. As far as Miguel knows, you're one of our agents. And we want to keep it that way, for your sake and ours."

"You asked earlier why we chose you," Mike went on. "One of the reasons was because you look a lot like one of our agents. He's outside right now and when the police arrive, he and I will do the explaining and answer any questions. Then, we'll be welcomed back at the agency as heroes. The capture of Miguel Espinoza will be a very big thing, for us and for America. I expect it to be front page news, if not tomorrow, then, the next day. And your role in it will appear nowhere."

Rico feels relieved. There will be no revenge from the Calexico gang and he will not have to sleep with one eye open for the next few months. That is, if he can believe Mike.

"Of course," Mike continues. "You must never speak of your role in this. Not even to your brother."

"But I told my brother I might use our cabin," Rico interrupts.

"We know exactly what you told your brother," Mike counters. "You asked him if it was occupied. That's all. He might ask questions but you should say nothing about our operation, no matter how much he pushes you."

After a brief pause, Mike goes on, "Actually, I suggest you call your brother on the drive back home tonight, or early tomorrow morning at the latest, and ask if you can use the cabin, maybe to entertain a girlfriend or something like that. Then, you'll be as surprised as he is to later learn of the events of tonight. Another little acting job to finish up your work with us. Right?"

Mike gives Rico his cell phone back, the one Caroline had taken earlier. Then, he extends his hand, saying as they shook, "Now, you need to move fast. Your car is right over there. Get in it and head right home. Hopefully, you'll never hear from me again."

Chapter 4

For weeks, Rico worried about some retribution from the cartel. Yes, their leader, Miguel, is in jail, but drug kingpins have notoriously long arms, certainly long enough to reach Rico. So, hopefully, Mike's ruse worked and Rico will never hear from any of them again.

Mike had certainly been right when he said that the story would be big. The morning after the shootout, the L.A. Times gave it one whole section. In it, there was considerable speculation about why Miguel risked coming across the border. For decades now, ever since Pablo Escobar tricked the Colombian government into letting him create his own luxury prison, drug lords have avoided going to America for fear that they would be captured there and imprisoned like an ordinary criminal. Which, of course, they would be.

Rico doesn't know why Miguel would travel to America either, but he does know that Miguel was planning to cook drugs in the U.S. Maybe the simple explanation is, as Miguel said, he wanted to choose his own "cooker" and he felt that the profit would be worth the risk.

As the months went by, Rico thought less and less about Miguel and more and more about his love life, which certainly could stand some work.

Outwardly, Rico looks the same; a short, friendly, slightly pot-bellied Mexican with jet-black hair. But, underneath, because of his impromptu undercover work, Rico feels he's a different guy now; a little more confident, more mysterious, perhaps. Now, all he has to do is get a woman to notice the difference.

Rico starts going to the singles bars again but, instead of two or three beers, he sips a martini. Also, now, instead of facing the bar, hunched over a beer glass, he turns around on his stool and confidently surveys the room. Rico may not be James Bond yet but that doesn't mean he can't act like him. Or, at least that's what he tells himself.

The new Rico now approaches a woman and, instead of the "Excuse me, but" approach he has used in the past, starts off boldly with, "Hi. I'm Rico. May I buy you a drink?"

And many women do, in fact, allow Rico to buy them a drink. A few even sit down with him and talk. But none agree to have dinner with him, or even coffee. So, although he has made progress, the bottom-line is still the same. Rico goes home to his bachelor pad, all alone. Very un-James Bond-like.

Something needs to change and Rico thinks he knows what it is. When he asks questions about a girl's background, her family, things right in his wheelhouse, the conversation goes well. But, when she starts to ask him questions about who he is, things go south, fast. So, Rico needs to find some way to make an average-looking, twice-divorced property owner, with virtually no hobbies, more interesting.

Just once, after Rico had run out of any other ideas, he lets it slip that he occasionally works for the government, in drug enforcement. But, of course, he can't talk about it, he says with a wink.

Suddenly, the woman takes an interest, listens to his small talk, looks into his eyes, and seems fascinated. More importantly, she quickly agrees to join him for dinner, something that hasn't happened to Rico in years.

At the restaurant, she continues to flirt and ask questions. Does he carry a gun? Has he arrested anyone? Has he worked undercover? She asks everything about his government work and nothing about his property management business. And, the more tight-lipped he is, the more curious she becomes.

A lightbulb goes off for Rico.

Then, out of the blue, she asks where he lives. Finding out it's nearby, and that it's recently been redecorated she says she just has to see it.

"Why? Are you a decorator?" he asks.

"What made you think that?" is her reply. Then, she smiles seductively.

In bed, she's insatiable and, after they make love the second time, she bombards him with more questions, not about his decorating or his properties, but about his life as an agent. What agency does he work for? Any foreign work? Has he ever been shot at? His answers are all vague at best. But she doesn't seem to care.

Her name is Margaret Smith; but she likes to be called Maggie. She's around forty, a perfect age for the fifty-year-old Rico. Her face isn't much to write home about, especially after Rico's second martini wears off; but her body is sensational. Breasts not too heavy. Reasonably petite waist. Well-proportioned legs. The kind of figure all girls exercise feverishly to get but which, in fact, only God can bestow.

Rico can't believe his good fortune. Even with the risks that come with it, he begins to believe that meeting Mike Andress, and agreeing to help him, is one of the best things that has ever happened to him. So, feeling really good about himself, and anticipating what James Bond might do in the same situation, Rico waits a week before calling Maggie back.

Big mistake. She is furious, calls him names he's shocked she knows, and hangs up on him. Every call he makes to her after that goes to voice mail. Rico has learned a valuable lesson. Only somebody who looks like Sean Connery can be as indifferent to women as James Bond, and get away with it. A short, pudgy Mexican like Rico better call back the next day.

Fortunately, Rico's business is going better than his love life. The neighborhood around one of his apartment buildings has turned into a magnet for young professionals. Two new restaurants and a playhouse have opened, to rave reviews. The old buildings around the area, like Rico's with its detailed stonework and crown moldings, are now coveted by single, upscale people who want to be where the action is.

As leases come due, Rico moves his old residents out, renovates a little, and raises rents dramatically. In some cases, he even renegotiates leases that are still in place. The increased cash flow finances the purchase of another apartment house that he feels is a good candidate for the same kind of treatment. No matter how dull the profession of property management is, Rico has become pretty good at it and his confidence continues to build.

Then, a few months after his meeting with Miguel Espinoza, Rico receives a very unexpected call, from his ex-wife, now Teresa Wilson, who is in town interviewing for a job. She tells him that she had been living and working as a hostess in Temecula, California, when the manager of an upscale Los Angeles restaurant walked in and offered her a job. So, she's here in town to try to seal the deal and asks Rico if he can meet her for a drink that very night. "Spur of the moment, I know, but I would love to see you again," she says. "For old times' sake."

Rico has mixed feelings. After all these years, he doesn't really know Teresa, and their parting long ago been anything but amicable. At twenty-years-old, he hardly knew how to make a gracious exit, but the truth was that, at the time, he just didn't think she would be an asset to him in America, which was where he wanted to live.

She represented much of what he was trying to escape, his upbringing, his neighborhood, his friends, and even the gang affiliations that he hoped had been wiped off his record by now. He didn't say any of this to her, of course. He just asked for a divorce, and, then, never looked back.

But now that she called him, he is more than just a little curious about how she turned out, and a part of him, not the best part, wants to show off his successful new life.

Teresa had loved him back then but he wasn't sure she respected him. Of course, how could she? He was just one of the many gangbangers hanging around the streets of their neighborhood, acting tough. But, now, he's a respectable entrepreneur and business owner. And he wants her to see how well he turned out.

So, Rico says yes, and suggests they meet at a bar he likes that is frequented by white collar Hispanics. It's a place he knows well and, more importantly, where they know him. If he's going to impress Teresa, this is the place to do it.

He arrives a half-hour early, chooses a table near the door, then, nurses a beer for fifteen minutes or so while he looks anxiously at every woman who enters the place. He's not really sure he'll recognize Teresa after so many years. How could he? She was just a girl when he last saw her.

He needn't have worried. She enters and recognizes him immediately.

"*Rico, mi premer amor. Como esta used?*" she says as she approaches, arms extended. Rico answers in Spanish and they hug warmly.

He's surprised and impressed by how she looks. He would have expected her to put on a few pounds, like most of the women back in the old neighborhood have. But she hasn't. He would have expected her to dress modestly. In fact, she's in designer clothes from head-to-toe, and they fit her so well, she could be a model in a fashion show.

Teresa Lopez, his ex-wife, has grown into Teresa Wilson, an elegant lady, with exquisite features, highlighted by big, brown eyes, and a sophisticated manner that belies their shared roots. In fact, she seems more Spanish than Mexican, which, as Rico knows, she actually is, several generations removed.

His first thought is that he chose the wrong place to meet her. He was trying to impress her but, ironically, now that he's seen her, she's actually too good for the place. When he tries to apologize for the choice, however, she immediately deflects his concern by talking about how charming the place is. And that it is so Rico.

He responds by telling her how beautiful she still is and how sorry he is that they have not kept in touch. She tells him that he hasn't changed at all, and that it's a good thing because, at his core, he still has the same innocence and irrepressible spirit she loved so many years ago.

They both talk about their second marriages; his to a California gold digger, hers to a businessman, twenty years her senior, who died two years before.

The conversation is warm, animated, and surprisingly familiar, given that, as adults, they really don't know each other at all. After an appropriate amount of catching up, her face turns serious. "It's great finally connecting with you, Rico, and wish I had done it years ago," Teresa says. "I also wish you had met my husband. He was a really wonderful man who loved me and treated me very well. I've had a good life."

"But," she continues, "there was another reason I had to contact you. I got a call from an old neighborhood friend a few days ago, who told me that some cartel thugs had been asking about you. She didn't know who they were but they weren't friends of yours. That much was clear."

Rico's face turns scarlet for a second, then, as quickly, the blood drains from it. His stomach turns and he feels like he's going to throw up. A wave of fear washes over him, completely unexpected, because he had put the meeting with Miguel Espinoza out of his mind weeks ago.

Teresa goes on, "I don't think any of our old friends helped them. Of course, what do they know, anyway? You haven't exactly stayed in touch. But, obviously, if I can find you, those men can. And, according to my friend, they should really scare you. Unless, of course, you're somehow connected to them, or their business."

"Believe me, Teresa," Rico responds, "I've changed. I don't hang around with those kinds of people anymore. So, you're right. I might be in danger."

"What can I do to help?"

"Nothing, really," Rico went on. "You need to go back to your life and not think about or contact me again. When this thing blows over, and I think it will, I'll get in touch with you. We'll probably laugh about all this then." With that, they exchange a kiss on the lips, their first in three decades, and go their separate ways.

Rico hustles out of the bar, drives home and immediately packs. He empties his safe and, with some cash in hand, drives to a nearby shopping center where he leaves his car and calls a cab. He isn't sure where to tell the driver to go but he certainly can't sleep another night in his house.

So, thirty minutes later, after driving through the infamous tent city of Los Angeles homeless people, momentarily envying their anonymity, he finds himself in the lobby of a downtown Hilton.

Rico registers under an assumed name, saying that he has lost his wallet and has to pay cash. Eventually, the manager allows him to do so and Rico prepays for two nights. Obviously, if he has to stay longer than that, he'll need to move to a more obscure, seedier hotel somewhere, one that he can afford without using credit cards.

The whole first day Rico doesn't leave his room but he stays busy. He calls a few friends to tell them he's out of town. He calls his lawyer and asks the guy to prepare all of his properties for sale. He orders room service, several times. He looks out of his window at the pedestrian traffic below, imagining his pursuers out there somewhere. He watches TV. He reads a book, grabbed off his night stand at home. But, mostly, he worries.

Rico thinks about calling Mike, *but why would the guy answer? And what could Mike do anyway? Send him to a safe house? That worked out really well the last time.* No, this is something Rico is going to have to work out on his own.

Then, the hotel phone rings.

Rico just looks at it. It rings again. Maybe it's the desk calling. But, maybe not. On the third ring, he answers.

"Rico. This is Mike," the voice on the line says. "Don't hang up. I know that Miguel has some of his people nosing around in Mexico. I also know that they haven't yet found any link to you but they probably will very soon. So, we have no choice but to hide you again."

"Thanks, but no thanks, Mike. Fool me once and all that," Rico says. "I don't know who I can trust but it sure isn't you."

"That's where you're wrong, Rico," Mike responds. "At the moment I'm the only one you can trust. Meet you in your hotel bar in fifteen minutes." And he hangs up.

Rico stares at the receiver. *Is Mike going to put him in danger again? Not if Rico can help it.* Except this time, he's already in danger. Once again, Rico thinks, *What can it hurt to listen? I can always say no.* Fifteen minutes later, Mike sits across from Rico, at an etched-glass table in the bar, and outlines his plan.

"So, here's what we're going to do," he starts. "First, we manufacture a new identity for you. Second, we clean up your investments and put the money into a blind trust under your new name. And third, we're going to send you to Mexico."

"I'm sorry," Rico says. "Did you say Mexico?"

"That's correct. I think we can kill two birds with one stone here," Mike says. "On one hand, we have an undercover operation underway in Mexico that could use somebody like you. Under your new alias, of course. On the other hand, the current Rico Lopez needs to disappear in a way that Miguel has no way to find you. A perfect scratch your back situation, if you ask me."

31

"You sure know how to mix metaphors, Mike; but, based on experience, I'm not confident you really know how to keep me safe, and I certainly don't want to go back to Mexico," Rico counters.

"Well, let's go over your other options, which are what exactly, Rico?" Mike is getting a little heated, or at least he seems like it. "Stay here at the Hilton for a year or so? Go home and wait for Miguel's guys to show? Catch a bus to Waukegan? Or some other god-forsaken place? And do it without access to your bank accounts, your credit cards? Start all over sweeping floors? I'm offering you the only viable alternative, Rico, you know it, I know it, and we're wasting time debating it."

Unfortunately, Rico thinks, *Mike is right. He wasn't able to disappear on his own, for even a day. Which was how long it took Mike to find him. He wonders why Mike is always just a few hours behind his every move. But it sure makes him believe Miguel Espinoza could be, too.*

Once again, Rico agrees to put his fate in Mike's hands.

Chapter 5

The flight to Mexico City is longer than Rico remembers, but largely uneventful. He's flying First-Class, of course, a perk of his newly-created position. His so-called staff, a motley crew of business-types and undercover narc-types, are accompanying him.

Rico is now portraying Felipe Cardoza, an ex-Marine, born in Mexico, but raised in San Antonio, Texas. His family traveled a lot during his childhood, which explains his obvious lack of a Texas accent. His Spanish is authentic, though, which, is more important. His cover story is that he's traveling to Mexico City to look at a proposed factory for his company, Lone Star Textiles Corporation (LSTC, on the National Over the Counter Stock Exchange.)

The real Felipe is an actual employee who has worked for the company for fifteen years and is now the Vice President of Property Management. He represents the company in sourcing new manufacturing sites in Mexico and South America. That makes him the guest of the Mexican government because they very much want Lone Star to build a plant in Mexico City.

In the beginning, it's estimated the plant will only employ several hundred workers but later, at full production, it will employ thousands. Mexico is willing to consider a number of tax and other incentives to attract the Texas firm.

Rico has slipped rather easily into the role of Felipe. Much of what he will do while in Mexico City he has done before, but on a much smaller scale, with city governments rather than federal ones. And, most importantly, without any of the danger he faces this time.

He'll be picked up at the airport by a representative of the Industrial Development Bank, an agency of the Mexican government. They will go directly to a cocktail party attended by the head of the bank. No business will be discussed there but Felipe (Rico) will be asked to informally present an overview of Lone Star, its products, its customers, and its channels of distribution. Rico has been preparing for that presentation for two weeks now.

The next day will include a site visit, a visit to two other fabric manufacturers and a brief meeting with government officials. Then, the whole Lone Star team will be given a free afternoon to tour Mexico City on their own. That's when the fun should start, because the second, more important, meeting will be with some prominent Batista drug cartel members to discuss how the proposed factory can fit into their drug distribution network.

This secret meeting is only exploratory at this point but Lone Star executives were advised a few weeks back that this off-line meeting is more critical to the approval and cooperation of the Mexican government than the meeting with government bureaucrats. When the Lone Star executives heard that, they realized they may be a bit too far over the tips of their skis, and they contacted their local drug enforcement agency, who, with the approval of higher-ups, decided to launch a new operation.

Shortly thereafter, Mike coaxed Rico to join his team.

Rico will be playing a much bigger role in this operation than he did in the last one; but he's well-supported by professionals. Todd Williams is the lead narc agent on the team who'll decide the plan of action at each stage. The team expects a pretty straight-forward discussion with the government officials, most of whom probably have no idea what's really going on behind the scenes. The tricky stuff begins with the second meeting.

At this point, the team doesn't know who from the Batista cartel will attend that meeting. So, the first order of business is to identify the players and the hierarchy of leadership. It would be highly unusual for them to learn much from the introductions, since most drug gang members don't like to identify themselves upfront, or ever, for that matter. So, the team has already spent a lot of time back in Texas studying photos and dossiers of suspected cartel members who might appear during the operation.

As with most meetings like this, they don't expect the one who seems to control the meeting to be the leader. In fact, there's a better chance that the guy who says nothing is the guy in charge. So, somebody will be watching each of the participants throughout the meeting, trying to read their nods and facial expressions.

A lot of possible scenarios have been "game-played" back in Texas as well. Everything from a perfunctory how-do-you-do meeting to a full-fledged raid. But, as it turns out, they're hardly ready for what actually happens.

The cocktail party, site visit, and tour of the two sewing facilities might have been interesting to the real Felipe, but all of them are incredibly boring to Rico. He feigns interest, something he happens to do very well, then, answers questions about how the project might proceed from a Lone Star perspective.

The meeting with Mexican government officials is, as expected, a lot of pomp and circumstance about nothing. Rico performs well, however, and the wheels seem to be greased for the project, at least from a government approval standpoint.

Then, the fun stuff starts. They meet the Batista cartel leaders at a warehouse on the outskirts of Mexico City, presumably one that's part of their distribution network. Only three gang members are visible, although there could be dozens more hidden throughout the building and grounds.

The Lone Star team isn't searched as they enter the warehouse but, if they had been, no weapons would have been found. Carrying a gun to this kind of meeting would be really stupid, an amateur mistake that narcs rarely make.

One of the Batista gang speaks, "For the record," he says, "this meeting never took place. We are here only to listen. What we hope to hear, however, is that, once the plant is operational, you'll cooperate with us." He pauses, then, goes on, "What form that cooperation takes is yet to be determined but, once established, we will insure…"

Suddenly, from outside, shots ring out.

The three gang members react quickly. They pull their guns and crouch in place, facing the warehouse doors. Three other drug thugs emerge from the shadows, guns in hand, pointing at the Lone Star team, most of which are already flat on the hard cement floor.

A few more shots are heard. Then, silence. Everybody looks around nervously. Seconds pass.

Then, through the door bursts a cartel gunman. His right arm is dangling uselessly from his shoulder. His left hand cradles a revolver.

"Pedro. What's going on?" A gang member asks him in Spanish.

"Federales," he answers, "or police. I don't know who or how many but we surprised them. They were trying to surround the building and stumbled into our hiding place. We dropped a few of them and the rest retreated. We need to get out of here right now."

With that, the cartel members take off running. They vanish into the bowels of the warehouse, leaving Rico and his cohorts lying on the floor, wondering what to do next.

Slowly, they rise to their feet and make their way into the office, where the only window in the whole building is located. Todd Williams looks out, trying to see who's out there. No one is visible. But he reflexively pulls his head back anyway and addresses the others in his party.

He explains that there are a couple of American snipers stationed outside, providing cover from afar. But they are fixed and stationary. Hardly responsible for the commotion.

So, it has to be Mexican soldiers or police who screwed everything up. They arrived on the scene, unannounced, and stumbled into a nest of Batista gang members who were providing cover.

One of the American snipers, who had been watching the activities, suddenly comes out of hiding and zig zags across the parking lot. The other one is close behind him. A minute later, both are inside the building, providing some protection, as several cars arrive to extract the whole Lone Star team. Todd coordinates everything and they are all gone within five minutes of the first shots.

They do not go back to their hotel. Instead, they separate and spread throughout the city, in homes and among families that are sympathetic to the cause. Rico is housed and protected by the family of an American narcotics agent stationed in Mexico. The next morning, he's booked on a flight into Atlanta and, from there, back to San Antonio where Mike is waiting at the airport.

"What a colossal fuck-up," Mike starts with. "We were obviously set up by the Mexican government to serve as bait. They had promised that this would be our operation from start to finish, with no interference. Then their troops show up. I'm sorry, Rico."

They walk in silence to a waiting car outside the terminal. Both get in the back seat and Rico's questions begin.

"Are you sure it was government guys?" he asks.

"They're denying it, of course, but there's no doubt some were wearing uniforms. Our guys saw them," Mike answers.

"Yeah, I overheard the Batista gang members in the warehouse saying the same thing. Who are the Mexican officials claiming it was?" Rico asks.

"They're saying it was a rival gang," Mike says. "But, until they provide proof, I'm not buying it. Unfortunately, this kind of thing happens all the time. We have to go to the source of the drugs. That's the nature of our business. But the source is always in some country where nobody can be trusted. That makes our job that much more difficult."

"What are you planning to do now? Is the operation over?" Rico queries.

"Hold that question until we get inside," Mike answers. They arrive at a very official-looking building, on the outskirts of the city, housing the offices of Customs and Immigration. Rico isn't sure if they are meeting here because the narcs don't have an official office in San Antonio or, more likely, that Mike isn't that comfortable with Rico hanging out with his fellow agents just yet.

They find an empty office and the questions continue. "So, what's the plan?" Rico asks again.

"That depends," Mike says, "All indications are that your cover, and that of our team, are both intact. The Batista Cartel seems to believe that the team from Lone Star Textiles was duped just as they were. In fact, inquiries are already being made, asking if Lone Star has been scared away."

Mike continues, "The problem for us is that the objective of our operation was to identify and neutralize the Batista leadership team, especially the top guy, who, unlike the infamous Pablo Escobar, abhors publicity. In fact, he changes appearances, aliases, and locations so much we don't really know where or who he is. We were hoping this operation would change that."

"So, what are you going to do?" Rico asks.

"For now, we wait. We have another small team going in, who, with the assistance of local agents, will try to determine the risks of another trip," Mike answers.

"How about I go back to L.A. while you sort things out?" Rico suggests.

Mike's reaction is quick and dismissive. "What are you thinking? Don't you get it? There is no L.A. for you, now or in the foreseeable future. It's too dangerous," he says. "I suspect Miguel's guys are already in Manhattan Beach watching your house, waiting for their opportunity to avenge his arrest."

Mike goes on, "For the time being, you'll stay in the role of Felipe Cardoza, hole up here in San Antonio, go to work every day at Lone Star, and bide your time waiting for further instructions from us, or, if we are lucky, a telephone call from Mexico. The company knows that they are not to bother you unless somebody they don't know from Mexico calls for Felipe Cardoza. Then, it's your job to answer and improvise. Otherwise, you're free to entertain yourself anyway you see fit."

"Sounds exciting," Rico says. "I always wanted to be an undercover agent, sitting in my office, chewing gum and reading magazines. Can I at least make some calls, check on my investments or something?"

Mike's face reddens and he stammers, "Are you crazy? Listen. You're no longer Rico Lopez. You have no investments in L.A. You are Felipe Cardoza, who lives in an apartment near Lone Star Textiles and tomorrow morning, as usual, you go to work. Outside is a car we've rented for you, a dark-blue Buick, I believe, with the keys to your apartment in the glove compartment. Enjoy your new life. I'll be in touch."

And, with that, Mike leaves the room. For a second, Rico feels good about one thing. No more kid-gloves. Mike is treating him as if he's a real agent, with just enough rope to fail or succeed on his own. And, although it feels good, it's also scary. Rico wonders if he's really up to the task.

The next morning, Rico arrives at the Lone Star Textiles building as instructed, expecting to be received with open arms. He's disappointed. Instead of greeting him warmly, the skeptical guard at the desk looks the unfamiliar visitor up and down, then, asks to see his employee card, which, of course, Rico doesn't have.

Rico tries to explain he's new, but the guard is having none of it. Then Rico asks to see Robert Smith, the CEO, which makes the guard even more suspicious. *This undercover stuff is not that easy*, Rico thinks. *I can't even get into the building where I'm supposed to be hiding.*

"Mr. Smith is not in yet. Is he expecting you?" the guard asks, getting more suspicious by the second.

There is a tense moment of silence when, fortunately for Rico, the real Felipe Cardoza comes through the front door, sizes up the situation quickly, and says to the guard, "I've got this, George. This guy's a new employee who doesn't have any paperwork yet. He can wait in my office until Mr. Smith gets in."

Once in Felipe's office, Rico explains that he's been ordered to hang out in a vacant office at Lone Star for a few days, just in case the Mexican government or the Batista gang calls. Then, hopefully, for both of them, Felipe will never see him again.

So, Felipe sets him up in a back office and Rico begins his eight-to-five grind just like any other working stiff, except he has absolutely nothing to do. He spends his time studying company handbooks and brochures, reading a paperback he picked up in the airport, doing crosswords, and watching the telephone sitting on his desk.

A day into his solitary confinement, the phone rings.

"Felipe Cardoza," Rico answers.

"Mr. Cardoza," the voice on the other end of the line says, "I represent the Batista cartel. They want you to know how sorry they are about the meeting last week. There was a bit of a communications mix-up between our guys and the government guys who arrived at the meeting unannounced. Unfortunately, these things happen in Mexico every so often, more than we would like, I must admit. But we are so glad you were able to escape unharmed and we offer our sincerest apologies for the inconvenience."

What a surreal way to address what happened in Mexico City, Rico thinks. *It was like they were apologizing for being a little late to an appointment instead of disrupting it with gunfire, and possibly killing somebody.*

"No problem," Rico says, matching the understated tone set by his caller, "What can I do for you?"

"Well, I just wanted to let you know that we are still interested in helping Lone Star establish a manufacturing facility in Mexico," the voice continues. "We certainly understand if your interest has waned a bit, but I want to assure you that ours has not. In fact, we're anxious to get things back on track."

"How do you propose we do that?"

"Well, differently than last time," the drug lord says, "no more presentations or cocktail parties. We want you to come to Mexico City alone this time. We will meet you at the airport, discuss things for an hour or two in a conference room we will reserve in one of the airline lounges, then, you can get on the plane and go home. How does that sound?"

Perfectly awful, Rico thinks. *No team. No cover. On their terms. On their turf. What should he say?*

"I'm not really authorized to make decisions on my own."

"We understand," the voice interrupts, "but I doubt your CEO will make the trip. So, you're elected by default. It won't take long. We just want to ask some questions about how your sewing facility will work so that we know how to work around it without bothering you. With that input, we should be able to propose a rent structure that works for both of us. Probably something with a base rate, and commissions on top, depending on how productively we can move product through your factory. Discounted by our security contract, of course. But I talk too much. Will you come?"

Rico hesitates. Lots of thoughts whirl around in his head, some professional, some personal. He believes that Mike will be ecstatic that there's going to be another meeting in Mexico but not so ecstatic that they want Rico there alone.

Of course, Rico is sure Mike will figure out some way to have eyeballs on him, no matter what. But, will that be enough? For Rico personally, the risks of helping Mike keep growing.

Chapter 6

"I think the meeting can be arranged," Rico hears himself say, "but I need authorization from my boss. How soon do you want to meet?"

"Tomorrow," is the reply, "and, of course, let your boss know. But, also, let him know that this isn't really a request. We do it this way or the deal is off. We'll call you back in an hour."

Rico stares at the receiver for a second, then hangs up, and grabs his cell phone to call Mike.

"Well, they called," Rico tells Mike as soon as he answers. "They want me to fly out tomorrow for a meeting at the Mexico City airport. But there's a snag. They want me alone."

"I thought that might be the case. Do you think you're up to it?"

"Will I really be alone?"

"Of course not." Mike answers, "We have an ongoing arrangement with the airlines to slip agents in among their employees anytime we consider it necessary. As soon as we find out what lounge they intend to use, we'll make sure that some of the people serving you are on our team. Other agents will be passengers in the lounge, and still others just outside, in the airport proper. You'll be as protected as last time."

"That doesn't exactly comfort me," is Rico's retort.

Mike has no appropriate response, so he goes on, "I'll check flights immediately. I suspect you will be on Southwest or American. By the time the cartel calls back, you'll know your airline, flight number, and can suggest a lounge. Then, let us know right away if they take your suggestion."

"Got it." Rico says, more confidently than he feels.

So, the next morning, Rico finds himself on a plane winging his way toward Mexico City, for the second time, although this time he's alone and crammed into a middle coach seat, the price of making his reservation at the last minute. He reminds himself again that he needs to go on a diet, although that's the least of his concerns at the moment.

Rico's having second thoughts about his decision to be the focal point of this operation. His earlier worry about a mid-life crisis has turned into worry about whether he will reach mid-life at all. He now knows from experience that anything can happen on these operations, especially when so much is out of his control. Or, more appropriately, out of Mike's control.

The precautions that Mike described are in place. Rico is sure of that. There will be agents all around him in the airport and in the lounge. And who knows? The raven-haired beauty now serving him orange juice on the plane right now may even be on his team, although, for ego reasons, he hopes that her flirtations are genuine.

Rico's butterflies grow as the plane begins its descent. A representative of the airline will meet the plane and escort him to the meeting room. Then, he's on his own.

The questions won't be a problem. Rico knows about the manufacturing plant, its production rate per line, how many lines they want to operate, and the capacity of the plant when fully operating. He's been well-schooled by the real Felipe Cardoza on those things. But, can he think on his feet when something unexpected arises? Which, of course, it most assuredly will.

As Rico strides off the plane, into the friendly handshake of the airline employee, a mystifying calm comes over him. He no longer has to worry about preparation. At this point, he can either do the job or not, and Mike seems to believe he can do it. That's enough for Rico.

The airline lounge is surprisingly luxurious, the meeting room even more so. Only when Rico enters is he reminded of what this meeting is all about and how serious it will be. Seated at the table are four tough-looking Latinos, two in chinos, two in denims, casually slouched in their seats. None of them were at the last meeting.

Two are young men, unshaven, who show little interest in the proceedings at hand. They may be smart but their dull, listless, half-lidded eyes give no indication of that. The other two, who are clean-shaven with alert, penetrating eyes, appear to be in charge.

Of the two, one is average height and weight but the other is a fairly large man who obviously likes to throw his weight around. Even seated, he's scary, not only because of his size but because of his eyes, which never leave Rico. He watches but makes no attempt to get up or to shake hands, or to make Rico feel comfortable in any way.

Rico sits down, without offering his hand as well, and stares back at the two men. He's decided to mirror the same sleepy-eyed, indifferent look the two thugs at the end of table have perfected.

This is particularly hard for Rico because he's naturally gregarious. Silence has always been his enemy. But, these four guys are more the enemy right now and something tells him that opening the conversation will be a sign of weakness.

Finally, the largest gang member speaks, "Thanks for coming, Mr. Cardoza," the guy says in a tone totally at odds with the cordial words he is saying.

He goes on, "Why don't we start by listening to your description of the sewing plant you want to build. We are particularly interested in what unused spaces may be available for our use, how you propose to hide our goods, and what loading docks will be made available to us, especially at night, when your workers have gone home."

Rico isn't surprised at the questions and launches into a well-prepared and rehearsed response. He's interrupted several times with other questions but, undeterred by their rudeness, he continues, and the two parties carry on a healthy discussion about how the partnership will work on a practical basis.

The two young gang members remain silent, as expected. They may be there just for muscle. But the other two are fairly animated as they listen to Rico, asking for clarification where needed, and responding quickly, when appropriate.

The Batista-produced product will be stowed below ground, in climate-controlled bins constructed specifically for that purpose. There will be portable lifts provided by Lone Star that will be of limited use in their sewing operations during the day, but invaluable after hours to put the product into the holds, or to pull it out and load it onto trucks. An electrically-charged wire fence around the perimeter will be provided by Lone Star, far enough away from the facility to discourage on-lookers. It will be the Batista gang's responsibility to provide security manpower both during the day and at night.

The conversation is surprisingly detailed and without much animosity. When they get to the matter of how much rent the Batista Cartel will pay, Rico takes a hard stance upfront, as he has been instructed to do.

"Given the extraordinary risk the company will be taking," Rico says, "the return on our upfront investment for the bins and docks has to be at least 40% per year. That translates into about two million dollars per year, which we will reduce by about half a million dollars for the security you're providing."

The large man who appears to be in charge objects to the high base rent and introduces the idea of a "performance incentive" based on how much product they are able to move out of the facility each month.

There is some discussion about the idea but, because Rico doesn't have final authority, no agreement is reached. They all do agree, however, on a deal structure, absent actual numbers, and, in order for Rico to catch his flight back, they decide to tie up the loose ends later.

The smallest of the gang members speaks up for the first time, suggesting they use a Colombian lawyer he knows to draft up the agreement. Rico counters that he prefers his company lawyers do the first draft, and the gang members agree.

Rico just barely makes his flight back to the States; the notes of the discussion and agreement tucked into the side pocket of his briefcase. He spends the next few hours on the plane, nursing a drink, and wondering exactly what was accomplished by this fairly impromptu trip.

There was no indication of anybody around that could have protected him. No listening devices were apparent. No video cameras visible. He felt incredibly alone in the meeting.

But, now, here on the plane to Albuquerque, seemingly safe, and with one drink in his belly and another on the way, Rico feels a kind of rosy glow of satisfaction, with his performance, yes, but also with the significant role he played in facing down some pretty tough hombres. For the first time, he even believes that he and Mike might succeed in bringing down the Batista cartel.

Of course, he has no idea what kind of intelligence may have been gathered and how it will be used. That is Mike's purview. But Rico did his part. And, at the moment, he feels it could be significant.

Once again, Mike meets his plane but this time he is in a much more celebratory mood. He congratulates Rico on a job well-done. There seems to be a smile peeking out from under his mustache, a rare sight. As before, however, when Rico starts to ask questions, Mike says, "Not now. Save it until we get to the office."

This time, they do drive to the small headquarters of the Drug Enforcement Agency right in the downtown area of San Antonio, and go immediately into a conference room. Finally, Rico has earned his stripes and feels like he is part of the team.

"Well," Mike begins, "nobody will ever know it but, Rico, you are a true American hero." He shakes Rico's hand again, then, continues, "I think that the man you sat across from in the Mexico City airport lounge was, indeed, the head of the Batista drug cartel, at least in Mexico. For the first time we have pictures of him and, even more significantly, we followed him so we now know where he lives. It is only a matter of time before we make our move on him."

"Are you sure he's their leader?" Rico asks, shifting his weight around in the chair to get more comfortable. "I know he's certainly a presence but, often the real leader is someone you least suspect, like Miguel, who had no presence at all."

"I have a confession to make," Mike says, rather sheepishly. "That was not really Miguel Espinoza that threatened you back at Lake Arrowhead. He was actually an agent with us, pretending to be Miguel."

"What do you mean?" Rico asks.

"It was all an act, a kind of training exercise for us and a test for you," Mike continues. "I needed to find somebody for this operation, to go to Mexico City and meet with high-level gang leaders. It couldn't be an agent, of course. They would see right through anybody I sent. It had to be somebody totally anonymous. Non-threatening. But also somebody who had the right background and the right set of balls."

Mike goes on, "We spent months looking for the right guy, and, lo and behold, you surfaced, a perfectly ordinary guy, with a little thirst for adventure. But, once we found you, I didn't think I could just walk in and ask you to leave your perfectly happy life to do something so inherently dangerous. So, I came up with the idea to use a simple one-day assignment that we make go wrong. We turn you into a hunted man, by a blood-thirsty drug lord, no less. At least, that was the idea. Then, getting you to hide out, by participating in our second operation, was pretty easy, as you might remember."

"I don't believe you," Rico blurts out. "The capture of Miguel Espinoza was big news, in all the papers."

"Not all the papers," Mike counters. "Just your paper. We had a whole section printed up and slipped into your newspaper before it was delivered. Oh, and by the way, we didn't put your real estate holdings into a blind trust either. We just had an expert watch over them for you. They will be there for you when you return."

But Mike doesn't stop there, "So, you aren't out much money and whatever our caper cost you, well, maybe that was just the price of admission for the fun ride we gave you."

"What a deceitful prick you are," Rico stammers. "A totally unprincipled piece of shit. Can I go now? Or do you have some other fanciful story you want to tell me."

"Not a story. A job offer," Mike answers. "My timing may be off but I was impressed with how you handled yourself in the field today. I'd like you to come work with us. Part-time or even full-time, if you wish."

"You gotta be kidding me. Why would I work for such a lying bastard?" Rico spits back.

"Well," Mike starts. But Rico interrupts.

"That was a rhetorical question. You don't need to answer. Anything else you want to say?"

"That's it. Obviously, you don't appreciate what we did for you and your exceedingly dull life. Not yet, anyway. Someday I think you will."

Rico stares at him, shocked that Mike doesn't understand how devious and duplicitous he has been. Then, Rico turns around and, without looking back, flips Mike the bird as he leaves.

Chapter 7

When Rico arrives back at his home in Manhattan Beach, it feels like he has been gone for months rather than weeks. The house smells musty from being all locked up. The lawn needs mowing. Everywhere he looks there's something to be done and he can't believe he has gone so quickly from being a star undercover agent for the Feds to just an ordinary guy with ordinary issues to resolve.

Welcome home, Rico.

There are multiple complaints from renters on his business answering machine, an overdue bill from the electric company on his desk, and, worst of all, a notice from the insurance company that they're raising rates on two of his properties. Obviously, they don't know who Rico is, or, more appropriately, who he was for a while.

At least, there's much to do, giving him little time to worry about the last couple of weeks and how he could have fallen for such a ruse? *What an idiot.*

Still, he feels good about the job he did in Mexico City. But, hero or not, it's back to the old grind for Rico. And, to make matters worse, he can't talk about what he did, to anybody. Of course, he has nobody to tell anyway. That's the really sad part.

Rico decides to join a gym, not only to meet people but also to get in better shape. His little pot belly, carefully-crafted over years of non-exercise, has started to spread a bit and he's beginning to look like one of those old men he used to see sitting around outside the taco shop in his old barrio.

So, Rico starts running, then, swimming, then, lifting. Anything to create a body that fits with the new image he has of himself. The workouts help to tone him up a bit. But he makes no new friends and, no matter how much Rico sweats or grunts, without more meaningful work to do, he still feels a void.

Rico begins to think about girls and dating again. More specifically, he begins to think about seeing Maggie Smith again, the woman who came home to his house that night a few weeks back. She would inject a little excitement into his life. That's for sure,

Unfortunately, as Rico so painfully remembers, the last time she wouldn't even return his calls. Still, Rico is a different man now, at least in his own mind, battle-tested under actual fire, confident, and self-assured. So, he decides to call Maggie and give it a shot. What the hell.

Surprisingly, she answers the phone, something Rico had not expected. He'd scripted a short message specifically for her answering machine but he had not been prepared to speak to a live person, especially one as alive as Maggie. Once again, using his newly-honed improvisational skills, Rico starts to wing it.

"Maggie. How great to hear your voice," he begins, gathering his thoughts as he goes. "Sorry I haven't been able to call lately. I was out of town on business." He pauses, then, in a slightly lower voice, "You know, government business."

"Oh," she says. He waits. Nothing more from her. But she doesn't hang up. It's a start.

"I wondered if you wanted to grab a quick drink sometime and catch up."

"You mean another night where we make love and, then, you never call. No thanks," is her reply. But, again, she doesn't hang up. Rico takes that as another positive sign and he rushes to fill the silence:

"I know. I would like a chance to start over, Maggie. I'm very sorry for not calling you right away last time. But if you remember, I did call your answering machine quite a few times."

"I know. That's why I picked up the phone this time," Maggie responds. Then more silence, but he's run out of ways to fill it. So, he keeps quiet. Finally, she says, "Okay. Where would you like to meet?"

And, just like that, Rico is back in the game. They meet for a drink. He keeps the mood light, relaxed, as best he can. He doesn't push her and calls her the next day to tell her how much fun the date was. And he calls her the day after. And he takes her to dinner the day after that, followed by roses delivered to her house the following day. No more James Bond coolness and finesse. Rico has learned his lesson on that.

Not surprisingly, Maggie continues to be interested in Rico's government work more than his real job. Property management is hardly the sexiest thing to talk about, but it pays his bills and is something he knows how to do. Still, every time he steers the conversation into the comfort zone of his regular work, she gets bored.

Rico now believes that Maggie is trying to live vicariously through him and his secret life. In her day job, she's an office manager at a mortgage company and that's kind of like being a property manager. Anything else seems exciting by comparison.

So, in the past, Rico has taken advantage of her interest by embellishing his other life a little. But, now that he has given that other life up, without telling her, is he living a lie that will come back to bite him?

Then, out of the blue, Rico gets a call from Teresa, his first ex-wife, checking back to make sure he is OK.

"How are you? I was worried," she says anxiously. "Were those guys really cartel guys who were looking for you?"

"No. That was all just a misunderstanding. They were looking for somebody else. It's all squared away now."

"Great," she says. "Say. Rico, this may be a bit forward of me but how about we meet again for a drink? I would love to bring you up-to-date on my new life, and some of the interesting people I've met. I'm thinking your experience here can be helpful to me right now."

Interesting people in L. A., Really? Rico thinks, but he doesn't say anything. Instead he replies, "Sure. When and where?"

"How about the restaurant where I work, Ricardo's?" she answers, "Say ten o'clock tomorrow night, when I get off?"

Rico responds, "I'll be there."

From famine to famine to feast. A few weeks ago, Rico couldn't get a girl to go out with him and, now, two attractive women are expressing interest, an unfamiliar position that Rico needs to play carefully. He sure doesn't want Maggie to get wind of Teresa coming back into his life, or that he has had two wives already; an inconvenient fact he has neglected to tell her. And Teresa finding out about Maggie might be even worse at this point. Rico needs to be careful, yes, but, at least, for the first time in a while, he has options.

Rico arrives at Ricardo's early, partially because he wants to see Teresa doing her job, but mostly because he has a better chance to stay awake here at the restaurant than at home. Ten o'clock is well past his normal bedtime.

Rico manages to slip into the restaurant unnoticed and grabs a stool at the far end of the bar. He orders a tonic, just a tonic, and then, turns around to find Teresa.

She's very easy to spot. One just looks for the most elegant, refined woman in the place and there she is. Teresa is dressed in a black cocktail dress, tastefully cut to reveal just enough of her slender figure. Her hair is up off her shoulders, exposing a neck that could only be described as regal. She is what a Rico, in his younger days, might have called a knock-out; and he is sure that no guy in the restaurant would disagree with that characterization. The irony is that, in his younger days, he didn't see that in her.

Rico tries to remember the gangly but pretty girl he married so long ago. But there is no hint of her in the vision before him. He's so entranced, in fact, that it takes a minute to realize she's actually looking back at him and giving him a shy, waist-high, girlish wave. Rico returns it, in a similar, fashion, not caring that he looks ridiculous.

Rico nurses a second tonic, waiting for Teresa to get off work and come to him. It is the longest wait of his life. *Perhaps*, he thinks, *he should have stayed home rather than wait at the restaurant.*

Finally, she sort of glides across the room and plants a big kiss right on his lips, making every guy in the place instantly jealous. Despite having been married to her at one time, Rico is still surprised by her overt show of intimacy. Flattered and proud as well.

Teresa grabs his hand and guides him to a table. The waiter appears. "You want another?"

To which he replies, "Yes, but please put vodka in it this time."

"And for you, Teresa?"

"Just a spritzer, please," she answers, and then launches immediately into what has happened to her since they last met, her job interview, her search for an apartment, her difficulty adjusting to the chaos and unfriendliness of L.A., and the people she had met; mostly men, but a few women as well.

Rico doesn't know any of them by name but he knows the type. They are typical Hollywood vultures, producers, writers, and the like, ready to pounce on any good-looking woman who happens on the scene. As Rico knows well, the "casting couch" is still alive and well in this town.

Rico realizes that he's begun to feel strangely paternalistic toward Teresa, even though she was once his high school girl friend and wife. He knows her family, background, and open, trusting nature, maybe better than anybody else in the world and knows she will have trouble holding her own in this town. Somebody has to protect her. Might as well be him.

In fact, just to underscore the point, Teresa starts talking about Carlos Silva, the handsome man she's dating, how wonderful he is, and how much she wants Rico to meet him.

Carlos is a successful businessman with his own transportation company, renting out truck trailers, railroad cars, and ships that carry all types of cargo. She then says how much she values Rico's opinion, a fact that disappoints him a little. He'd prefer she was interested in him, not just his opinion.

Then, they talk about old times and some of his friends in the gang.

"Whatever happened to 'Santa,'" she asks, referring to Santiago Sanchez, a childhood friend of Rico's.

"You remember he was jailed for stealing a woman's purse?" Rico says and Teresa nods.

"Well, we kind of drifted apart after that."

"I'm glad. I didn't like you hanging out with him anyway. Or any of that gang, for that matter."

"I know. You kinda made that clear at the time."

"And your brother Roberto?" she asks.

"He's doing great. Left Mexico shortly after I did, and now works for an e-commerce business near Santa Barbara," Rico answered.

They talk about their early days as a couple. Teresa's memories of their marriage are surprisingly fresh and positive. He remembers the struggles. She remembers the fun.

Importantly, Rico detects no lingering resentment over the way their marriage ended. In fact, Teresa tells him that, in the long run, it had probably been for the best. He'd always felt that way himself, but, right now, looking into her exquisite face, he isn't so sure he made the right choice.

After an appropriate amount of time, Rico bids her adieu, assuring her they will get together again soon. He doesn't feel it's his place yet to warn Teresa that she could be heading toward an emotional bruising, at the hands of one Carlos Silva, the same kind experienced every day in this town by girls much younger, and less experienced, than she is.

Driving back to his place, Rico's thoughts drift back to Maggie and their relationship. He realizes that he once thought he was too good for Teresa and now the shoe is on the other foot. Teresa is obviously too good for him and more importantly, too attached to her new love, to be a factor in his life.

But Maggie is a factor in his life, Rico acknowledges, and he needs to focus on her first or he'll be left with nothing. No Teresa. No Maggie. No love interest of any kind.

After a few months of dating, Maggie has moved in with Rico, partially to save money and, also, because they thought it would be good for their relationship. It wasn't long, however, before they begin to behave like a normal married couple. Not a good thing.

She goes to work every day and he goes up to his second-floor office to deal with his tenants and pay his bills. They see each other over dinner, with few words and even fewer sparks. And absolutely nothing happens after dinner, which is pretty disappointing for Rico. But he does nothing about it.

The real problem in their relationship, at least for him, is the little white lie he told her, that he was doing exciting things he couldn't disclose to her.

That was no longer the case, of course, and he would have to unwind that lie sometime. *But when and how?*

Fortunately, Maggie has stopped asking him about his other life anyway. She's no longer interested in anything Rico is doing, and he needs to do something to get things back on track. He needs to inject a little excitement back into things.

So, he calls Mike.

Chapter 8

"Mr. Lopez on line two," Mike Andress' secretary says through the intercom. Mike isn't surprised. He had expected Rico to call, just not this soon.

"Hello, Rico. How are things going?" he says cheerfully, as if their last parting had been amicable.

"Just fine," Rico answers, "business could be better but, otherwise, I can't complain. Listen, I've been thinking about your offer to become a narc agent. I still have my qualms but maybe we could discuss it further some time."

"What qualms?" Mike abruptly asks.

"Well, you know, the lying and misleading and all that stuff. Not exactly a great way to start a relationship."

"Well, Rico, we *are* in the lying and misleading business," Mike counters. "If you're not comfortable with that, I doubt you'll make a good agent. But, let me ask you this, have you told your girlfriend about your work with us."

"Kinda."

"What does kinda mean?"

"She knows I've done work for the government. Secret stuff that I can't talk about."

"And her reaction?"

"She seemed impressed."

"Did you tell her you no longer work with us?"

"Not really. Not yet."

"Isn't that misleading?" Mike asks. Rico doesn't answer but he gets Mike's point. The knife cuts both ways.

Mike goes on, "Listen, Rico, I know, better than anybody, how good you are at lying and misleading and deceiving, among other things. That's why I want you as an agent. The trick is to be good at those things and still basically an honest person, especially as it relates to the people around you, those who work with you."

"I was working with you when you misled me," Rico replies. "Making up a drug lord? That's a pretty big lie."

"You weren't really an agent at the time, so you were fair game," Mike says. "As soon as I decided I wanted you on the team, I told you."

"Listen, I know from experience you wouldn't have cooperated had I been totally straight with you." Mike goes on. "Maybe I was wrong to do that but, if you choose to join us, you will be surprised how straight-forward, honest and trusting we can be, once you're one of us." Mike pauses. "Do you still want to talk?"

They meet at a coffee shop in Manhattan Beach near Rico's home, a concession to how important Rico's recruitment is to Mike. Once the introductions are over, Mike gets right down to business.

"I have to tell you that what we're proposing here is a little unusual for us," Mike starts. "We like to hire young men who are smart and motivated; then, train them ourselves. I started that way. So did almost everybody else at the agency. But, times, they are a'changing. More and more, we need people who did not grow up in this business, who can walk into situations, not with the swagger we do, but with the wariness that real life experiences bring."

Mike continues, "One other thing. Our home-grown agents are just too easy to spot. You're exactly the opposite. Don't take this in the wrong way but you are one of the least memorable people I have ever met. And, right now, that's valuable to us. Oh, and your ability to think on your feet helps."

Rico shifts in his seat, not sure how to take the candor. *Least memorable?* He decides to own it, until Mike speaks again.

"But," Mike continues, "on the flip side, you're flabby, unobservant, and far too trusting. You have sloppy work habits, probably because you never had a boss. You're incredibly naive about the world you're entering. Those are traits we'll have to change, or mold, without, of course, affecting the anonymity that makes you so valuable to us."

Mike pauses, then goes on, "Not an easy job, I admit, but I have two good trainers that can work with you over the next few months. They'll shape you up both physically and mentally if you'll commit to about four hours per day, with no distractions. Can you do that?"

Rico hesitates. He doesn't really want to do that at all. He had been thinking he might do a gig for Mike, here or there, like a part-time musician, and then go back to his regular job.

Until now, he was viewing this sidelight as a way to add some excitement to his life and pick up a little extra bread along the way. Nothing more. Mike obviously sees it differently. But Rico is smart enough to keep his feelings to himself. At least for now.

"Sure. Why not?" he hears himself say.

So, a couple of days later, he finds himself at an unfamiliar gym across town, facing two solidly-built, in fact, hard-as-a-rock trainers, one of whom he actually knows. It's Todd Williams, the lead agent on his last operation, the one who so adroitly got Rico and the rest of the team out of Mexico City when the meeting with the Batista gang members went south.

Todd looks differently than Rico remembers. He still has a sort-of hang-dog look to his face, with puffy cheeks and bags under his eyes, but the whole package beneath his doughy face is much more impressive than Rico remembers. Of course, he hasn't seen Todd in gym clothes before.

Still, as chiseled as he is, Todd looks puny next to the 6'4" blonde-haired giant standing beside him; an Adonis of a man who would stand out even among guys on the American Gladiator show. He introduces himself as Alfred Blankenship, a name that fits him about as well as a size forty coat would. Todd says to just call him Big Al, which seems much more appropriate to Rico than Alfred.

Todd and Big Al take about a half-hour to explain the program. They're not going to turn him into a body-builder, as if they could anyway. No, they just want to get his body in shape enough so he can react quickly if attacked, and to run fast enough to get away from most pursuers. Also, they will teach him a few basic escape holds and one or two chokeholds to use in an emergency.

Most of the program will actually be more mental than physical, they explain. He needs to study up on the drug trade, of course; such things as varieties of street drugs, gangs, the players, distribution channels, how to case a joint, and such as that. He needs to learn some of the protocol that all agents need to follow. He has to be taught how to respect and handle a gun, something that, thanks to his gang experience, is not totally foreign to him.

Rico is also told that some of the training materials they intend to use are similar to those at the Harvard Business School, employing case studies and real-life situations that he might face in the field. He will learn a lot, sure, but, more importantly, he'll be trained to quickly use what he's learned.

When Rico gets home from his first day at the gym, he goes right to bed. Every muscle in his body is tired, including the one in his head. He doubts he would have been cut out to be a narc agent even when he was in his twenties, and in better shape. But now, in his fifties, getting to look and act like Big Al, as an example, seems impossible. Still, he sure isn't going to quit the very first day.

An hour or so later, Rico hears Maggie come in the front door. His mind decides to get up and meet her but his body will not listen. She comes through the bedroom door, stops abruptly, and says rather dramatically, "What the hell happened to you?"

"It's confidential," is his lame response, then, after an uncomfortable silence, he struggles to sit up in bed. "I have to get in shape for my next assignment. So, I started to work out."

"I thought you already worked out."

"I thought so, too," he answers, "but obviously not."

"I'm proud of you," Maggie replies, giving him a peck on his cheek. And that one small sign of support, reinforced almost daily over the next few months, gets him through the program.

When Rico sits down with Mike, one week after he finishes his training, he isn't sure what to expect. Todd and Big Al were effusive in their praise of what Rico had accomplished in a few short months. His body, though hardly chiseled, looks considerably fitter. His paunch has disappeared. His confidence level is off the charts.

But Mike doesn't care about any of that. He looks Rico directly in the eye and asks, "You ready to go, partner?"

To which Rico responds, "Ready to go, boss."

"Okay. Here's the situation," Mike starts. "The operation you were part of was theoretically discontinued after you left but, in truth, it was just renamed. We now call it Operation Felipe in honor of the guy you impersonated, who, by the way, quit Lone Star a month ago and joined a competitor. He's completely out of harm's way now."

Rico is surprised. He didn't know Felipe well but he thought the guy seemed like a Lone Star lifer. Still, he remembers that the Mexican sewing factory was the third project in a row that Felipe, and Lone Star, had not finalized. Not his fault, of course, but the lack of success may have caused Felipe to fall out of favor at Lone Star. Who knows?

Rico tunes back into what Mike was saying, "Turns out the guy you met with in Mexico City *was* the boss of the Batista cartel there. But we now believe somebody in the United States has actually been pulling the strings. It appears the big boss here communicates through various couriers, one of whom lives fairly close to you, in Hermosa Beach, in fact."

"Really? He's an American?"

"Of Mexican heritage, yes. We want you to befriend the guy and keep us posted on his whereabouts, especially if you learn he's traveling to Mexico, or, even better, if he does anything that can lead us to the real boss. Unfortunately, despite putting a lot of resources into it, at this point, we have no idea who the guy really is. We can guess. But we don't really know."

Rico stares back at Mike, glassy-eyed, realizing for the first time that he is going to be thrown right into the espionage pool, deep end, with no water wings. He had thought a more experienced agent would tag along for a while, maybe even Todd, whom he had grown quite fond of over the last few months, but Rico never dreamed he would be on his own right out of the box.

"Are you OK?" Mike notices the surprise on Rico's face and finally says, "Can you do this?"

"Of course," Rico answers, with a confidence he doesn't really feel.

Mike hands Rico a file clearly marked *CONFIDENTIAL*. Rico wonders aloud whether he is cleared to read it, to which Mike answers, "Yes, of course. But we don't have your *SECRET* or *TOP SECRET* classification yet. To get that, you'll need to interview with an FBI or CIA agent sometime in the next few days."

Rico is immediately concerned.

"Do I need a classification that high?" he asks.

"Absolutely. Don't worry, though. The agent will come to you. I doubt it will take more than an hour. Just be yourself and you'll be fine."

Rico begins to worry about his early rebellious teen days in Mexico City. And the struggles he encountered when he first moved to the States. *What do they already know?* The idea of him being an agent may be a risk he can ill-afford. But Rico decides he'll cross that bridge when he comes to it.

Mike goes on, "But, in the meantime, the information in that file should give you all you need to get started on your assignment. I trust you to formulate a plan to meet the courier somehow or, worst case, just try to follow him and keep track of who he contacts. Did Todd teach you how to shadow a suspect?"

"Of course," Rico says. And, with that, his work as a narc agent begins.

There isn't much in the file folder. The guy Rico is supposed to find and follow is named Edgar Vegas and he does, indeed, live in Hermosa Beach, one community south of Manhattan Beach. Rico has his address, his home, his cell phone number, his place of employment, and the fact that he's divorced, with a 10-year-old daughter living with his ex-wife.

There are a few pictures of Mr. Vegas, one taken when he was a senior in high school and three other grainy images taken from a distance with a zoom lens. More useful is a description of his car, a blue Ford Mustang. And the license plate number, *1M16B2.*

Not much to go on, Rico thinks. He wonders if there will be more information in the other files when he's authorized to see them, but he can't wait to find out. At least, that's what Mike intimated. Rico feels he needs to develop a plan of action right away. In fact, he's anxious, indeed, excited to get at it.

Once home, Rico spreads his meager intel out across his desk as he has seen police officers do in countless Law and Order episodes. Of course, they always have much more than one half-page of information, and a few photos, to work with, but it's a start.

Rico reviews his options. *Should he concoct a scheme to meet Mr. Vegas? Just call him up and talk his way into a business meeting?* He looks up Edgar's place of employment, a metal shop in downtown L.A.; not exactly Rico's area of expertise.

Maybe he should come in as a customer; but, then, thinks better of that idea. It wouldn't be believable anyway. *Maybe he should try to meet the guy somewhere around his home?* Finally, he decides to do a stakeout of Edgar's home early the next morning, just to see how Mr. Vegas spends a typical day. Maybe that'll help him with his plan, and it does.

Edgar Vegas pulls out of his driveway promptly at 6:30 am, with Rico tucked in, a safe distance behind him. From what Rico can see, he's a large, very dark-complexioned Latino, with a serious expression seemingly frozen onto his face. Nothing very distinctive except he has a bluestone stud earring in his right earlobe; an affectation that Rico does not understand. It seems incongruous that a guy who would work hard building such a massive body, would wear a sign advertising that he was actually a gentle soul, or something else. *Talk about your mixed messages.*

Rico has rented a compact car for the day so he can be inconspicuous and untraceable as he darts in and out of traffic behind the blue Mustang, keeping it in sight as best he can.

He is just pulling around a car to the left, trying to get closer, when Edgar takes a right turn into a mid-sized shopping center. Rico nervously doubles back and, fortunately, finds Edgar's car parked near a *Planet Fitness* workout facility. He parks his car several rows away from the Mustang and waits, another agent skill that doesn't come naturally to him.

An hour later, Rico sees Edgar come out of the gym, get into his car, and drive away toward the freeway leading to downtown. Rico is able to keep up with him on the local streets but, when Edgar enters the freeway, he gets away.

Obviously, Rico doesn't know as much about tailing a car as he thought he did. His confidence falters a bit and the thought of whether he can do this, creeps into his head. But, as it turns out, losing the courier doesn't really matter because Rico knows the address of the place Edgar works. He just drives directly to it and there, parked conspicuously in front, is the blue Mustang.

So, a little shaken by his amateurish beginning, Rico decides not to follow Mr. Vegas anymore that day and returns home instead to plot his next move. After wrestling with several options, Rico decides to use the gym, *Planet Fitness*, as his point of initial contact with Edgar.

But, to do that, he needs to be a member. So, he drives over to the gym, makes a down payment, checks out the equipment, and gets everything ready for the more difficult part of his plan, which, in agent vernacular, is called the "intercept." Hopefully, that will go better than his tailing of Edgar's car went.

Chapter 9

The next day dawns cloudy and a bit misty, a rare kind of gloomy day for Los Angeles. Rico opens the window shade and sighs, hoping the weather isn't a harbinger of what is to come.

He gets out of bed carefully, so as not to disturb Maggie and have to answer her questions. Even the parts of his new job that he can talk about are hard to explain, and it's too early in his assignment to brag, especially when, at this point, he has such self-doubts.

It had been a sleepless night. Rico's thoughts vacillated between optimism and sheer terror, as he mulled over what could occur in the next few hours. Any clumsiness, in the introduction or follow-up, could raise Edgar's suspicions about who Rico really is, and put the plan in jeopardy. Or worse.

Rico arrives at the gym a little after the time he assumes Edgar will be there. His luck is holding. A large hulking man, in sweats, is already there, pedaling and sweating, alone on a stationary bike in the back row. Rico is sure it's his target but checks the sheet at the desk, anyway, and sees Edgar's name on it. *So far, so good.*

Rico chooses another bike on the back row, one not right next to Edgar's, gambling that no one will be between them when he makes his move. Rico doesn't want Edgar to think he's stalking him, even though, of course, that's exactly what he's doing.

"Excuse me, sir, but, how does this thing work?" Rico asks Edgar. "I'd like to watch the news while I work out, but it doesn't look like there are any local stations available."

Edgar looks perturbed but he responds, "Move the wheel, there on your right, up. More stations will appear."

"Oh. I see. Thanks."

Nothing is said for a few minutes. Then, Rico breaks the silence, "Can you believe the Lakers got LeBron and Anthony Davis?" Rico thinks he hears a grunt from Edgar, although the big man doesn't take his eyes off the bike's display, or acknowledge the question. He just keeps pedaling.

Rico continues, "I think they'll be good on down the line. But it might take some time."

"Sorry. I don't follow basketball," Edgar says, this time turning to look directly at Rico. His expression says, "Leave me alone" more clearly than his words do.

But Rico, playing the part of an affable, harmless fool, which actually doesn't take much acting, continues, "Now, those Rams, they look like they can be competitive. They might actually rekindle my interest in football."

Edgar turns toward Rico, as if to dress him down, then surprises him by responding, "I kind of feel sorry for the Chargers, though. Nobody here wants them."

Rico's heart jumps. *An opening*, he thinks. But he waits a bit before responding, "I just joined this place. Anything I should know?"

"Not really," Edgar says. "*Planet Fitness* is more for the ordinary guy, just trying to fit a little exercise into his life. No bells or whistles. No grunting. That's the company mantra. So, body-builder types go to the bigger, better-known gyms that have the selection of weights they need."

"Well, this is right for me, then," Rico says. "I'm certainly not a body-builder, in case you hadn't noticed."

No response from Edgar.

They pedal along in silence for a couple of minutes before, surprisingly, Edgar says something more, "You know, on Thursdays, the management orders in free pizza for everybody in the late afternoon. You might want to come. It'll give you a chance to meet the manager and some of the regular members."

"Okay," Rico responds. "Are you going to be there?"

"Hadn't planned on it. But I might. I haven't attended one for a while," Edgar says.

Rico remains quiet and finishes his workout off with a flourish. Then, grabs his towel. The successful "intercept" behind him, he has even more energy than he had at the beginning of the workout.

"I'm Rico," he says to the target who's still pedaling away,

"Edgar," the big man responds without even looking up.

"See you Thursday, Edgar," Rico tosses over his shoulder as he heads to the showers. Edgar doesn't respond; but Rico hardly expects that. It's a promising start to, what he hopes, will be a productive relationship.

The next day, Rico decides not to go to the gym. He can wait until Thursday before doing anything more with Edgar. His gut tells him he should leave well enough alone for now. Also, he's falling way behind in his paperwork and he can't just ignore the place where his bread is buttered.

Rico is half-way through reading a lease agreement when the telephone rings. He answers and is surprised to hear Teresa's voice.

"Hey, Rico," she says. "How ya doin'?"

"Fine, Teresa," Rico answers. "Everything OK with you?"

"Yes. Of course," she says. "Better than OK. You remember when we met, I told you about Carlos and that I wanted you to meet him?"

"Carlos?" Rico asks without thinking.

"Yes, the guy I'm dating," Teresa goes on. "You remember, right?"

He didn't really but, in typical Rico fashion, he answers, "Sure, how's old Carlos doing?"

"That's why I'm calling. He's having a small dinner party at his house in Brentwood on Friday, just a few people we know, and that would be a perfect time for the two of you to get acquainted." She says, "It's no big deal. You can dress casually, come around 6:30 pm. Oh, and are you dating somebody? If so, she's certainly welcome as well."

"No, no," Rico says without thinking, "I'll be there alone."

"Looking forward to it," from Teresa.

"Me, too," from Rico, and they hang up.

He immediately starts worrying about what to tell Maggie. *Another white lie*, he supposes, something that's becoming uncomfortably easy for Rico these days. Maybe he'll make a good agent after all.

The phone rings again. It's an FBI agent asking if Rico can drop by their offices that afternoon. The guy explains that he needs to finish up a background check he's doing on Rico and all that's left is the interview. To Rico, everything seems to be moving incredibly fast and he supposes that's a good thing. Still, his dalliance with a neighborhood gang, when he was a kid, might step up and bite him in this interview, something new to worry about.

It turns out, however, that Rico needn't have worried. His early days in Mexico City are not discussed at all, nor are his two marriages. The agent, who seems congenial throughout, is most interested in Rico's business life, something Rico enjoys discussing anyway.

There are some probing questions about one of his tenants but the agent seems satisfied with Rico's answers. When he finally walks out of the FBI offices after about an hour, Rico feels confident that he will get the necessary clearances; another step on his path toward becoming a full-fledged agent.

The next morning, after another sleepless night, Rico heads over to *Planet Fitness*, arriving at 6:30 am, as planned. Edgar is already there, getting ready to ride his normal stationary bike. Rico waves at Edgar from the desk and, then, walks over, this time choosing a bike right next to the one Edgar is using.

"Good morning, Edgar," Rico says. Edgar grunts a reply, maybe trying to remember the name of this nondescript, but pleasant, man he talked to a couple of days before. But it's more likely that he's just expressing his disinterest, something Edgar does very well.

They pedal in silence, which is particularly difficult for Rico, but necessary. He doesn't want to push the relationship too far too fast and Edgar's body language is like a big "Do Not Disturb" sign anyway. Still, Rico will not be deterred.

"I know that you don't like basketball," he starts, "but the Lakers looked real good last night. I was impressed." Edgar does not respond.

Rico goes on, "I think the Lakers are on the right track."

"I don't watch basketball," Edgar replies curtly.

Rico isn't surprised. Edgar indicated as much earlier. *Still, what kind of guy in L.A. doesn't follow the Lakers?* This is going to be more difficult than Rico imagined. Finally, he asks, "Are you coming here for pizza tonight?"

Edgar turns, looks Rico in the eyes, and, deciding he's harmless, says, "Not sure I am but, if I do, I'll probably stop by about five o'clock."

That's all Rico needs to know. He finishes his workout in silence, takes a shower, and says to Edgar as he leaves, "Hope to see you tonight." Once again, no answer.

But Edgar is there, at five, as he said he might be, pizza slice in one hand, beer in the other. He's much more talkative drinking beer than he is on the bike, which is not saying much.

Rico gets him to discuss his job, local politics, and even what he likes to do on his vacations. Edgar is divorced, between girlfriends at the moment, and enjoying the free time. He seems to appreciate Rico's company and Rico decides not to push his luck. All he wants is a casual relationship and he's accomplished that.

"Well, got to go," Rico says, "I'm meeting somebody." Then, he winks and says, "Wish me luck." Edgar smiles back, a not totally unpleasant look, Rico notices. *Maybe there's a person in there after all*, he thinks.

The next morning, Rico calls Mike to update him on his progress but, if he expects kudos from his boss, he's disappointed. Instead, Mike berates him for the lack of actionable intel.

"Is he traveling to Mexico soon?" Mike starts, "Who are his friends? Any names? Is the metal shop a cover-up operation?"

The barrage of questions unnerves Rico. *Does Mike really believe an undercover agent can introduce himself, act friendly for a few minutes, and, then, out of the blue, just ask when the target is going to Mexico next?* Rico may be inexperienced as an agent but he knows people. He wonders if Mike can say the same.

Mike goes on, "Our contacts in Mexico City believe that a meet has already been scheduled for the week after next. They're not exactly sure who will be flying down from the States but they're betting on your guy, Vegas, since he hasn't been down there in a while and they think something is brewing that the real boss needs to weigh in on."

Rico says, "I see." But he doesn't really. *Why did Mike neglect to tell him there was a deadline? And what does Mike want him to do anyway?*

"Let's go over the mission again," Mike sighs and continues. "We are trying to identify the leader here in the U.S. and we think Vegas, as his most trusted courier, may be a key to finding out who he is. If you can find out when, and where, they're going to meet before the trip, we can cover the meet and identify the big boss, the guy who gives Vegas the package of instructions. That would be plan A. You with me so far?"

"Yes," says the chastened Rico.

Mike goes on, "But, absent that, we absolutely need to know when Vegas is flying to Mexico City so we can grab the package from him as he arrives and, also, squeeze him for the name of his boss. That's plan B. But, Rico, let me be perfectly clear here, neither plan works if you don't do your job, hopefully, in the next few days."

The weight of Mike's instructions broadsides Rico. This is not just fun and games anymore, a little diversion on the side, as Rico has been treating it. He's not only in the big leagues now but he's the ace pitcher, albeit with little time in the minors to work on his curve ball. Still, Rico's analogy doesn't really work. A star pitcher who is off his game goes to the showers. An undercover agent goes to the morgue.

So, bottom-line, the clock is ticking. It's Friday already, and Rico has no idea when, or even if, Edgar will work out over the weekend. So, Rico needs a back-up plan. He has a week to do his job and, to Rico, that may not be enough time to be subtle, which is his strength.

He considers asking Mike for help when Mike says, "You'll think of something. Don't be afraid to take chances. We need more information and you're the only person in a position to get it. Good luck." Then, he hangs up.

So, Rico is on his own. He needs to think like an agent, like Mike, maybe. Well, that may be a bit much. Nobody thinks like Mike.

His phone rings and interrupts his thinking. It's Teresa reminding Rico of his dinner engagement that night, something that had totally slipped his mind.

So much for being a full-time agent, he thinks, *I have other obligations. Mike is important. Edgar is important but Teresa is really important.*

Then, it dawns on him. Maggie is important as well, and he has forgotten to tell her about his dinner plans. How will he finesse that? Suddenly, there is much to do before 6:30 pm.

Chapter 10

Rico arrives at Carlos Silva's house right on time. He's left a furious Maggie at home, his explanation for this "innocent" dinner with an old friend falling on deaf ears.

Surely, he thinks, *Maggie will understand when she calms down and can listen to him rationally. It has been decades since he was married to Teresa. She has a good life in America; a new job, a rich boyfriend. Their relationship, if you can even call it that, is strictly platonic. Whereas he truly loves Maggie.*

Or words to that effect. He will hone his message better later. Maybe even believe it. But, for now, he needs to focus on the task at hand.

Unlike the way he imagines the owner to be, the home of Carlos Silva in Brentwood is tastefully understated. Large, yes, but still just a two-story, Colonial that could be located in any upscale neighborhood in the Midwest as easily as here in California.

It has shuttered dormer windows and a battle-gray clapboard exterior, with white trim. The houses on either side, a French Provincial beauty and an ivied, Spanish-influenced villa, are elegant but far from palatial. In fact, all of the houses in the neighborhood are located on lots that seem far too small for the size of the houses, or for their cost, which must run into the tens of millions.

Obviously, Carlos is doing well with his transportation business. Too well, perhaps. But he has chosen not to be flamboyant about it. Where he lives whispers rich rather than shouts it. But the fact that he lives here at all speaks to a wealth that only titans of industry, celebrities, and the occasional crook, can achieve.

Teresa meets Rico at the door, Carlos right behind her. Rico takes an immediate dislike to the guy. He's too perfect; strong jawline, dazzling white teeth, sparkling brown eyes, and an imperious manner that's off-putting. His hair is well-coiffed and sprinkled with gray, not because he's old, which he isn't, but more probably because his hairdresser has convinced him it's a good look for him.

"Rico," Carlos says, arms outstretched, as if they are old friends. "Welcome, *amigo*. I have really looked forward to meeting you. Please come in." They shake hands. A demure Teresa steps forward and gives Rico a peck on the cheek, then, takes his hand, and they follow Carlos into the foyer.

Another tall, slender, dark-skinned man is there, waiting. He doesn't come forward or offer his hand. Instead, he waits patiently for Carlos to introduce him, an indication that he is either humble, important, or both.

"Please, meet Pablo Cerritos," Carlos begins. "He's a friend of mine who will be joining us for dinner. Unfortunately, his wife took ill and will not be with us tonight. How is she, by the way, Pablo?"

"Could be worse. I think she picked up a bit of a cold. I have our housekeeper, watching out for her," Pablo replies. Then, he turns to Rico, smiles broadly, and says, "Nice to meet you, Rico," followed by a firm handshake.

There's something vaguely familiar about Pablo but Rico can't quite put his finger on it. Unlike Carlos, Rico likes Pablo immediately. There's something almost regal about him, but in a very understated way. It makes him seem approachable. Pablo has friendly eyes, with laugh lines around them that make his face open and non-threatening.

Rico gladly follows Pablo into the dining room, eager to hear who he is and how he came to know Carlos. Teresa falls in behind them, with Carlos following her. Both stay uncharacteristically quiet, so their two guests can get acquainted.

"So, what do you do?" Pablo asks.

"Property management. I have my own small firm," Rico answers. Carlos and Teresa still say nothing, in obvious deference to Pablo. *He must be a man of consequence*, Rico concludes.

"It's not much to speak of. Some apartment buildings, warehouses, office buildings," Rico continues. "Just enough to keep me out of trouble." *Until I met Mike*, Rico thinks. *Now, nothing but trouble.*

"I own some warehouses as well," Pablo says, "but mainly I am in the import/export business. I only buy buildings when I have to, in order to adequately support my business activities. Frankly, I much prefer to rent. We should talk about that sometime."

There is a pause, and Pablo goes on, "But not tonight. This is an evening of celebration. Here's to the engaged couple, Teresa and Carlos." He downs his drink and signals Carlos that he needs a refill. He's obviously used to being served.

Rico is surprised to hear the news that Teresa and Carlos are getting married. He's especially surprised that she never mentioned it to him. But why would she? He just re-entered her life and, really, has no role in it.

Above all, however, he's disappointed in her decision to marry Carlos. He may look the part but, to Rico's way of thinking, the guy isn't in Teresa's class. No way, no how.

"I'm so sorry Alicia couldn't be here." Pablo turns to Rico and adds, "My wife," then back to the others, "since she introduced the two of you, she feels responsible for your relationship. She's funny that way."

Although he has never met Alicia, Rico is already upset with her for bringing Carlos into Teresa's life. It shocks him to realize what a proprietary interest he still has in Teresa, a woman he so casually discarded all those years ago. But this is a very different Teresa, one that Rico feels particularly close to, and wants to protect. Which, given his history with her, is pretty ironic.

The evening plays out very well, thanks largely to the garrulous nature of Pablo. He talks more and more as the wine flows but, at least to Rico's mind, he's never boring. He talks of running with the bulls in Pamplona, Spain, falling down once without getting hurt and, even more fortuitously, he says, meeting a pretty *senorita* in the process, a woman he enjoyed running with a lot more than the bulls.

He talks of the Paleo, the famous horse race in Siena, Italy, and how he got so drunk at the pre-race party that he missed all of the festivities the next day. He talks of the Mardi Gras in New Orleans, which he attended with Carlos, and the Bogota Carnival and how great Rio used to be, before the petty criminals and gangs made it so dangerous.

"What a pity," he laments.

Rico is fascinated by Pablo's ability to throw around places and events without sounding pompous. He just seems like somebody who fully embraces life and encourages his listener to do the same. It's obvious, however, that Pablo has money and knows how to enjoy it, in an inclusive rather than exclusive way.

The evening flies by and its midnight before Rico realizes it. He rises from the table, a little wobbly, then, thanks his hosts, tells Pablo how much he enjoyed his company, and makes his departure.

Rico's drive back to Manhattan Beach is more difficult than the drive here was. He enjoyed his dinner, the company, and especially the wine, way too much. So, Rico stays off the freeways as much as he can, to avoid the cops, of course, but also to avoid other drivers like him.

Somehow, Rico successfully wends his way home through unfamiliar backstreets and, once in his driveway, breathes a sigh of relief. Then, he takes a minute to steel himself for the confrontation that undoubtedly awaits him inside.

But, fortunately, because of how late it is, Maggie is already asleep in bed.

So, immediately, Rico thinks of Edgar, the other problem in his life right now, and how to find out when, and if, he's flying to Mexico. But, as Rico tries to sort through alternatives and develop a plan of action, he makes the best decision of the night, which is not to decide anything until morning. So, he sets his alarm to get to the gym before Edgar arrives, and, then, tries his best to sleep.

Edgar doesn't show up to *Planet Fitness* on Saturday morning, as Rico had hoped he would. Rico also strikes out at Edgar's home, and at his office. *Maybe the guy went away for the weekend*, Rico thinks, *hopefully not to Mexico earlier than Mike thought he would.*

Back at his now-empty house, Rico is contemplating his next move when the phone rings. He's surprised to hear Pablo's voice on the other end, saying how much he enjoyed the previous evening, and asking Rico to join him for a cocktail at a restaurant on Sunset Boulevard that very evening.

Rico quickly agrees, hangs up, and then, wonders what in the world Pablo Cerritos could want. *He had said something the night before about doing business together but what would be so urgent that it required a get-together right away, on a weekend, no less?*

Oh well, Rico concludes, *maybe Pablo is just a guy of action. His stories from the night before would suggest that he can be impulsive. He probably just wants to find some warehouse space and why not start right away, with his new best friend from last night?*

Rico decides not to read too much into Pablo's surprising interest in him until he's heard him out.

The rest of the afternoon is spent catching up on work, making calls, paying bills, and the like. Rico's mind keeps going back to Edgar and how he might re-connect with the guy. Finally, he decides to stake out Edgar's house early the next morning and go from there. He gives no further thought to Pablo until late in the afternoon, when he realizes he's running late for their appointment.

After a quick shower, Rico dons a fresh set of clothes, and ably negotiates the 20-minute drive up the freeway to the restaurant, arriving only five minutes late. Pablo is already there, seated at a table in the back of the bar.

"Mr. Cerritos," Rico greets him formally. "I'm sorry to be late. More traffic than I anticipated."

"Don't think a thing about it," Pablo says. "And, please, don't call me Mr. Cerritos. Pablo is fine. Have a seat. I took the liberty of ordering you a martini."

"Thanks," Rico responds. "That's my go-to drink."

The two men look at each other briefly. Then, Pablo breaks the silence. "I enjoyed our conversation last night. You seem like an enterprising guy who makes things happen."

Rico waits, still not sure what to expect.

"I have a proposition for you," Pablo continues. "As I mentioned last night, I occasionally buy properties to help me in my import/export business. But real estate isn't a priority of mine and I've found I'm not very good at managing rental properties anyway. After meeting you last night, I got to thinking, maybe we should consider merging our properties. We could work out some kind of partnership deal. Pool our assets, I provide the capital going forward, and you provide the expertise. Of course, you would receive a nice salary for handling the management end. But the real money would be in growing the value of our shared properties. What do you say? You interested?"

Rico is taken aback. On its surface, this seems like the break he has been hoping for all of his life. With the small properties he owns, and the meager cash flow they throw off, he was always going to be small-time. And he's been OK with that. Now, out of the blue, this, a chance to break out of his comfortable rut and, just maybe, become wealthy in the process.

Something makes Rico pause, however. *Why me? Why now? Teresa had probably given Rico a good recommendation, of course. But what did she really know? And was her recommendation enough for Pablo to offer up a partnership? Without much investigation? Probably not*, thinks Rico. *There must be more going on here than meets the eye.*

Pablo goes on as if he is reading Rico's thoughts, "Of course, you don't have to decide anything now. Why don't we both sign confidentiality agreements, exchange financial information on our properties, and go from there?"

"I know this might seem a little impulsive," he continues, "but I like to do things quickly. Always have. Also, I have a pretty good instinct about people and I know you would be a partner I can trust. I'm guessing we look at things the same way."

Rico answers, "OK. I'll send the information over tomorrow morning."

Pablo immediately responds, "I'll do the same." They exchange cards, Pablo downs his drink and, then, gets up to leave. "Sorry but I'm late for a dinner engagement," he says as he heads toward the door, "We'll talk in a few days."

Rico is left alone, to nurse his half-full martini, and ponder what just happened.

When he gets home, Maggie is waiting. Fortunately, Pablo has provided Rico with his cover story.

"Teresa was just bringing the two of us together for a business opportunity," Rico says, then pushes his luck. "Why do you worry so much? You know you can trust me," he says.

"I know, darling. I'm sorry," she responds, then shows him how really sorry she is with a passionate kiss, leading them both upstairs for a rare evening of adult recreation. Afterwards, Rico lies there thinking how incredible he is at slipping punches, forgetting for a moment the critical role luck played, once again.

The next morning, Rico gets up early and spends a couple of hours at *Planet Fitness* hoping to run into Edgar. He's unsuccessful, but the extra time on the bike gives him some time to think.

Rico wonders if he is really cut out for this narc agent stuff. It seemed like fun in the beginning but now, with Mike hounding him to find out more about Edgar, he realizes he doesn't know how to go about it. *He's planning a stakeout, and that might work, but, even if Rico is able to intercept Edgar, how would he broach the subject of a possible trip to Mexico? And why would a reticent Edgar confide in him anyway?*

Mike seems to think that Rico is more capable of this kind of espionage work than his training and experience would suggest. The easy thing is intercepting the target. The hard thing is what to do then.

Rico decides to call Mike and beg off the assignment, maybe even the job. He has too much to do right now to give Edgar his full attention anyway. He has to send out rent notices, pay some bills, and work on the deal with Pablo. Especially, work on the deal with Pablo, which could change his life forever.

Just to make things even more complicated, when Rico gets home from the gym, another situation is brewing. Somehow, Maggie has figured out that he was once married to Teresa, a fact he never got around to telling her. And she is furious.

This time, he realizes he can't talk his way out of the situation. Her bags are packed. She's sitting, stiff-backed. on the sofa, just waiting around to let Rico know it is over.

She seems to take a perverse pleasure in breaking the news to him and nothing Rico says, in his admittedly weak defense, can dissuade her.

So, he decides to play his hole card, the fact that he is working on a very important top-secret government assignment and it has distracted him momentarily. But the subterfuge doesn't work this time. Within minutes, she's gone and Rico is left standing in the hallway, all alone, a little unsure about what to do next.

He picks up the phone and dials Mike.

Chapter 11

"Are you crazy," Mike asks as soon as he understands what Rico is trying to say. "You can't quit now. That would cripple our whole operation. Edgar knows you, seems to trust you, and he's our only link to the leadership of the Batista cartel. We need you now more than ever."

But that argument falls on deaf ears. Rico couldn't care less about their operation and how much they need him. This was always going to be a part-time gig for Rico and he has other priorities now.

He's certainly not being paid enough to give up his day job, and even more importantly, with the upside Pablo is promising, property management is becoming much more interesting, and lucrative. He doesn't need the side diversion of going undercover anymore. Nor is there a Maggie to impress.

But Rico doesn't say any of that. Instead, he goes in another direction.

"I'm just not good enough to do this kind of work," Rico responds. "It's a young man's game, a patient man's game, and this particular case deserves the full attention of a trained and experienced agent, which I'm not. Even you would admit that."

Mike detects a steely resolve in Rico's voice that he hasn't heard before. Maybe he misjudged the extent of Rico's gullibility. So, he decides to modify his approach.

"Listen. You're right," he says, "I made a mistake putting you on Edgar alone. Nobody could do that job, let alone a new agent. I'll assign another guy to work with you starting immediately. He'll run the stakeout, maybe even with a junior agent tagging along. Then when, and if, he feels your relationship with Edgar can be useful, he'll contact you."

"In the meantime," he goes on, "you go on about your own business and forget all this nonsense about quitting. That won't be necessary. We'll accommodate your needs and your schedule. You're a very valuable asset to us and we don't want to lose you. OK?"

Rico is surprised by Mike's conciliatory tone, flattered by the compliments, and he certainly welcomes somebody else helping him on the case. So, without hesitation, he decides to give this drug agent thing another chance, knowing full well he can quit anytime he wants to anyway. Or, at least, that's what he thinks.

"OK, Mike. I'll give it a try," Rico responds. "You want Edgar's contact information? Or do you already have it!"

"We're all set," Mike answer. "You go take care of your personal affairs and one of my agents will be in touch in the next few days. And, Rico, thank you. You're doing the right thing, for me, your country, and yourself."

Rico isn't so sure about that but, for the time being, he's still on the government payroll, still in the spy business, and, most importantly, it's on his terms. He feels good about that.

So, with the Edgar problem behind him, Rico concentrates on his pending merger. There's much to do. He has to get Pablo some financial information, hire a lawyer, and, when he receives the necessary information, review Pablo's properties. Rico is amazed at how the opportunity to make more money excites him. Maybe, at his core, he is more capitalist than drug agent after all.

In the meantime, Mike is busy, too. He re-connects with the agents assigned to follow Edgar Vegas and tells them about the latest development. Not surprisingly, the agency has had eyes and ears on Edgar the whole time and, despite his trepidations about it, Rico has never been acting alone. Mike is too careful for that.

"Change of plans," Mike says to the lead agent in charge of tailing Edgar, "Rico's getting cold feet. I can get him back into the game if we need to, but, in the meantime, Edgar is your baby. I want to know the name of everybody Mr. Vegas talks to, even his paperboy. I still feel he'll be in contact with somebody important, either directly or indirectly, before he gets on that plane to Mexico City."

The next day, unencumbered by agent duties, Rico forwards the information about his properties on to Pablo and, surprisingly, receives an immediate response. Pablo wants to meet the next day to discuss a deal. He's prepared to show Rico financial information, recent property sales in the area, and major customers. Also, he suggests that Rico put together a package of information as well.

The speed with which Pablo works is pretty shocking, and, so far at least, the guy seems to be working alone. Not so for Rico. He has asked two friends, one a broker and the other a lawyer, to look over everything he's given to Pablo. And also accompany him to the first meeting.

They arrive at the address given to them, an unimpressive, two-story office building just off Wilshire Boulevard, promptly at nine. Pablo's offices are located on the first floor, behind a door containing an opaque, frosted window with a small logo that says "Global Trading, Inc." Once inside, a dour, middle-aged woman escorts them into a small conference room with no windows. The furnishings are spartan but functional.

Pablo, dressed in chinos and an open-collar shirt, joins them five minutes later and seems quite disappointed that Rico isn't alone.

"Look," he says to the two men in suits accompanying Rico, "At this point, this is only a personal discussion between me and Mr. Lopez. It's far too early for you guys to be involved. I would appreciate it if you would wait out in the reception area while we discuss the framework of a deal. Or, better yet, why don't you go home and wait for Mr. Lopez to call you."

Rico immediately jumps in, "Pablo, hold on. I invited these men here because I don't feel comfortable making this decision on my own. This is my life's work and I want to make sure everything is in order before I sign. It's only normal on such an important transaction."

"Rico," Pablo responds in a tone of voice Rico hasn't heard before, "we are not just talking about a sale of properties here. We are talking about an ongoing relationship that will be very unfair, yes, but in your favor. The thought is that we will pool our assets, at some agreed-upon comparable price, create an LLC, with partnership interests equal to what we have brought into the deal, and then, I will offer you a very lucrative contract to manage all of the properties."

"Yes, but..." Rico begins.

"I haven't finished," Pablo interrupts impatiently. "The best part of the deal is that I'll bring in the necessary capital to grow our partnership and, with no additional investment on your part, we both benefit equally going forward. What could be fairer than that?"

Pablo pauses, looks at the other two men, then continues talking to Rico, "And, frankly, I'm not comfortable talking about any of this in front of these gentlemen. I hate to be blunt but either they leave or we have nothing more to discuss."

A very tense silence follows. Rico correctly understands that he's unwittingly triggered a deal-breaker condition right off the bat. He's either going to have to assess the framework of this deal on his own or walk away from it. But it doesn't take him long to decide. There's no way Rico is going to walk away from this kind of opportunity, especially here and now, at the very beginning of discussions.

"Guys, thanks for coming," he says to his two friends, "but you won't be needed today. I'll call you in a few days."

Rico doesn't see the small, wry smile that creeps onto Pablo's face, but the two others do and wonder about it. However, it's less a smile of victory than one of pride. Rico has passed his first test. There will be others, Pablo knows.

Once alone, the two men discuss everything in a much more calm and friendly manner. There isn't much to discuss, though. Pablo is offering him an incredible opportunity, with a salary higher than his current net cash flow, with a larger base of properties, and three times the number of customers.

Also, if he understands Pablo correctly, he'll have access to additional capital as other properties became available, without having to involve any banks, or pay any interest. He just has to return the capital when the properties are liquidated.

There's one hitch, though. Pablo wants voting control so he can approve whatever properties Rico identifies. Since it is mostly Pablo's money at risk anyway that seems reasonable to Rico, and he quickly agrees. They decide to try to finalize the deal within a week. The two men shake on it and Rico goes out of the office a very happy man.

Back home, with Maggie gone, there's nobody around with whom to share his joy. In fact, the house seems incredibly empty. Her departure has created a void in his life that for years before he'd hardly noticed. But, now that he has experienced life living with an excitable, and exciting, woman like Maggie, there's a noticeable emptiness.

So, instead of celebrating, Rico busies himself with paperwork. There are checks to process and bills to pay. He answers a few emails and one irate letter from the neighbor of one of his properties. When he finally gets around to checking his messages, he's surprised to find three, all from Teresa, all this morning, and all asking him to call as soon as possible.

"Rico," she says when he reaches her, "I just broke up with Carlos." There is a long pause, as she struggles to get her emotions under control. "It was kind of ugly," she finally continues. "Any chance I could get together with you to discuss it." Rico doesn't answer right away. He's processing what he just heard.

"I hate to bother you with this. But I don't know where else to turn," Teresa goes on, and, not unexpectedly, she starts to cry. "Everybody I know in this town, I met through Carlos," Teresa goes on. "And I don't really trust anybody enough to confide in them. I feel so alone."

Rico finds his voice. "Sure, Teresa. I'd be glad to meet. Where?" he says.

"Do you mind if I come over to your place?" she asks in a little girl voice Rico hasn't heard in decades. "I don't really want to go anywhere public. I'm a mess."

"Okay. When?" he replies.

"I'm on my way." Teresa says and hangs up.

When the doorbell rings, Rico isn't really ready for guests, especially Teresa. He had tried to tidy up a bit but his mind wasn't really into it. Too much to think about. He wasn't sure how he should take the news. He's glad, of course, that Teresa is done with Carlos, if that is truly the case. But Rico remembers all of the times Teresa broke up with him in the old days. As he recalls, she used to be fairly good at breaking up; and even better at making up.

Still, this is a different time, a different Teresa, and there is something in her voice he hasn't heard before. She seems frightened.

Rico opens the door to a wholly unexpected sight. Teresa's hair is disheveled. Her face is tear-stained and her mascara is running down her cheeks. There's a look of helplessness in her eyes that he has never seen before. She's a total mess but still, to him, a beautiful mess.

Teresa throws her arms around his neck and collapses into his arms, sobbing. He half-carries her over to the couch, lays her down as gently as he can, and caresses her face. She keeps crying, her chest heaving in and out as the tears flow uncontrollably. He just holds her without saying anything.

When she finally begins to calm down, Rico asks if she wants anything; a glass of water, perhaps. She declines, sitting up straighter on the couch and looking him directly in the eyes.

"That man is evil," she blurts out, "pure evil. Nothing he told me about himself was true."

Of course, Rico is not surprised, although he thinks of Carlos as more suave, pompous, and self-absorbed than someone truly evil. He's anxious to hear why Teresa has such strong negative feelings toward the guy.

"That man is a total fraud. He acts like such a big shot but somebody else is pulling his strings. I'm sure of it. I don't even think he owns the business he's so proud of, or the house you visited. He spends much of his time socializing with bad people," Teresa blurts out, "and, worst of all, he has a number of other girlfriends. I don't even know how many but a lot. I've heard he sometimes calls them his harem. I'm better than that."

Rico now begins to understand the intensity of Teresa's feelings. She's been misled, yes, but, even more maddening to her, she's been used, and embarrassed. Carlos took advantage of her naivety, then flaunted her beauty just to make him look good. Teresa added to his mask of respectability, nothing more. Welcome to L.A.

The more immediate problem for Rico, however, is how the breakup will affect his pending merger with Pablo. He cares for Teresa a lot, but he needs to protect himself, too. As soon as he can get Teresa calmed down, and on the way back to her apartment, he will need to call Pablo. It's probable that, with the breakup, his sweetheart deal will be over too.

Pablo answers on the first ring.

"Mr. Cerritos," Rico began, "I suppose you heard about the fight between Teresa and Carlos?"

"Yes," Pablo answers somewhat hesitantly.

"It looks like they may be breaking up," Rico says, "and I was wondering…"

"Whoa," Pablo replies. "I hadn't heard that they were breaking up. It's probably just a lover's spat. Right? I'm sure they'll patch it up."

"Sounds like more than that to me, and I'm curious about whether it will affect our deal?"

"Why would it?"

"Well, Carlos is a friend of yours," Rico clarifies.

"Listen, Rico. I've known Carlos for some time now. He has a weakness for pretty women," Pablo went on. "He likes to collect them, romance them, and dump them. Not my style, certainly. Probably not yours either, I dare say. And I'm not surprised your Teresa doesn't want to be part of his collection anymore. I respect her for that. But why should that concern us, or affect our relationship in any way?"

"Well," Rico hesitantly begins, "we met through Teresa and Carlos."

"I know," Pablo interrupts, "but that didn't have anything to do with why I wanted to work with you. In fact, meeting you through Carlos was probably a negative at first. But you were able to overcome that pretty quickly the other night. Actually, I've been looking for a property manager like you for some time. I liked you immediately and I just felt that you were the guy. It had nothing to do with Carlos, or Teresa, for that matter."

"Glad to hear that," Rico said.

"Well, then, let's see how everything works out between Carlos and Teresa, but from afar," Pablo goes on. "Frankly, I hope she has nothing further to do with the guy. In the meantime, however, let's get our deal done and get to work. There's a property I want you to look at right away."

Rico is, of course, pleased with Pablo's response. In fact, the more he works on the paperwork for the deal, the more excited he gets about it. After reviewing everything, his advisors share his enthusiasm for the deal. They portray it as a "win-win," with Rico enjoying both sides of the win.

Chapter 12

Several days have passed since Rico last talked to Mike, a welcome reprieve from the pressures of being a part-time drug agent. Edgar hasn't even entered Rico's mind, and that's a good thing. *Who wants to think about Edgar unless it is absolutely necessary?*

Then the phone rings and Mike's voice brings him back to reality. "I think we've got something," Mike says breathlessly. "Can you come over to the office right away?"

"Can't you just tell me over the phone?" Rico asks. He has a meeting soon with his lawyers and doesn't want to slow the merger process down, even if it's only for a few hours.

"This is not the kind of news I can deliver over the phone," Mike says with a slightly exasperated tone. There's an audible sigh and Rico can even picture Mike's eyes roll, something he's seen Mike do hundreds of times. *These Feds can be so dramatic*, Rico thinks.

"Okay. Be right over," he replies.

Mike meets Rico in the parking lot, a first, then escorts him right past the reception desk, and into the main conference room. The other agents are already there, looking over some grainy photos taken by the two-man surveillance team.

"Edgar finally varied from his routine," Mike begins. "He went to this office building off Wilshire Boulevard, was in there for about thirty minutes, and came out carrying what looks like a locked canvas courier bag."

One of the other agents takes over the narrative from there, "We think this is the pick-up we've been waiting for, but we can't be sure. There are three businesses in the building but none that have been on our radar before. We're doing a search of the names of the owners as I speak. Edgar could have just picked up the bag in the lobby for all we know. But whoever gave it to him is probably the guy we want."

Mike jumps back in, "So, Rico, we know Edgar is booked on a flight to Mexico City day after tomorrow. We were hoping that you might 'accidentally' bump into him at the gym tomorrow and ask him about it."

Mike stops talking because he sees Rico is no longer listening. Instead, the newly-minted agent is looking closer at the surveillance photos.

"Where did you say this building was?" Rico asked.

"Off Wilshire."

"On Manning Avenue?"

"Yes, I think so. I have the address here in the file. Why do you ask?" the agent replies.

Rico looks Mike in the eye and says, "Because I think I know who your drug lord is."

Nobody says anything for a second. Finally, Mike responds, "How can you possibly know that?"

"Because he asked me to go into business with him."

Rico can't be sure, of course. But the building in the photo looks very much like the one that houses Pablo Cerritos' office, the one off Wilshire where Rico went to talk to Pablo about buying his company. He can't recall the name of Pablo's business offhand but it's something like Global Trading, Inc., which, upon closer inspection, is one of the names shown on the small sign outside the building.

As Rico thinks about it, all of the pieces of the puzzle fit. Pablo's import/export business. His wealth. The warehouses Pablo owns and his desire to own more. The access to free capital. The travel to cities in countries well-established in the drug business. And, above all, the deal Pablo wants to make with Rico, the one too good to pass up. With unlimited cash to make other deals.

The only thing that doesn't fit is Pablo himself.

The stereotypical gang boss is like Escobar and El Chapo, bigger than life characters with even bigger egos. Flashy, charismatic, and possessed of a sociopathic capacity for violence.

But Pablo? He is so understated and kind, a gentleman, a businessman, and, yet, he does have a steely underbelly, which Rico has seen only once or twice. But, could he kill?

Mike just continues to stare at Rico, probably not sure what to believe.

He ponders the situation. *Is it really possible Rico was cozying up to the boss man himself while we tried to get him close to a lowly courier?* That's way too weird to be believed, and, bottom line, Mike doesn't believe it.

More probable is that Rico was wired into the cartel all along, which, if true, makes Rico way more dangerous than he seems. What if the woman who recommended Rico to Mike in the first place was close to the cartel as well, and was just trying to get Rico embedded? That would explain Mike's frustrating lack of success so far, but, still, it's hard to believe that Rico could be that duplicitous.

Meanwhile, Rico has begun to weigh the fallout from the realization that Pablo might be the cartel leader. *Is Teresa involved in some way? And what about his merger with Pablo? That would be the first casualty, of course, and what bad luck that would be for Rico if his patron saint turns out to be a really bad guy.*

"What's his name?" Mike asks.

"Pablo Cerritos."

"Never heard of him."

"Well, that is kind of the point, isn't it?" says Rico. "Obviously, this guy works hard to make sure you don't know who he is. Still, a lot of signs point toward him."

Mike stares at his so-called agent skeptically, "OK. What signs? Tell me everything you know about this guy."

So, Rico starts with Teresa and her relationship with Carlos and their dinner together at Pablo's house. He describes Pablo, what he learned about his business, his travels, his lifestyle. He tells Mike about the deal that Pablo has offered him and how disappointed he is that it will now go away.

As Rico talks, Mike's suspicions about him subside. Instead, a new opportunity presents itself. "Wait a minute," Mike says. "Why does it have to go away?"

Rico is visibly confused. *Did Mike misunderstand what he just said?* But Mike's mind is spinning. He turns to one of the agents sitting at the table.

"Ben, you were involved in the Mendocino case, right?"

"Yes," was the reply.

"Didn't you put an agent underground who made a business deal with the gang leader?"

"Yes," again.

"Tell me how that worked," Mike asks.

Ben looks at Rico uncomfortably. Like Mike, he's not sure the property manager can be trusted. If Rico isn't already affiliated with the Batista Cartel, he's about to be through his merger with Pablo's business, and the spoils of that deal far outweigh anything they can offer.

"He's one of us, for God's sake." Mike goes on, reading the agent's mind. "If we're going to make this whole thing work, he has to know everything we know."

Obviously, Mike has decided to trust Rico.

"OK," Ben starts slowly, "We created a legal shell company, got a judge to bless it, then, sold it to the Mendocino family. Our agent was the fictitious head of the company who worked directly with one of the Mendocino brothers. He gathered enough information in a few months to put the whole family behind bars."

"What happened to the company?" Mike asks.

Ben thinks a minute, then replies, "We liquidated it. Surprisingly, the company made a small profit in the few months we ran it. We treated the profits as if they were confiscated goods."

Mike goes on, "How does that apply to this situation?"

Ben answers, "I'm not sure, Mike. I think Rico could sell his properties into the merged company controlled by both him, and what was the other guy's name, Pedro?"

"No, Pablo Cerritos," Rico clarifies.

Ben goes on, "Anyway, we could keep a second set of books so that, after we successfully arrest Mr. Cerritos, if he is the guy, Rico would get his original properties back plus the net profit the properties had earned while the operation was underway. The rest of the properties and profits would be booked as confiscated goods."

"Sound OK to you, Rico?"

Rico is surprised by the question. He responds, "I'm not ready to talk about that. Tell me why I should want to go ahead with this deal at all. I've identified the guy who might be a cartel head here in the States; you can now follow him, gather evidence to your heart's content, and, then, even arrest him; while I go on my happy way with the properties I still own, living off the same income I've always enjoyed. Clean, simple, and, at least for me, entirely risk-free."

"Well, not entirely," Mike counters. "How long do you think it will take the cartel to figure out your connection to the arrest? And how long before they go after your properties? Or you? You need us on your side, Rico. That's just the way it is, partner." He smiles mockingly.

Rico blanches. Mike has a unique way of making him feel uncomfortable about any choice but the one Mike is promoting. But Rico knows from experience that Mike will say or do anything to get what he wants. And right now, Mike wants Rico to take an enormous personal risk by becoming an informant for the Feds, against Pablo Cerritos.

"And you think I'll be safer after I trick Pablo?" Rico counters.

"I think you'll be safer when we dismantle the whole Batista distribution network in the United States, and jail its main players," Mike says. "There will be nobody left to go after you. The Mexicans will be too busy trying to find somebody else to move their drugs. And there won't be any American cartel members left who care about avenging Pablo's arrest. They all will be positioning themselves to go undercover or fill the vacuum."

Rico can't argue with Mike's logic but he isn't sure how his deal with Pablo would increase the DEA's chances to take out the whole Batista U.S. operation.

Mike evidently senses Rico's concern. He goes on, "And having you on the inside is critical to building the evidence we need, not only to help us convict Pablo but, also, to get rid of his cohorts."

Rico wonders whether Carlos is one of Pablo's cohorts. Taking that guy out might be worth the risk all by itself.

Mike continues, "Just knowing who the leader is doesn't count for much if we lack the evidence to convict him. If you quit now, Rico, we'll have to find some other way to get Pablo. We could raid his office but I doubt he's stupid enough to have anything of value there. We could pick up everybody around him and squeeze them. That's worked some in the past. But the most effective plan has always been to place an agent inside his organization, just like we are now blessed to be able to do with you."

Mike pauses again. "Through a lot of luck, and some skill on your part, we have you perfectly positioned," he goes on. "When you originally said you would work with us, what was your goal? To get the bad guys, right? Well, together, we have a chance to get one of the baddest of them all, and his bad buddies to boot. If you bail on us now, we have to start building our case all over again. Just think of the number of young kids that'll die from drug overdoses in the meantime."

The room goes silent. Rico weighs his options. He's very reluctant to put himself at further risk. He could still go back to his old life and probably die an old man, with a nice nest egg to show for it.

"You became an agent for what reason?" Mike makes his final plea. "For the money? I don't think so. The excitement? perhaps. To give your life purpose? To stretch yourself? To do something heroic and worthwhile? Well, all of that is here, right before you."

Mike steps closer to Rico, "I can't guarantee you this operation will be a success. I can't guarantee you that you'll be honored for what you do. But I can guarantee you that, if we get this guy, ten years from now you'll wake up in the middle of the night, smiling at the ceiling, because you'll know, in your heart, that your life made a difference."

"Okay. Okay. Anything to get you to stop preaching at me," Rico says. "What do you want me to do?"

Chapter 13

It has been a very difficult week for Rico. What was a labor of love in the beginning, as he tried to put his own life-changing deal together, has now become something quite different. Every contract detail, every move he makes, every negotiation point he argues, is fraught with peril. It's no longer just a matter of money. There's much more at stake.

Rico meets with Pablo twice during the week and continues to be impressed with the man's professionalism and energy. He looks for signs of the dangerous man Pablo must be, but sees no evidence of anything other than an authentic desire to get a deal done.

In fact, the more Rico works with Pablo, the more he begins to doubt that he's actually the cartel leader he, and the Feds, have suspicioned he is. Pablo is smart and tough in his negotiations, yes, but always the gentleman. He knows just when to apply pressure and when to back off. He's patient and detail-oriented. His advisors, now that he has hired some, seem legitimate.

Mike looks up the ownership of Global Trading, Inc. It belongs to a trust that seems legit as well, but also obscures the identity of the real owner. He rechecked the address of the building Edgar visited and it is, indeed, the one where Rico met with Pablo the first time. So, either that's an amazing coincidence, or something else.

But, in Rico's mind there's still a chance that Pablo is clean, and he really wants to believe that.

With the DEA lawyers involved behind the scenes, the negotiations are considerably more complicated for Rico than if he was doing the deal on his own. They want him to form his own trust rather than put the ownership directly under his own name. They draw up the trust papers so that it will be simple for Rico to get his properties back once the arrests are made. Then, they plan to dissolve the trust entirely, making it difficult for anybody to trace Rico's involvement.

Pablo has no objection to the use of a trust. In fact, he tells Rico he's doing the same thing. They thought about calling the partnership RIPA

Investors, using the first two letters of their first names but, because they now have two trusts as owners, they decide on Double T Investors. Surprisingly, that name is available.

When the papers are finally drawn up to both parties' satisfaction, Pablo and Rico meet at a restaurant to have a celebratory signing dinner. After dinner, with the deal inked and the advisors dismissed, the two partners sit alone, a bottle of Silver Oak Cabernet between them, and talk about the successful days that their partnership will enjoy in the days ahead.

Pablo then discloses the details on the properties he wants to buy, two warehouses he sometimes uses to store his goods. He thinks that, given how important his business is to the owners, they'll entertain a low offer.

There is a warmth to the discussion that makes Rico uneasy. He can't let his guard down no matter how friendly Pablo gets. There's a big difference between being a drug agent and a drug informant. One gets killed more than the other one, for instance.

Still, as they talk, Rico gets with the program. He acts every bit the enthusiastic partner he had planned to be before Pablo came under suspicion. He has had a rapport with Pablo ever since they met and he sees no reason to change that at this point. He just has to be more cautious.

Back home, with the glow of the wine still warming him, Rico decides to call Teresa. Thankfully, she's feeling much better, and profusely thanks Rico for the sympathetic ear he gave her a few nights before. Carlos has called several times, she says, but she's not taking his calls.

More importantly for Rico, she says that, with time to think about it, she has decided the relationship is over and she has no regrets. She's ready to get on with her life.

I hope I am part of it, Rico thinks but doesn't voice. He needs to be a sympathetic ear to Teresa for a little bit longer before disclosing his true intentions, which aren't really clear to him anyway.

Ironically, the next day he receives a call from Maggie. She's been rethinking things and, although she doesn't want to move back in, she wonders if they might grab a drink some time.

Rico knows that the best thing would probably be to let bygones be bygones, especially with Teresa potentially back in the picture, but something won't let him do that. He misses the passionate nights he once spent with Maggie and, although he feels nothing resembling love toward her at this point, he still wants a woman in his life, at least until his feelings toward Teresa become clearer.

So, Rico makes a date with Maggie for Saturday night.

Instead of just a drink, however, he invites her to have dinner at, what was once, their favorite Italian restaurant, *Sandini's*. Nothing fancy about the place but it oozes with good memories for both of them. If their passion is to be rekindled, *Sandini's* is the place to do it.

In the meantime, Rico busies himself with work. Given all that he was required to do to complete the merger, his paper work is now more up-to-date than it has been in years.

But Rico has fallen behind in maintenance. He calls his team, his handyman, plumber, and carpenter, with assignments for the coming week. Then, he gets in touch with a couple of delinquent renters, encouraging them to pay by the end of the week. He even squeezes out time to drop by his apartment buildings, talk with some of the people who live there, and do the periodic inspections that are so crucial to his business.

The bulk of his work, however, involves acquainting himself with the new properties that are now part of his portfolio. Pablo has given Rico full authority to review the maintenance contracts in place and deal with them as he sees fit. He plans to terminate most of them, because their prices are higher than they should be. He can just add to the workloads of his current contractors, pay them a little more, and still save money in the process.

For two days, Rico visits Pablo's various properties, which surprisingly need a lot of work. Pablo's attention must have been elsewhere and, wearing his agent hat, Rico thinks he knows where. The drug business is infinitely more profitable than the warehouse business.

Still, for the time being, when Rico visits Pablo's warehouses he doesn't look too closely at what's stored there for fear he will discover something he has to address. Ignorance is bliss in the short term and, more importantly, can be helpful to the relationship he wants to build with Pablo.

Mike would probably agree with that. What is stored in Pablo's warehouses is a conversation Rico needs to have but he has to control when and how that conversation will take place.

The dinner with Maggie goes much better than Rico could have ever imagined. Absence does make the heart grow fonder, or at least Maggie makes it seem that way. She's all over Rico, like she had been at the beginning of their relationship, and, for a few hours at least, he doesn't think of Teresa at all.

They end up back at Rico's place for a nightcap, which turns into a midnight swim in his small pool, then, a few hours of sleep between bursts of passion, topped off by bacon and eggs at 9:00 am the next morning.

Maggie never asks about Rico's work, which surprises him a little. Maybe she's beginning to appreciate the man he is rather than the one he concocted for her. Maybe she's choosing Rico Lopez over James Bond, which would be a bit surprising, to say the least.

After breakfast, Maggie leaves for work, tossing a cryptic, "see you later" over her shoulder. Rico is left to wonder whether she will just show up after work, bags in hand, or whether she just couldn't think of anything else to say.

Still, Rico finds himself hoping for the former rather than the latter. Then, he has second thoughts, as the prospect of a relationship with Teresa creeps back into his head. Romance sure can get complicated at times.

The next day, Sunday, Pablo calls to ask about Rico's tours of his new properties. Rico is careful not to bring up anything that might raise concerns for Pablo. But he did notice, during due diligence, that Pablo's own business, Global Trading, represents almost 20% of the revenues Pablo is bringing to the table. He asks Pablo about it.

"Frankly," Pablo answers, "a big reason I had my warehouses in the first place was to accommodate the unique requirements of Global. I expect our storage needs to grow and, hopefully, the new warehouses we buy and even some of the warehouse space you brought to the table will go toward that increasing need. I don't expect Global to use more than 15% or 20% of our overall space but I do want to keep some extra space in one or two of our warehouses available for emergencies. Of course, Global will pay for that space, even if it's empty, plus a premium for lost opportunity cost. I hope you don't have a problem with that."

"Of course not," Rico replies, as if he had a choice. "But we need to keep everything with Global on an arms-length basis. I have to be free to establish pricing without undue pressure from you or anybody else."

"You got it," Pablo says and they go on to discuss other less-controversial elements of their relationship. Still, it's clear to Rico that the accommodations Pablo asks for are things that might benefit the cartel if, in fact, Pablo is running it. Not only will they be able to move shipments in and out quickly but the increasing revenues from Global would help them launder money. Mike might be getting his evidence even quicker than he imagined.

At the end of their conversation, Pablo asks Rico to join him for dinner on Tuesday night. He says that his wife will be preparing a chicken Kiev dish that is her specialty and, given that she missed Rico last time, she's really looking forward to finally meeting him this time.

"Will you be bringing Teresa?" Pablo asks. He sees the hesitation on Rico's face. "Or do you want me to invite her?" Rico could have kissed Pablo. What an elegant solution to an indelicate situation.

"Yes, please do," he says, "I would love to see her again. Carlos won't be there, too, will he?"

"No. Now that would be awkward, wouldn't it?" Pablo says with a wink. "It will just be the four of us. Unless, of course, you're bringing someone."

"No. That would be awkward, wouldn't it?" They both laugh.

Under normal circumstances, Rico would really be looking forward to dinner with Pablo, and especially Teresa, but these are hardly normal circumstances. Any time spent with somebody as powerful as Pablo carries a risk, but that risk is far greater now that Rico is essentially undercover.

Rico not only has to be careful about what he says at dinner but, also, to remember whatever Pablo says, so he can report everything back to Mike. To make that easier, Mike promises to be waiting back at Rico's house to debrief Rico right away,

But no martinis tonight, Rico decides.

As it turns out, the decision is not Rico's. As before, Pablo has already mixed martinis for both of them and he serves Rico a healthy one, with olives, right when he arrives.

As Pablo sets the glasses down, the two exchange pleasantries like old friends. Rico talks a little bit about the business and, then, Pablo begins to tell Rico about the first time he met his wife, Alicia.

The story is touching, with Pablo falling for Alicia immediately and, then, despite very little encouragement from her, spending months wooing her with flowers and presents. As Pablo tells the story he becomes animated, like a little kid, and very proud of what he had to do to land her. "The single biggest accomplishment of my life," he calls it.

When Alicia finally enters, it's easy to see why. She's a naturally beautiful woman with a friendly, flirtatious manner that belies her age. She rushes immediately over to Rico and, despite having just met him, gives him a big hug.

She talks about how much Pablo loves Rico, how he respects Rico's business acumen, and how anxious she has been to meet him. She pooh-pooh's the story Pablo has been telling, saying that she fell for Pablo right away but hid that from him because, as she put it, "Ladies have to do what ladies have to do."

Rico is a little surprised that Alicia doesn't appear to be Hispanic. She is pale, blonde with freckles on her face and shoulders that she doesn't bother to hide. If Rico were to guess, he would think she was Scandinavian but, of course, he can't be sure of that.

He knows one thing, though. Although Pablo and Alicia are both tall and slender, they are quite a mismatch, not only color-wise but also personality-wise. He talks slowly and carefully, weighing each word and phrase. Alicia's words burst out of her mouth staccato-like, as if each word is eager to pass the one before. Rico is both entertained and entranced, forgetting for a second that he's there on agency business.

When Rico eventually thinks to look down at his drink, it is only half-full. *Oh-oh*, he thinks. *That vodka didn't just evaporate. He better be careful.*

Teresa arrives a little after Rico and greets him like an old friend, which, of course, he is, if you can say that about an ex-wife. She also greets Pablo as if he is an old friend, which, given what Rico now knows about Pablo, worries him some. Drug lords don't normally have old friends.

Teresa immediately compliments Pablo on the decorating of his house but, as is Pablo's manner, he takes no credit. "All Alicia," he said. "She calls it Mediterranean with a touch of Asian tossed in for spice."

"Well, it is beautiful," Teresa says. Then, she repeats the compliment when Alicia arrives. That starts a conversation about different pieces Alicia has acquired, when she got them, and from where.

Rico and Pablo just listen quietly and nurse their drinks, smiling conspiratorially at each other as the women babble on about things that interest the two guys not at all.

After a while, Pablo asks Rico if he wants another one. When Rico politely declines, Pablo heads to the bar to open a bottle of wine, with Rico close behind.

"Where did you grow up?" Rico asks.

"Guadalajara. Wrong side of the tracks," Pablo answers, "You?"

"Mexico City. Wrong side of the tracks as well. Teresa and I were married there. Divorced within a year or so."

"That's right. I remember now. Carlos told me," Pablo said. "Why would you break up with somebody who looks like that? Are you crazy?"

"Young and crazy. I wanted to try to make it in the States and I thought she would be a liability."

"Some liability."

"Well, you know. I'm not proud of my thinking back then, on Teresa and a lot of other things. I'm curious, Pablo. How did you get to the States?" Rico asks, trying to guide the conversation back away from him.

"Went to school in Berkeley, on a football scholarship."

"Really? How did you manage that?"

"I played soccer in Guadalajara and my senior year I discovered I could kick field goals. Missed only one the whole year. Missed quite a few more in college, though. I was a little distracted," Pablo chuckles. "But I was good enough to get a full ride and, more importantly, keep it."

"How did you get into the import/export business?" Rico asks innocently.

"Why do you ask?" Pablo replies, a sharp tone edging into his voice for the first time.

Rico wonders if the conversation is drifting too close to Pablo's drug activities. Is he over-probing? Has the martini made him careless? Or is Pablo testing him, something Mike had warned Rico about earlier.

Whatever it is, Rico detects a slight chill in the air all of a sudden.

But, then, Pablo gives him a big smile.

"Just curious," Rico answers.

Pablo calls to his wife in the next room, "Is dinner about ready, dear?"

Chapter 14

Mike doesn't disappoint. When Rico opens his front door, and turns on the light, there Mike sits, one leg up, sprawled on Rico's living room couch, his face filled with curiosity. "How did it go," he asks right off the bat.

"It was a very pleasant evening," Rico says. "I found out Pablo grew up in Guadalajara, went to Cal where he played football, and is married to a wonderful and charming wife named Alicia. Is that helpful?"

"Yeah. Sure. How did he get into the import/export business?"

"He wasn't very forthcoming on that."

"Do you think his business is just a front that allows him to move drugs in and out of the country?"

"I don't know."

Mike pauses, then looks Rico right in the eye, saying, "Listen, Rico, we don't have time for idle chit chat. Edgar leaves for Mexico City in about ten days. We have to decide if we're going to have our agents raid that meeting, arrest whatever Mexican gang members are there, and put pressure on the whole operation."

"Or what?" Rico asks.

"Well, if we're one hundred per cent convinced Pablo is the head guy in the States, we'll just bug the meeting in Mexico City, not raid it," Mike continues. "Then, that'll give you a few more days to gather whatever evidence on Pablo you can. In the meantime, we'll get ready to sweep up the Batista gang in Mexico City, at the same time we pick up Pablo and his cohorts here."

Mike pauses again, probably weighing how much more he should tell Rico.

"Your judgement on Pablo is critical," Mike goes on. "The only thing we have to link Pablo with the Batista gang is the visit by Edgar to his office building a week or so ago. We can't arrest somebody based on that. We need more. Can you get us more?"

"I have an idea," Rico offers. "I now have access to all of Pablo's warehouses and can disarm the alarms and cameras."

"Yes. Where are you going with this?"

"What if we get some drug-sniffing dogs in there, late at night, and see what we can find?"

"Good idea," Mike responds. "Now you're thinking like an agent. We need a few days to get a qualified dog team here. How about we do it on Wednesday night?"

"Great," Rico answers.

The next few days Rico pays particular attention to the shipments in and out of Pablo's warehouses. He's surprised at the volume, more leaving than coming. By Wednesday, the warehouses are only about three-quarters full, something Rico has never seen before.

Perhaps it's a seasonal thing, Rico thinks, but he's surprised at how quickly it's happened. Shipments are only staying in the warehouses for a week or two, as opposed to several months. Maybe there's a reason but Rico is suspicious.

The undercover operation on Wednesday night goes off without a hitch. The two-dog team arrives at the first warehouse a little after midnight and leaves the last warehouse just after 3:00 a.m.

The only problem is that the dogs find no drugs.

"They aren't fool-proof," Mike says when the team gathers back at the office, "but it isn't very often that, when we suspect something, the dogs find nothing. If I had to guess, and I probably do, I would think that Pablo is using these warehouses for something other than transporting drugs. Which puts us back at square one."

"He could just be using your business to launder money, Rico," one of the other agents said. "We will see how fast he pumps cash in. That will tell us a lot."

"Or he could have kept a warehouse or two out of the deal," another agent posits, "until he trusts you more. Or maybe he moved his drugs out into reserve space while he sizes you up."

Rico isn't sure what to think. It's clear that some goods, maybe not narcotics but something else, has moved out of the warehouses. But nothing in Pablo's behavior or demeanor suggests he is a drug lord. In fact, just the opposite.

Later, Rico is surprised by a call from Pablo asking him to come by the Global offices that very afternoon. There are some things in the daily cash flows that concern him and he wants to talk about them.

Maybe Pablo has seen the same outgoing shipments that Rico did earlier. If so, that would be some impressive forensic work for a guy supposedly disinterested in the business,

When Rico arrives, the small parking lot in front of the Global office building is completely full and Rico has to park a couple of blocks away. When he finally reaches the entrance, he is shocked to run into Carlos Silva coming out, looking as natty as ever. *What the hell is he doing here?* Rico thinks.

Carlos greets Rico warmly, saying nothing about Teresa or their breakup. He talks, instead, about Rico's partnership with Pablo, which seems to please Carlos no end. In fact, Rico is surprised by how much Carlos knows about the deal. It seems obvious, all of a sudden, that Carlos and Pablo are more than just casual friends, which is a bit worrisome.

Then, Carlos gets into his car and leaves.

Pablo meets Rico at the door and leads him into the same conference room where the two negotiated their deal a few weeks before. When they are comfortably seated, Rico asks about Carlos.

"I see Carlos was here visiting you, Pablo," he says.

"No. I haven't seen Carlos in days," Pablo surprisingly answers. "Why? Did you run into him?"

"Yes. Just outside."

"He must be back from Mexico. I understand he went there to forget Teresa, with the help of several of the girls he keeps down there."

Pablo notices the puzzled look on Rico's face and goes on, "Oh, I guess you don't know. Carlos' transportation company is located in this building as well. That's how I met him, in fact. I offered him a sweetheart deal on rent. We come and go here all the time, but seldom run into each other. In fact, most of our interactions these days are social, way away from here."

"I'm surprised you're so close to Carlos."

"He certainly is an acquired taste but he's always been straight with me. Or, at least, I think he has. But, enough about Carlos. Why do you think we're losing business all of a sudden? I notice almost all of my old warehouses are way under capacity."

"I could ask you the same thing," Rico counters, "Remember, I just got into your part of the business."

"Touché. I just wondered if some of the clients who pulled inventory out in the last few days might have said something to you."

"I doubt that they even know how to reach me," Rico responds.

"Then, you better get in touch with them, right? We can't live very long with warehouses half-full," Pablo says, the edge back in his voice. Every so often he shows a little hint of temper, making Rico wonder.

Still, on his way back to his car, Rico is almost giddy. First, a drug lord, with millions pouring in, would not care so passionately about the cash flow of a small warehouse business. But, more importantly, if Carlos had his business in the same building, what if Edgar picked up the courier bag from Carlos, not Pablo? What if Carlos is the real drug lord? That makes a lot more sense to Rico.

Once he reaches home, Rico ignores the five messages on his voice mail and calls Mike first.

"Hello," Mike's voice sounds drowsy. Rico then remembers that they were up most of the night before and Mike may have been napping, something Rico wishes he had done. But Rico isn't really tired, probably because he's still running on the adrenaline created by the news about Carlos.

"This is Rico. I have what I consider great news. Pablo might not be the drug lord in the U.S. after all. It might be a guy named Carlos Silva who has an office in the same building."

Mike answers more quickly than expected, obviously wide-awake now, "Why is that good news? We have you on deep cover with Pablo Cerritos. He trusts you. You are his partner, for God's sake. And we're perfectly positioned to gather the evidence that will break up the cartel once and for all. Now you tell me this? Who is Carlos Silva anyway? And why should I care?"

Rico had not looked at it that way. He was so pleased that Pablo might not be a cartel boss that he lost sight of how Mike might see things. Not only does Rico not have a relationship with Carlos, the odds are high that Carlos actually dislikes Rico.

"Besides, I wouldn't discard Pablo so quickly," Mike goes on. "Why is he in the import/export business? Where does he get all the cash he needs to grow your business? Why does he need so much warehouse space? I would say, at this point, he's still more of a suspect than this Carlos Silva guy. But, believe me, we'll check this new guy out and see. In the meantime, you stay close to Pablo. He's still our best bet to end this thing quickly and quietly."

Rico hangs up, completely deflated. All of a sudden, the exhaustion he should have felt hours ago hits him. He can't even keep his eyes open long enough to check his voice mail. He just barely makes it to bed.

It may have been a good thing. The messages are all from Maggie, each progressively more heated. It is Deja vu all over again. After a wonderful night of love-making, Rico has once again neglected to call Maggie back right away. The first time it was a strategic move on his part, albeit one that backfired. This time, she just slipped his mind.

Rico's world is getting more complicated, even as he sleeps.

The next morning, he's awakened by a phone call from Mike, who had obviously spent a good part of the night mulling over the new information Rico had provided. "OK, sleepyhead," he says, "I have one of our best men tailing Carlos. The other two guys we need to watch are in your job jar," he said.

"What other two guys?"

"Pablo, of course, and Edgar."

Rico is surprised to hear Edgar's name thrown back into the mix. *Now that they have Pablo and/or Carlos in their crosshairs, why do they need Edgar? Hasn't he provided all of the intel they were going to get out of him?*

"What do you want me to do with Edgar?" Rico asks.

"Well," Mike says slowly, "His trip to Mexico is now only a few days away. And Edgar is still the only one here in the States that we know for sure is affiliated with the Batista gang. Maybe you could run into him at the gym, chat him up and see what you can learn?"

"Just chat him up? Really?" Rico replies.

"Look," Mike goes on, "It's now clear that we're not going to have anything actionable here before Edgar leaves. With the introduction of Carlos Silva into the mix, things are murkier than ever. That makes Edgar's trip the most important thing we have going."

"I couldn't agree more."

"I think we need to know what's in that courier bag," Mike continues, "I have a plan but it involves somebody being on that plane with Edgar. And, for reasons I'd rather not talk about on the phone, I'm thinking that somebody should be you."

"Oh, great," Rico groans. "Like I have nothing else to do."

Mike pauses, then, goes on, "Rico, I think you need to be more thoroughly briefed. Can you come by the office tomorrow around 11 am? You need to know what the rest of us know."

"That would be a first," Rico replies. Then, he says, yes, of course he will do whatever Mike wants. After he hangs up, he thinks, *What in the world did I get myself into now?* Being in partnership with a drug lord is one thing. Being the point man on a pivotal operation, one that could turn violent, is quite another. Rico needs answers and he sure hopes the meeting the next day will provide them.

Then, his mind turns to Maggie. It will take tact and cunning to do what Mike wants but it might take even more for him to turn Maggie around at this point. Rico briefly wonders whether she's worth the effort but then, remembering the recent night they spent together, he reaches for the phone.

"Hello. This is Maggie. Speak your piece at the tone."

Rico keeps his message brief. He will be at the Pancake House near her house at 9 am tomorrow and would love to see her there to explain himself.

There's one little problem Rico realizes as he hangs up. He isn't sure how he can explain himself, for the second time in a few weeks, and make her believe him. One thing is clear, though. The truth won't work.

Chapter 15

Rico is up early the next day, anxious to get on with things. Unfortunately, nobody else is so eager. Edgar doesn't show up at the gym and Maggie isn't at the Pancake House. The best laid plans, as they say.

It's probably just as well, Rico thinks. He has no idea what to say to either of them, anyway.

The rest of the morning, Rico busies himself with paperwork, mostly related to his new partnership with Pablo. Having twice the number of properties to watch over seems to generate four times the work, something he had not expected. But, at least, that partnership is paying some dividends.

His partnership with Mike is another matter altogether. The pay isn't much, the thrill of helping America catch the bad guys has worn off and, above all, with Maggie gone, he has nobody to brag to when something goes well. Mike certainly isn't going to fill that void.

Rico arrives at the DEA offices promptly at 11 am, dead-set against going to Mexico City, no matter what arguments Mike might make. *There is a limit to what he can, or will, do for the agency. And, being undercover, stalking, and, then, tricking a homicidal thug, is way over that limit.* At least, those are Rico's thoughts as he waits in the conference room for Mike.

But Mike doesn't show up. Instead, the lovely woman who once escorted him to his safe house walks in. *What was her name again?* Rico thinks. *Was it Caroline? um…Pendleton? or Pendley?*

"Mr. Lopez," she says, "So delighted to see you again," extending her hand. Rico is ready for the strong grip this time.

"Ms. Pendley, the pleasure is all mine," Rico says warily; not only because he isn't 100% sure it is her last name, but also because he's well aware of the role Caroline played in the scam perpetrated on him so many months earlier. Her looks and seductive manner were disconcerting to Rico then, and even more so now.

"Please, follow me," she says, turning on her high heels to leave the conference room. Like the puppy dog that he is at times, Rico falls in behind her.

They walk through a bank of cubicles, mostly unoccupied, and down a long corridor to a door having only one prominent feature: a finger-print detecting lock. Caroline puts her thumb onto the face of the lock and the door clicks open immediately.

The room behind it is quite large and bathed in a pale, blue light. There are several agents in the room, sitting at desks, peering at computer screens, looking like blue men from another planet. None look up or even acknowledge their presence.

At the back of the room are two huge, back-lit, diagrammed charts hanging on a wall, with photos of Hispanic faces scattered around on them. One has a lot of photos on it and the other just a few photos. Rico recognizes Edgar's face just below a silhouetted face with a question mark in the middle of it. He sees that the first diagram is marked "Mexico" and the second, "United States."

Rico also notices that, on another wall, is a map of the western states of the U.S. and Mexico, all aglow, in luminescent greens, reds, and yellows. Certain areas of the map stand out because of all the electronic pins that are posted there. *Do they represent targets? Or victims?*

Both charts are beautiful but Rico suspects the statistics they portray are less so.

Caroline waves her hand in the direction of the charts, dismissing them for now. "We will get to those shortly. In the meantime, I want you to meet one of our very important, behind-the-scenes support people."

"Rico, meet Jim Adams," she says to Rico. "Our lead data guy." Then, she turns to Jim, "Rico is one of our field agents. He's never been in this room before and it would be helpful if you could outline what you do here and why."

"Sure. Be glad to," Jim answers. "This room is command central for our battle against the Mexican drug gang known as Batista. I understand you have had some interactions with them. There are similar rooms throughout the building that target other gangs. We like to post the data from computer reports, news items, wiretaps, and any other intel that flows into this room to keep a continuous visual record of how we're doing. As you can imagine, the gangs are recruiting constantly and changing methods, distribution channels, even product. The more we can keep up-to-date on who they are and what they're doing, the better decisions we can make. Any questions so far?"

"No," Rico says. He's surprised and impressed with the sophistication of the operation. He really had the impression up until now that Mike and his cohorts were operating mostly by the seat of their pants. Rico certainly knows he was, but to see the actual resources dedicated to help him do his job is pretty humbling.

"OK," Jim goes on. "We don't graphically display everything. Over there are computers dedicated to our current organization, with backgrounds on our field agents, and current assignments. That information, of course, is not accessible outside this room and I'm not at liberty to show any of it to you now. However, everything we have on you, and everybody else working out of this office, is in there and available, on a 'need to know' basis." Rico nods.

Jim goes on, "Those computers in that corner contain operation files which can only be accessed from here as well. They aren't available on any other computers. The status of each operation, and the projects within it, appear on a dashboard report available to all personnel who have an appropriate clearance. Each operation is named and, then, marked in color to portray how active they are. For closed files, there is another color portraying how successful the project was. Completed projects are cross-referenced to the personnel files so that each field agent's file shows the success or failure of his completed projects."

"I'm curious," Rico interrupts. "Is the job I am being asked to do next week an active project?"

Jim Adams looks at Caroline for direction. When she nods, he says to Rico, "Yes, it is. The project is titled 'Edgar Trip' under the operation we call 'Batista, U.S.A.' You are working with Caroline on that one."

Caroline sees the puzzled look on Rico's face and interrupts, "I'll explain later. If all goes well, you won't even know I'm around."

As if that was possible, Rico thinks.

Rico notices another small chart on a side wall entitled "The World's Most Deadly Wars." There are colored circles for dozens of wars—large for the World Wars, much smaller for Iraq and Afghanistan—the size of the circles, obviously, representing the number of fatalities suffered during each war. In the center, dwarfing all of the other wars, is a huge black circle depicting the fatalities from the drug war. The point is easy to see. The agents are engaged in a war that is more important, in terms of fatalities, than any of the other wars the U.S., has been in, combined.

Finally, Jim turns toward the tree diagrams Rico noticed earlier. It's easy to see that, on the Mexico side, almost all the members of the Batista gang are identified. The two he remembers from his trip to are there, one a key lieutenant and the other the gang leader in Mexico. On the U.S. side there are very few photos, especially at the top of the organization.

When Rico points to the question mark at the top of the hierarchy, Jim responds, "We hope to replace that with a photo of the cartel leader the day after you return from your trip. Either Pablo, or Carlos, or both."

"We need to talk about that, Rico," Caroline says. "That's enough for you to process for one day. Let's go back to the conference room where Mike is planning to join us for lunch."

When they reach the conference room, it's empty, but there are cold meats, bread, and condiments laid out on a side table. A variety of soft drinks are cooling in a bucket of ice next to the condiments. There are only three places set at a conference table that could handle sixteen people easily, not exactly an intimate setting, but Rico hardly expects that from the DEA anyway.

Mike ambles in as Caroline and Rico are sitting down with their plates and sodas. They all exchange pleasantries. Then, Mike asks Rico about his reaction to the Batista operation command center.

"Pretty impressive," Rico responds, "You have a lot more going on here than I expected."

"Yeah, a lot of flash with very little substance," Mike agrees. "In fact, we've only made one arrest so far in the whole operation. A low-level runner in Mexico City. He was able to identify many of the people in Mexico you saw on that side of the chart. No such luck on the other side. Our side. But you know that."

Rico has many questions but he decides to hold back for now. He isn't even sure he wants to be involved in the project entitled "Edgar Trip" and he feels it is best to wait and see what Mike has in mind first.

"So, Rico, here's my thought," Mike begins. "We don't know what's in the courier bag Edgar will be taking to Mexico. Hell, we don't even know if he'll be taking it. But, given the security mechanisms, and the markings we saw on the bag, I doubt Edgar will be leaving it at home. We made a duplicate of the bag and it's already in the hands of TSA officers at the L.A. airport. When Edgar goes through security, one of their officers will follow him to the security line he chooses and switch the bags."

Rico is surprised. "They can do that legally?"

"I didn't ask. Anyway, the officer will give the real bag to Caroline who will take it to a near-by room, empty the contents, and photocopy everything. If time allows, we'll have Caroline switch the bags back again, right in the boarding area, before Edgar gets on the plane. Hopefully, that works and you will have taken a flight to Mexico City for no reason."

99

"And if it doesn't work?"

"Well, Caroline gives you the real bag before you board and, if Edgar goes to the bathroom, you just switch the real for the fake while he is in there."

"And if he doesn't go to the bathroom?"

"Then it gets tricky," Mike explains. "We'll have an agent meet you as you come off the plane. You're sitting at the front of the plane so you'll be off before Edgar. Give our agent the bag and he'll make the switch with the bag Edgar is carrying when he gets the opportunity."

"How will he get the opportunity?"

"That's the most important part of your assignment," Mike answers. "You need to accidentally bump into Edgar, drop your bags, and get him to shake your hand, or help you gather up your bags. Or ask him for a light. Or hug him. Or anything you can think of to get him to put the fake bag down on the floor so our guy can switch it out."

"Sounds sketchy," Rico says.

"I agree. It isn't foolproof," Mike surprises Rico by saying. "If you can think of a better plan, I'm all ears. Maybe buy Edgar three beers in L.A. before you board. Then, he will surely have to pee on board." Mike looks Rico in the eye, sees he isn't smiling, and decides to stop being so flippant. "Just kidding."

He goes on, "It will probably only take fifteen minutes or so to copy what is in Edgar's bag and I'm sure Caroline will get it back in his hands before he boards. But, if not, the backup plan is that Edgar will have to pee on the plane. Right? It's about a 4-hour trip. You just make the switch then. Bottom-line, you meeting Edgar in the airport is just the backup plan to the backup plan. I don't remember when we've ever had to go to plan C, do you, Caroline?"

Her silence tells Rico all he has to know.

Chapter 16

When Rico finally checks his voice mail, he's surprised to find a message from Maggie. She apologizes for missing coffee that morning and suggests that they meet for a drink; either that night or the next. Rico calls back immediately and leaves a message that he will meet her at *Armando's* at six. It's already past three.

Rico arrives at the restaurant well before six, and immediately begins to question his decision to meet there. In his memory, *Armando's* was a very nice place and, if he was still thirty, single and looking for a kind of boozy ambience, I guess it could be.

Now, though, in his fifties, with many more dining experiences under his belt, so to speak, the half-hearted attempt to class the place up has just cheapened it.

Wall colors are more muted than he remembered in the old days, which could be a good thing, but they look faded rather than elegant. The few pictures on the walls don't help and, at this time of day, with not much happening in the kitchen, Armando's smells more like a bar than a restaurant.

Even worse, the dining section is entirely empty and the bar is populated only with slightly-inebriated guys, looking into their glasses, trying to find answers that have eluded them for years. As if on cue, they all look up furtively, when he enters, hoping, perhaps, that Rico brings some salvation; which, of course, he does not.

Rico isn't sure if Maggie actually got his message but, thankfully, she walks in promptly at six. At least she didn't stand him up again. She slides into the booth next to him, a good sign, but avoids his attempt to kiss her, a not so good sign.

"I'm meeting you against my better judgement," she says, in a slightly combative tone. "I've concluded that, to me, you're more bother than you're worth. You have other priorities. I get that. But I'm not even on your radar."

"Yes, you are," Rico feebly interjects.

"Your actions say otherwise. Look. I know you're busy managing your properties, and being some kind of spy, but our relationship can't be a sometime thing, at least from my standpoint."

"I thought you liked me doing the government thing."

"That isn't the point. I did like that you're doing something exciting. It makes you fun and more interesting to be around. But if you're not around."

"I'll make sure I'm around more."

"Actually, just being around isn't enough," Maggie counters, "I want you around and engaged and entertaining, like the old Rico. You're so serious these days. I don't know why. Since you don't talk much, it's kind of hard for me to help you,"

The waiter interrupts to take drink orders. Rico orders a vodka martini. Maggie passes.

"In fact, I'm doing most of the talking again," Maggie says. "I came here to hear your side of the story. So, have at it."

Rico is unprepared to speak. As a general rule, he's much better at countering arguments than presenting them. So, he considers his words carefully.

"I know I haven't been much of a companion lately, or a friend, or a lover."

Maggie nods in agreement.

"But," he continues. "Frankly, I'm a little confused about what you want me to do. I can talk about my property management business but you have no interest in that. I can't talk much about my government work, for obvious reasons, and I'm not sure you would find it all that interesting anyway. We can't talk politics or religion. You don't really want to talk about your work. So, I'm at a bit of a loss."

"You can talk about how much you love me," Maggie interrupts. "Or how much you enjoy being with me; or where we might go together next weekend; or what shows I might want to see or what I want out of life. Things like that."

She recognizes the futility of talking to Rico any more, rises from the booth, and, as she prepares to leave, says, "Here's the bottom line, Rico. Living separate lives while under the same roof doesn't interest me anymore," she pauses. "If you find a way to squeeze some time out of your precious life, or I should say your precious two lives, give me a call. But, until then, I have my own life to live."

With that, she spins on her heels and marches out, leaving Rico alone with his thoughts and his martini.

She's right, of course. Life does seem more serious to Rico these days. His worries multiplied considerably when Mike knocked on his door, and what started out as a fun avocation has become just the opposite. It is work, worry, and not that much fun.

He stares at the empty martini glass for a few seconds, then, orders another one.

Appropriately lubricated, Rico finds it much easier to make decisions than he could just thirty minutes before. He will change his attitude, he decides, go to Mexico City, enjoy the ruse. And, even if the switch fails, Mike will figure something out. There's no reason for Rico to worry so much. That's Mike's assignment.

The important thing, Rico decides, is that, going forward, he will treat his little side business more like a game, the way he did in the beginning. He can only prepare so much. Then, the referee throws the ball in the air and the game starts. After that, Rico's job is to react and win. Pretty simple.

Rico's mind goes back to his conversation with Maggie. There's one good reason he can't tell her what she wants to hear. He now knows he loves Teresa, not Maggie. And Teresa is the antidote he needs for his life to get back on track.

On impulse, Rico pulls out his cellphone and begins to dial Teresa's number. *Why not share his revelation with her*, he thinks. Then, slowly, through the vodka fog, it dawns on him what a bad move that would be. He isn't sure what he wants to say but, more importantly, whether he can actually say it.

So, Rico makes a really good decision and stops dialing. He'll wait until morning to call Teresa. Instead, he calls the waiter over to order dinner and, in another wise decision, orders a pot of coffee to go with it.

The next morning, Rico wakes up earlier than he intended, his mouth dry, his head throbbing. His first thought is to turn over and go back to sleep. But his second thought is to drag himself out of bed and go to the gym to work some of the poisons out of his body. Also, he might run into Edgar, a good thing because he needs to make sure Edgar remembers him when they meet in Mexico City in a few days anyway.

Fortunately, Edgar is at the gym when he arrives. Rico grabs the bike right next to Edgar and is greeted just as enthusiastically as he has always been in the past, which is not very. Rico asks, "How's it going?"

"Not bad." No follow-up comment.

"Are you going to come by for pizza later in the week?"

"Nah. I have to be out of town," Edgar responds. "You?"

"Out of town, too," Rico answers. He isn't sure how to inquire about the trip any further. If Edgar tells him he is going to Mexico City, Rico will have to say that he is, too, and the surprise element of his interception will be lost. So, Rico quickly changes the subject, "Say, I never asked. Are you married?"

"Divorced."

"Me too. A couple of times."

"I can't imagine that," Edgar says. "My first divorce was so awful I swore off marriage for life."

"Do you have kids?" Rico asks.

"Yeh, a girl. She lives with her mother in El Centro."

"What do you do for a living?" Rico continues.

"I own a machine shop. Work mostly on parts for old cars. You?"

"Real estate and property management," Rico answers. "Nothing big, but it keeps me busy."

They chat amicably for another few minutes, then, Edgar moves on to lift some weights and work on the mats. Rico waits an appropriate amount of time before heading to the showers, his mind already back on Teresa.

After he gets home, he picks up his cell to call her but reaches her voice mail. He quickly decides that what he has to say shouldn't be left there and he hangs up.

It's probably a good thing. All Rico knows for sure is that he wants to invite Teresa out for dinner or something. But he realizes there are many complicating factors to consider. Not only is there a chance Carlos is back in the picture but, even if he isn't, Rico has no idea how close Teresa is to Pablo.

If Carlos is the head of the cartel, and Pablo is not involved at all, it could all work out just fine. But there is so much unknown at this point. Rico finally decides not to call Teresa until he gets back from Mexico City.

So, putting his personal issues aside, Rico sits down at his desk, now once again overflowing with paperwork. Fortunately, business has picked up a little since the DEA's middle-of-the-night raid a week or so back. There are a lot of bills to pay, yes, but it looks like the incoming cash will cover them easily. He sorts out the bills, pays them, then, sets aside the few incoming checks he has received. He will deposit them later that afternoon.

His bigger business problem right now is how to deal with the two properties Pablo wants him to buy. He reviews the P&L statements and balance sheets. They look OK. The customer contracts are not as long-term as Rico normally likes but the renewals are solid. So, given no unforeseen changes, the revenue should be steady.

In fact, a couple of the long-term customers are companies owned by Pablo anyway, so those revenue streams should be entirely secure. He decides that, from his point of view, the acquisitions make sense. The returns should be excellent, especially since, as far as Rico knows, they will be buying the warehouse at affordable prices, with cash that can be recouped fairly quickly through rental income. Where Pablo will get the cash to buy the companies is another matter; of more interest to Mike than Rico.

Coincidentally, while Rico is educating himself on the new opportunities, Pablo calls, "Have you had a chance to look at those financials I sent you yet?"

"Yes. They look OK to me," Rico answers, "but, obviously, the success or failure depends on retaining the business of a couple of companies you own. If that cash flow were to go away it would be a little dicey."

"Why would it go away? It's in my best interest to make sure it doesn't. Right?" Pablo pauses. "But let me be honest here. I chose you because you have experience managing properties like this. Keeping them in place and happy is part of your job. Right?"

Again, Rico detects a new, sharp tone in Pablo's voice. He sounds like a boss. Normally, that would concern Rico, but nothing about this deal is normal anyway. So, he doesn't react. Instead, he says, "Of course, Pablo. That's what I do."

Chapter 17

While Rico is worrying about his business and his love life, Mike is thinking about the trip to Mexico City, and how much depends on its success. He calls his Batista team together for a meeting, without inviting Rico.

"How do you feel about Rico at this stage? Can he handle an assignment like this?" Mike asks the group. There are some uneasy looks exchanged. Mike isn't the type to get input on any decision and, given that Rico was his brainchild, there is some risk in answering honestly.

Caroline is the first to speak up, "Some of the same qualities that have made him effective so far work against him going forward. He's simple, trusting, but, frankly, a little too wet-behind-the-ears to be effective in the clutch. He has been believable as an ordinary guy, yes. But our work requires more than that."

She pauses, waiting for some support, which, surprisingly, she doesn't get. So, she continues, "Frankly, if the shit hits the fan, I don't know that we can rely on him. This bag exchange seems simple on paper but, as we all know from past experience, I doubt it will go down the way we've imagined it. Do we want an operation as critical as this one coming down to Rico's ability to think on his feet? I think not."

Todd Williams is the next agent to speak, "Some of you might not know that I was involved in Rico's training a few months ago and I disagree with Caroline. Rico is friendly and personable, yes, but, underneath, there is some steel, and lots of determination. Of all the agents I trained, and that includes some of you here, he was the most tenacious and disciplined. I'm sure that comes from his desire to please but it also comes from an internal drive that you wouldn't guess just by looking at him. He looks like an ordinary guy, and that's a strength for us, but I think he has the makings of a great agent as well."

Todd pauses and looks at each of the faces around the table.

"I agree that he's naive," he goes on, "and an amateur, without much experience in the kind of things we face every day. So, putting him in a pivotal role in an operation this risky should give us pause. But, tell me, who is better-positioned to throw Edgar off his game? He knows Edgar. And Edgar knows him. The rest is us are total strangers to Edgar, thank God. I think Rico will do fine."

Mike nods. "I agree with Todd," he says. "But Caroline is voicing something I'm sure you all feel. Can we really be comfortable that, in a tough spot, Rico will have our back? How about we focus on this thought: Let's make sure we have his back. We should 'game-play' a few scenarios, think about what we do, not what Rico does."

"Well, under almost any scenario, somebody has to be on that plane with Rico," Caroline says. "We can't very well back him up if we are not there."

"Good point. You volunteering?" Mike said.

"You're damn right I am. Who better to distract Edgar if Rico can't? I might be a stranger but he'll have trouble ignoring me. I'll make sure of that."

"Another good point," Mike replies.

And with that, they start talking out the various scenarios, using a flip chart to make sure they're on the same page. By the end of the meeting, the team feels a lot more comfortable with the operation than they had been when the meeting started.

Still, Caroline asks to meet with Mike alone, in his office. Once the door is closed, she again attacks the decision to have Rico as a point person on this operation.

"I can do it without Rico," she begins. "I'm sure I'll be able to return the bag before Edgar boards the plane but, in the unlikely event I can't, I'll take the bag onto the plane and make the exchange there. I can assure you that we don't need Rico, or his chance meeting with Edgar in the Mexico City airport, as back up."

"I don't doubt what you say," Mike replies. "However, what harm will it be to have Rico on board and available? He can certainly distract the guy for a few seconds, if necessary. Besides, I want to see how Rico handles the pressure and responsibility of an operation like this. It will make him even more valuable to us on down the line."

Mike gives Caroline a chance to respond but she doesn't. Probably thinks she's said enough already.

Then, Mike continues, "If Pablo is our main Batista guy in the U.S., Rico's relationship with him can prove quite valuable. Pablo trusts Rico. Even if Carlos is the guy, Rico knows him as well. He doesn't have the same kind of relationship, perhaps, but he has the access, which should be worth something. If Rico chokes, if he can't operate independently, think on his feet, we'll have to go in an entirely different direction. I agree with that. But we need to know that earlier rather than later."

Caroline realizes there's some logic to the argument. Mike continues, "Yes, this is an important operation but it isn't that complicated. You pointed that out earlier. And if, worst case, we don't get the original bag back to Edgar, the fake one he's carrying contains papers that will at least confuse everybody for a while. Then, when Edgar returns, we just pick him up and squeeze him for information. Remember, that was what we were going to have to do anyway, before Rico conveniently found himself right in the middle of our operation. We have to take advantage of Rico's positioning. That's all."

Then, Mike delivers the clincher, "But, above all, Caroline, this bag switch is worth the risk because you're involved. I wouldn't attempt it with Rico alone. I see him pretty much the way you do. I'm telling Rico it's his operation but you're key. You know that, right? I trust you to make the switch happen. And I trust you to help me decide what to do with the information when we get it. The final act to our play is just beginning. I'm the producer. You're the director. Rico is just a bit player who we hope can remember his lines. The Batista cartel is going down and you and I are the ones that will make it happen, not Rico."

Caroline walks out feeling much better about things. She realizes now that she has the opportunity of a lifetime and she's damn well going to take advantage of it. The flight to Mexico City is only the beginning. Pablo, or Carlos, or whoever, will be going to jail, and Caroline will put them there.

Meanwhile, Mike goes back into the meeting room and looks over the various scenarios sketched out on the flip charts. After some more thinking about what might happen, he calls Rico and asks him to come in the next morning. Rico may be a bit player but the role he'll play going forward is critical. Starting with the bag exchange. Mike wants to make sure he's fully prepared.

Mike needn't have been concerned. Even as Rico has been wrestling with his business paperwork, his mind has been on his upcoming assignment. Rico's operational experience may be limited but he's been around long enough to know this operation will probably not go down the way it's planned.

So, Mike's call is actually a relief to Rico. He's been thinking about calling Mike anyway before he steps onto the plane a few days from now. Rico's goal is to have fun with this assignment but it doesn't mean he should go in unprepared.

The next morning, Mike really runs Rico through the paces. *What if he's sick, the day of the flight? What if Edgar doesn't have the bag?* The various scenarios are limitless but Rico surprises Mike by having a good answer for most of what Mike, and his team, had game-planned the day before.

Mike decides not to tell Rico that Caroline will be on the plane but he's pleasantly surprised to hear Rico suggest she have a ticket just in case something happens to him. So, at least, Rico will not be surprised to see her board, probably at the last minute. Mike has already arranged with the airline that the flight will not leave until she's on board.

Mike is thrilled to hear Rico question things unrelated to his part of the operation. *How many copy machines will they have waiting in the back room? What about thumb drives? Will there be anybody other than Caroline reviewing the material? What will they copy first?*

Obviously, Rico is taking ownership of the operation and that's a good thing because, despite the concerns voiced earlier, Mike believes that Rico can be a really good field agent over time. The success of this operation may not rest entirely on Rico's shoulders, but it's a perfect chance to test Rico's mettle without too much risk. Mike is betting that he'll be fine.

Rico leaves Mike's office feeling better about the planning and eager to get on with his assignment. There might be another sleepless night or two before he climbs onto the plane but, at least, the worrying will soon be behind him. There is only so much preparation a guy can do.

Chapter 18

Rico is nervous on his drive to LAX and, as he gets closer, the traffic, noise and confusing signs around the airport add to his discomfort. There's always a little knot in Rico's stomach when he flies, not just because of the chaos of the airport, but because he knows he's about to lose control of his life, something Rico fears above all else.

He knows that, what happens to him over the next few hours depends on a giant, mindless, uncaring air traffic bureaucracy that has very little regard for the inconveniences it may cause him and others. All it takes is a "flight cancelled," or "flight delayed" next to his flight number on the big console to put him in a long line of people needing to be rerouted, with only a distressed clerk between him and hours spent in an airport lounge.

Today, at least, he can take comfort in the fact that there's a whole team of DEA agents waiting for him at the terminal, all with the single assignment of making sure Rico and his team succeed. They may not be visible. In fact, they better not be visible. But he knows they are there, ready to assist him in any way necessary.

Still, Rico is even more nervous than normal about this trip. The consequences are far greater than usual.

While standing in the security line, he looks for Edgar even though he would be surprised to see him since Rico is here three hours ahead of flight time. But, one can never be too careful.

Once through security, Rico disappears into the throngs of travelers scurrying around trying to find their gate and, as quickly as he can, finds a seat at his gate, near the window, facing away from the hubbub, and buries his head in a newspaper. No shopping. No coffee. Not even an occasional peek at the faces going by to see if Edgar has arrived.

It's surprising to Rico how much his heart is racing. If Edgar happens to see him, he'll act surprised and happy but it will scuttle any thought of a surprise encounter on the other end. *That probably won't be necessary anyway*, Rico thinks. Caroline will get the exchange done way before that.

While Rico is making himself as inconspicuous as possible, Caroline and her associates are preparing for the main event. A tail is put on Edgar from the time he leaves his house and, simultaneously, two DEA agents in the airport are dressing up in TSA uniforms and positioning themselves where they can reach the right security line in seconds. They're the ones who will make the actual switch.

They have the "fake" courier bag hidden near them, ready for a quick grab. The exchange, something that they've already practiced over a dozen times, should be quick as well, and not visible to Edgar. The bag to be exchanged is identical to the one being carried by Edgar; but it's loaded with dozens of fictitious reports and memos that, hopefully, will confuse everybody for a while.

The secure room where they will be copying documents is about fifty yards away. Caroline is there, with several copying machines, a computer, and a team of assistants. They estimate that they can copy the materials within fifteen minutes, easily enough time to replace the original bag before Edgar boards the flight, assuming, of course, that they can find some way to do it inconspicuously.

Caroline is in charge of the exchange at LAX and, once Edgar is on board with the right courier bag, her responsibilities are over. The flight to Mexico City will be for pleasure only. However, if the exchange can't be made before Edgar boards, Caroline will have to bring the original bag on board with her for exchange there or in Mexico City.

She's decided to be as inconspicuous as possible for the trip, with a gray-streaked black wig, a baggy A-line dress, and padding that makes her look like the dowdy middle-aged dowager she most definitively is not. If he were to look closely, Rico could recognize her but nobody else will have a clue that an attractive DEA agent is in there somewhere.

So, everything is ready. All they need now is Edgar. According to those tailing him, he left his house in plenty of time to reach the airport an hour before flight time. But, a stop at Starbucks and an unexpected traffic jam on the freeway has put him a little behind schedule.

Caroline is prepared for that eventuality. She has one of her men parked in the garage Edgar has used in the past. The agent is occupying a space very close to the terminal and will exit that space just as Edgar arrives. They can't afford to have Edgar reach the security line late or, even worse, miss the flight.

The first part of the operation goes smoothly. Edgar finds the right parking space, reaches security about forty minutes before his flight boards, seems totally focused on his flight as he goes through security and settles comfortably into a seat near his gate, the "fake" courier bag firmly in hand.

Meanwhile, Caroline and her cohorts are busy picking the lock on the real bag and copying what appears to be a treasure trove of information inside. She doesn't have time to study everything but she can see lists of names, addresses, travel schedules, boat and charter plane schedules, and a lot of other stuff that will provide solid intel for raids they might want to conduct in the near future.

She doesn't see anything that would link Pablo or Carlos to the syndicate but it could be there somewhere, hidden in the body of one of the memos or letters. The important thing at the moment, of course, is not what's there but how quickly they can copy it and return the bag to Edgar.

If they're able to make the exchange undetected, the information will be that much more actionable. At the very least, with dates and registration numbers, they'll be able to intercept the traffic coming up the coast, something that, because of the number of boats, has only been marginally successful in the past.

The copying done, Caroline hurries to the appropriate gate with the original courier bag in hand. She sees Edgar right away and positions herself outside his sight line.

The good news is that she has at least fifteen minutes to make the exchange before the flight is called. The bad news, however, is that Edgar is clutching the "fake" bag to his chest, like a three-year-old girl might with her teddy bear. He looks strange doing that, of course, but stranger than normal? How he looks has never been a concern of Edgar's and, at this point, protecting the bag is much more important to him.

Caroline reluctantly decides to go to Plan B, which is to get on the plane herself and try to make the exchange there. She sees Rico is boarding. But, fortunately, it looks like Edgar doesn't see him. So far, so good.

Rico's window seat is in the second row of coach so he can exit quickly and be positioned to "run into" Edgar in Mexico City. The only risk is whether Edgar sees Rico as he goes down the aisle looking for his seat. But Caroline has every confidence that will not happen. Rico is wearing a wide-brimmed floppy hat, covering his face, and he will be looking out the window while the passengers board.

Of course, Caroline will board last and have to pass Edgar to get to her seat. But he doesn't know who she is and, even if he did, she's virtually unrecognizable in her wig and formless gray dress. She's carrying a large, flowery, bag, within which, of course, is the locked courier bag, ready to be exchanged back.

As Caroline passes Edgar, she notices he's positioned the targeted bag at his feet, under the seat in front of him. Any exchange on the plane will be difficult. The only possibility is that Edgar leaves it behind when he goes to the rest room or stretches his legs. Hopefully, that will happen but, given Edgar's body language, Caroline isn't counting on it.

It's going to be a tense flight for Caroline. She has to be ready to move at any time but, even if Edgar leaves the bag alone, she isn't sure she can make the switch without attracting attention from the passengers around him. It's beginning to look like option C will be their best bet. Unfortunately.

As it turns out, there's one chance for Caroline to make the exchange on the plane. About fifteen minutes before the plane begins its descent, Edgar goes to the rest room, leaving the bag behind. But, unfortunately, the person sitting beside Edgar, in the window seat, is wide awake, reading a book, when Caroline wanders down the aisle. The woman will see any exchange. Caroline realizes that they should have purchased both seats next to Edgar and left them empty. But it's a little too late for second-guessing their game plan now.

Caroline continues on up the aisle to where Rico is sitting and shakes her head, signaling to Rico that it's up to him now. He has to distract Edgar enough in the terminal that Caroline can make the switch.

Rico is actually thrilled to see Caroline shake her head. He's been nervous about this trip for weeks but, now that he's here, he wants a chance to do his part, minor as it might be. He's well-rehearsed and he can't imagine just climbing back on the next flight to L.A. without contributing in some way.

As the plane makes its descent, Rico plays out various scenarios in his head. The best case would be: Edgar putting the bag down to shake Rico's hand. That seems unlikely. Rico's next move will depend on which of Edgar's hand holds the bag and how friendly his greeting is.

Maybe he can buy Edgar a beer. Or get him to sit down for a minute in one of the chairs lining the terminal. But, more likely, Rico realizes, he will have to divert his attention in some way that is more disruptive.

Rico is the first passenger off the plane, and the first to reach the terminal area. That gives him just enough time to steal a half cup of coffee off a nearby table, and get back into the crowd waiting for arrivals before Edgar exits.

Fortunately, Rico blends in quite nicely. He looks like any other Mexican family member there to welcome their prodigal son or daughter back home from America.

When Edgar comes out, Rico sees that Caroline is right behind him, holding her flowered bag with both hands. How she has been able to catch up to Edgar so quickly is a mystery to Rico, but not a surprise. Caroline is a professional and she has put herself in the perfect position to make the exchange.

"Edgar. I'll be damned," Rico blurts out as he greets the big man, startling Edgar a little. Rico notices the bag is in Edgar's right hand so maybe a simple hand shake will work. "I thought that was you," Rico says, extending his right hand toward Edgar, who, unfortunately, keeps a tight grip on the bag with his right hand and awkwardly offers his left instead.

Rico acts confused by the move, starts to lift his left hand in response, and, in doing so, spills his cup of coffee all over Edgar's right hand and arm, causing him to drop the bag.

Rico is immediately all over Edgar, patting his wet shirt sleeve, and hand, with the paper napkin he's holding, and apologizing most profusely. But, mainly, he's keeping Edgar from reaching down for the bag. Then, Rico holds Edgar's hand for a few seconds in an effort to see how badly it's burned, asking somebody to find more napkins. It's an act worthy of an Oscar.

"So sorry, Edgar. I'll pay the cleaning bill; you can be sure of that. Is your hand OK?"

Edgar is obviously confused but he quickly gathers his wits, looks around for his bag, finds it behind him, grasps it with his left hand, and brushes Rico off with a quick, "Yea. OK. Gotta go. See you later." He also apologizes to the hefty woman he runs into as he turns to exit, the one with the brightly-colored, floral-patterned bag. She gives him an exasperated look, then, steps aside.

Once Edgar is gone, Caroline turns back toward Rico and starts laughing, "You sure can act like a bumbling fool when you want to. Or was it an act."

"Let's just say I have a lot of experience to draw on," Rico responds, "I assume you got the job done."

"With the act you put on, I could have switched it back and forth several times while enjoying a cup of coffee myself," Caroline says. "Nice job being a stumblebum." Which was the nicest thing she had ever said to him.

Rico blushes a little, shuffles his feet, looks down, acting like an embarrassed little boy. Rico is not used to compliments, especially from Caroline.

Chapter 19

Caroline and Rico have a mini-celebration on the flight home, enjoying two cocktails apiece as they toast their success. What they did in Mexico City may not have seemed like much but it was as effective as if they had used force. Maybe more so, because, in this instance, the suspect had no idea what happened.

"That's Mike's style," Caroline explains. "He's more cerebral than most and loves to play games, the more complicated the better. Above all, he tends to keep people in the dark, even those he's working with, if it serves his purpose. For Mike, the end always justifies the means and, because his track record is so good, nobody argues with him.

"The only problem with Mike's style," Caroline goes on, "is that he can't really train anybody because, of course, who can be trained to think like Mike anyway?"

Even with the two drinks in him, Rico decides not to mention how Mike tricked him into becoming part of the team in the first place. He isn't sure Caroline was clued in on that scam, anyway, but he suspects, and hopes, she wasn't. She was probably just doing her job, without asking questions. Like she always does.

He's learned one thing, though. He's really glad Caroline is on his side. She knows how to handle herself in tough situations.

While Caroline and Rico are exchanging pleasantries on the plane, back in Los Angeles, a team of research experts is busy, going through all of the materials the operation yielded. The papers may not have looked like much originally but, to these experts, they're a gold mine of intel.

There are operational orders, telling different drug runners where to pick up and drop off their packages. There's a changed source for their meth and fentanyl. There are purchase orders for bulk shipments, which look so official, they could easily be mistaken for those coming from drug store chains.

Again, the only real disappointment is the absence of information on an organizational structure. Occasionally, there's a code name or a boat registration number, either of which might lead to somebody's name eventually. But, as a general rule, the people at the top of the organization remain as opaque after the operation as they did before.

Mike decides to call a meeting of the operational team to update them on what has been discovered. So, he tells his support team that he needs a Power Point presentation prepared by the next morning. He also wants all of the charts in the war room updated with the latest information, not realizing or caring that it will take them well into the wee hours of the morning to do it. Meanwhile, Mike himself gets a good night's sleep and arrives for the meeting well-refreshed; one of the perks of being the boss.

"First, let me compliment everybody involved in the switch in Mexico City," Mike opens the meeting. "As far as we can tell, it went off without a hitch. Edgar is on a plane back to L.A. as we speak and some of the orders he delivered are already being carried out. So, we don't believe that the Mexican cartel members suspect anything."

"We noticed Edgar was carrying the same courier bag back with him on the plane when he returned. It probably has some more valuable information in it but we can hardly work the same trick twice. So, we need to tail him again when he lands, see who he delivers the bag to, and, then, put a tail on that person. Jack and Ken, you have that assignment."

The two agents nod.

"In addition, we'll station you, Jim, at the Global office building where Edgar picked up the bag a few days ago. He might go there right from the airport. You need to know who's in the building when, and if, Edgar comes there to drop the bag off."

"By the way," he continues, "we intend to bug the entire building tonight. So, starting tomorrow, we should understand a lot better how deeply Pablo is involved in this thing. Or Carlos."

Rico asks, "What about Edgar going forward? Should I just be a no-show at the gym for the next few days?"

"I don't think so, Rico," Mike replies. "You need to be there tomorrow morning to see how Edgar acts toward you. I don't think your chance encounter with him in Mexico City raised any alarm bells but if it did, his behavior at the gym could tip you off."

Mike then turns to the research guys in attendance, "OK, let's hear it. What did we learn?"

The lead analyst pulls up the first slide which shows an inventory of the various documents they reviewed. "We aren't going to go through all of these

116

in detail," he starts. "But, for the sake of this discussion, we grouped them into four categories: organization, product, distribution, and customers."

For the next two hours, the agents in the room discuss what is happening within the cartel, how it is changing, and what they may have to do in response.

For example, they learn that, although few new names have been discovered, the organization has grown dramatically larger since their last briefing. Mike uses this info to light a fire under his team. "Every day that we fail to shut down the cartel," Mike explains, "the job gets more difficult. Like an amoeba, the gang just continues to morph into something more dangerous and more effective. The cancer cells just keep multiplying."

As an example, Mike tells everybody about a new sales operation that is operating in Puerto Vallarta, Mexico. Somebody nicknamed Shine has recruited a group of young people, mostly women, who mingle with the well-heeled Americans arriving by private yacht. They start by coming on to the target romantically. They party with them, then, they get them their drug of choice, at a reasonable price. After that, they convince their targets to take larger and larger stashes for their friends back home. Like a pyramid scheme, eventually, each new recruit gets paid to bring in other recruits.

The cartel hopes to have a whole fleet of expensive, luxury boats, operated by spoiled, rich kids, running up and down the West Coast with relatively small amounts of very expensive drugs on board. They call the owners of these boats, "influencers" because it's felt that they will get all of their friends hooked and open up a whole new market for the cartel, with products designed, and priced, specifically for that upscale market. Part of the appeal will be convenience. Like Amazon, they will guarantee same day delivery anywhere in the areas they are serving.

"Hopefully, Amazon doesn't get in the drug business, too," somebody says, only half-facetiously. "What a nightmare that would be."

"Another reason not to legalize drugs," somebody else chimes in.

Then, the analysts explain how the product is changing. Just like consumer products companies, they say, the cartel is experimenting with new formulations and rebranding them, all the time. The benefits may not be dramatically better but you wouldn't know that from their marketing.

Blue Lightening is now Blue Horizon. A new brand called Camelot has been created. Customers are being put on to automatic delivery and payment plans based on their need and their ability to pay, just like a finance company; only with a dunning system, the last notice of which could prove fatal.

The cartel is doing more research on the effect their products have on different types of users. They are including personalized usage directions in each of the shipments so that the risk of an overdose is substantially reduced. They're well aware that drug deaths are rising precipitously and that dead customers don't buy a lot of product.

The cartel is even charting death rates by product, channel, and customer groups, just to get some accountability into their system. The illegal drug business, once infamous for how many deaths it causes, is now trying to prevent them, a sign of how smart and sophisticated the cartels have become.

After the power point presentation is over, Mike talks about the actions the team will take in response. In concert with the Coast Guard, they will step up their boarding of boats coming up the coast. They now know numbers, routes, and drop-off points. Since their goal is the elimination of the cartel leaders, producers and dealers, not just the couriers, the plan is to use their new information judiciously so as not to set off too many alarm bells.

Assignments are made. Mike says that every boarding over the next month or so will include at least one drug agent who will question the captain and crew of the targeted boat first, before any other law-enforcement people get involved.

Additional agents are assigned to drop points along the coast. Almost everybody seems to have an assignment, except Rico and Caroline.

Rico is happy about that. He's anxious to get back to his real life and isn't really interested in how the sausage is made in the drug industry, so to speak. The updated charts around the room, with the new information highlighted in green, tell a depressing story. To his eye, nothing has changed all that much. The gangs are still pushing. Americans are still buying.

He looks out the window at a half-empty parking lot, wondering why there are so few cars for so many agents. *Do they all car pool? Maybe there is a garage in back*, he thinks. *He should check it out next time he has a chance.*

It's a nice day, Rico realizes. *Normally he would be taking advantage of this kind of weather to get out and about, to visit one or two of his properties. Hopefully, he'll have the chance to do that in the next few days.*

Then, he thinks of Teresa and the possibility of them dating again. He wonders if she's ever thought about that. *Probably not. Will it surprise her that he has interest in her once again? Will it ruin the platonic relationship they are enjoying now?* His mind bounces from one inane subject to the next while Mike drones on.

Suddenly, he hears his name. Mike is saying something about a special assignment involving Caroline and him. They are to leave on Sunday morning. But Rico doesn't hear exactly what he's supposed to do. He looks at Caroline. Her face is expressionless and she's taking notes, something he realizes he probably should have been doing all along.

Rico wants to object to the assignment, but he can hardly do that when he doesn't even know what it is. He feels a familiar wave of anxiety pass over him, just like back in high school. *Why didn't he listen? Some things never change*, Rico says to himself.

Mike finally seems to be finishing up. He asks for questions, answers a few, then, dismisses everybody and leaves the room. Rico has to scramble to catch Caroline before she leaves.

"Caroline, I'm sorry. Did you catch what we're supposed to do?" he asks.

"You're kidding, right?"

"Not really. I was counting cars in the parking lot."

Caroline rolls her eyes and says, "We're going to Puerto Vallarta on Sunday. We have an undercover assignment to find out what we can about this guy called Shine, and his harem. You and I are to pretend we are the spoiled, grown-up relatives of a business mogul. Just two lost souls looking for a good time. Any of this ring a bell?" Caroline says with a touch of sarcasm.

"I remember something about Shine, but why are we involved?"

"I don't know why you're involved," Caroline replies. "Maybe Mike is impressed with your performance in Mexico City. As for me, this is what I do. One minute I'm a middle-aged dowager, the next a bored bikini babe. I play roles and get people to talk to me. I find out things that others can't, and relay them to Mike. Then, he does with it whatever he wants. That's the way it works around here."

"Okay. I can do that. I'll be ready on Sunday. Are you making the plane reservations?" Rico queries.

"Boy, you really weren't listening," she says. "Mike is trying to get an acquaintance of his to loan us his name, his boat, and his captain. If the guy agrees to do it, we will sail down to Puerto Vallarta with his crew, and a healthy expense account."

"Sounds better than our last assignment."

"You got that right. We party, have some fun, and wait to be contacted by one of Shine's people. Then we wing it from there. Our objective is to identify the players and shut the whole operation down before it gets legs."

Caroline looks him in the eye and asks, "Got it this time?"

She's clearly upset by the baby-sitting job Mike has assigned her once again. And, even though Rico is growing quite fond of his young partner, the feeling doesn't appear to be mutual.

Later, when Rico gets home, he checks his voice mail and finds that Mike has already called him, saying that it's a go for Puerto Vallarta. He should expect a guy named Marcel to come by with outfits to pack. Also, a briefing book is being couriered to him along with a passport and driver's license. Mike finishes by thanking Rico for volunteering for this very important assignment, something Rico is pretty sure he didn't do.

It's obviously too late for Rico to talk his way out of the assignment now, so he decides, once again, to just embrace it. *A few days on a boat partying with his petulant, but pretty, partner Caroline? There are worse assignments. Right?*

Chapter 20

Before focusing on his sailing trip, though, there are some things Rico needs to do.

First, following Mike's orders, Rico gets up early and heads to the gym, hoping to run into Edgar. On the way, he plots his strategy.

Obviously, he'll have to explain to Edgar why he was in Mexico City but, with relatives still living there, that shouldn't be too difficult. A sick aunt or a birthday party or a family get-together ought to do it. Also, he'll apologize for his clumsiness but, if Edgar is at all suspicious, and why wouldn't he be, more questions should follow.

That is the only thing that really worries Rico at this point. Edgar has always been remarkably incurious but, if he is different today, if he asks a lot of questions, that'll raise warning flags for Rico.

Fortunately, Edgar is in his normal spot, on his favorite bike, pedaling away. *Edgar is such a creature of habit*, Rico thinks, which makes his job so much easier; something to remember if he is ever the pursued rather than the pursuer. Which, when he thinks about it, may come sooner than he would like.

They exchange pleasantries and pedal together in silence for a few minutes. Rico is hoping that Edgar will initiate the conversation but, as he might have anticipated, that doesn't happen. Still, given the circumstances, Edgar's lack of interest in Rico is comforting.

Finally, Rico says, "So, Edgar, what a coincidence running into you in Mexico. Sorry about spilling my coffee on you. I am such a klutz at times."

No comment or acknowledgement from Edgar. He just stares straight ahead. But, eventually, without turning his head, Edgar mutters, "No problem. I was surprised to see you, though."

"Yeah. I was visiting relatives. You must know how that is. Is that what you were doing?"

"No. Business. Just a quick trip in and out. You didn't stay very long either, obviously."

"My mother was sick. I left as soon as we got her home from the hospital."

"She OK?"

"Kind of a false alarm. Chest pains but no heart issues. Because of her age, they kept her in for observation."

Normally, Rico would engage Edgar further, especially given the big man's surprising willingness to talk a little bit. But he's worried that Edgar may ask him some more difficult questions. So, after about fifteen minutes of silently exercising together, Rico dismounts and heads for the showers.

Later, on the phone to Mike, Rico reports that, "Edgar is less surly than normal but he didn't take much interest in our chance meeting in the Mexico City airport. So, that much is good, right, boss?"

Mike is suspicious, "If I were his boss, I would tell him to be friendly but careful, just like he was."

"I didn't feel he was under orders to talk to me," Rico counters. Then adds, "Maybe my charm is wearing him down."

"Doesn't sound right," Mike responds. "But miracles do occasionally happen. Have a safe journey and enjoy the scenery." Then, he abruptly disconnects. Mike only has so much tolerance for idle chit-chat.

Rico can't always tell when Mike is just having fun at his expense, or when he's serious. But Rico decides to take the safe journey comment at face value. He will do all he can to make the holiday in Puerto Vallarta pleasant and enjoyable, recognizing, of course, that Shine controls that way more than he does.

While talking to Mike, Rico notices there are a couple of calls from Pablo on his call history. He's not surprised. Rico has been too busy lately to connect with his business partner and he knows Pablo gets nervous when Rico doesn't call. So, he dials him up immediately.

"What have you been up to?" Pablo starts, "I miss you, amigo."

"Nothing much," Rico lies. "Some maintenance issues I had to attend to, and a couple of customer complaints. Nothing major. Also, I'm trying to fill the vacancy in the building on Prospect. We have had some callbacks from our ad but I haven't been able to close anybody yet."

In truth, Rico had stopped running the ad because he knew he would be too busy with his trip to handle the incoming calls. And, as for the maintenance issues, he hadn't called the contractors yet either, but he certainly needs to do that before leaving for Mexico. He wants them working while he is away.

Then, Pablo complicates things further, "Say, Rico, some of my old customers have been asking about you. They want to meet the new boss. Can you work that into your schedule?"

"Of course. Which ones?"

"Well, one of our biggest customers is Savory Food Distributors. You might start there," Pablo answers. "The President is an old friend of mine, Hank Thompson. Really good guy. Why don't I call him and set it up?"

"Sure, but I'm going sailing with a friend next week. Can we do it when I get back?" Rico asks.

"I would rather not wait that long. Let's shoot for tomorrow morning? Can you be at their offices around 9 am?" It sounds more like an order than a request.

So, despite all Rico has on his plate, the next morning, he finds himself in the reception area of Savory Food Distributors, waiting for a secretary to escort him back to Hank Thompson's office.

Looking around the room, Rico is surprised at how lavishly it is decorated; leather couches, oriental rugs, fine art. In his experience, it's rare to see such extravagance in the offices of a distribution business. The successful ones keep their expenses really low. *Savory must be different for some reason*, he surmises. *But, still, obviously good at what they do.*

When the elegantly attired young lady arrives to collect him, Rico is struck by something else as well. Not many presidents of distribution businesses have secretaries these days, especially not ones paid well enough to dress the way this one does. Savory is either the most successful distribution company on the planet or something else is going on here.

But Rico's biggest surprise comes when he enters Mr. Thompson's office. There, sitting on the couch facing Hank's desk is none other than the ever-so-charming Mr. Carlos Silva.

As usual, he is well-coiffed, dressed in chino pants, legs crossed, an expensive polo shirt stretched tightly over his chest, and very short sleeves showing off his biceps. He has the same unctuous smile that turned Rico off the first time he met the man. His arrogance is visible and off-putting. Carlos makes no attempt to rise or shake Rico's hand. He just smiles that smile, pleased as punch with himself.

But, as Hank starts the introductions, Rico makes the first move. He goes over to where Carlos is seated, extends his hand, and forces the drug kingpin to rise or be totally rude. The smile disappears.

"Yes, I know Mr. Silva," Rico says. "How are you, Carlos?"

"Fine. You?"

With that opening shot, a kind of silent combat ensues, both men staring at each other for an uncomfortable minute or so. Hank Thompson doesn't notice and keeps talking. He explains that Carlos Silva is both a customer and an investor who has particular interest in how Savory inventories, moves, and protects its merchandise.

According to Hank, Mr. Silva has interviewed all of the companies in Savory's supply chain and, although Carlos is a friend of Pablo's, he wants some assurances that the practices promised by Pablo will continue under Rico's management.

Rico assures Mr. Silva and Mr. Thompson that they will, thinking that will placate them. No such luck.

"Do you know what practices we mean," Carlos says pointedly.

"Not off the top-of-my-head, but I will find out from Pablo as soon as I get back to the office."

"We want our merchandise to be stored separately, under lock and key. We now hold one key and Pablo the other one. We don't want anybody else to have access to our goods, you or your managers, ever. Is that clear?"

"Clear but unacceptable," Rico pushes back. "Isolating your goods is not a problem but you'll be charged a fee on top of the regular rent. That's standard procedure."

"Limiting our access to your goods, however, is a non-starter," Rico continues. "First, fire code prohibits it. Second, we have to make periodic inspections to make sure everything is secure. What if critters get in? Or the temperature rises unexpectedly? It's for the protection of your goods as much as it's for us."

"Talk to Pablo. This is nonnegotiable."

"I'm not negotiating. I'm telling you what the situation is. You have the choice to accept it or take a hike," Rico says, getting angrier by the second. "Pablo is not part of this."

"Listen, punk," Carlos counters, "obviously, you don't know who you're dealing with. I give orders. I don't take them, especially from somebody as far down the food chain as you. Check with Pablo. Maybe it's time for him to explain things to you."

Hank tries to jump in, erroneously thinking the situation can be defused by words. Carlos and Rico pay him little heed, shouting expletives at each other as if they are bullets coming out of a machine gun. Finally, Rico gets up and storms out of the room.

In the car headed home, Rico immediately regrets his actions. His Latin temper has gotten the better of him again. He should have just listened to Carlos, agreed with whatever the guy had to say, then, taken his grievances up with Pablo. His affection for Teresa and his animosity toward Carlos probably clouded his judgment a bit back there, he realizes.

What makes it even worse for Rico is the fact that Carlos could be one of the leaders of the Batista cartel. He certainly behaved that way, as if he has the power, disposition, and wherewithal to make things uncomfortable, if not deadly, for Rico.

It isn't smart to confront a guy like that, especially if you're working undercover for the DEA, so, Rico comes to the conclusion that he'll have to swallow his pride and set things right. But, first things first.

Chapter 21

Rico realizes now that he needs some clarification from Teresa. *Is her fling with Carlos really over? Or did they just have a lover's spat, one that may already be history?*

At this point, dating Teresa will greatly complicate things but Rico knows he has no choice. He's in love with her and he isn't about to walk away from her a second time, not to placate Carlos or to help Mike.

So, his first call is to Teresa, not Carlos. After exchanging pleasantries, he says, "So Teresa. I'm curious. How are things between you and Carlos these days?"

"Are you kidding? There are no things between us. As I told you before, I'm done with him. He's a creep."

"Anybody else in the picture yet?"

"No. Why?"

There is a brief pause. Then, Rico takes a deep breath, exhales, and says, "How about you and me get together for dinner sometime, like Saturday night for example?"

There's no hesitation on Teresa's part. "I thought you'd never ask," she responds. "I'd love to."

Rico is so surprised by her immediate positive response that, for a second, he can't think of anything else to say. Finally, he stammers, "Well. OK, then. I'll pick you up at six."

Rico takes a minute to let his heart stop pounding, Then, he calls Carlos. His apology, although not really heartfelt, sounds sincere enough, Rico thinks, ending with an assurance that he will try to accommodate Savory's needs.

The call is short, sweet, and ends with what sounds like a genuine thanks from Carlos. Maybe it clears the air. Maybe not. But, for the moment at least, Rico feels a little safer.

Then Rico calls Pablo, explains the situation and asks for guidance, something he doesn't often do. Pablo is sympathetic, but says Rico needs to

126

agree to whatever Carlos wants. Don't confront him. Carlos is big on threats upfront but not that good at follow-up, and Rico can go on managing Savory's business the same way he handles other customers. That's what Pablo has done for years and he's never been called on it.

Feeling better, Rico turns his attention to Teresa.

Rico is not about to make the same mistake with Teresa that he made with Marge. No seedy bar this time. No old haunts. Not for this, his first real date with a beautiful new girlfriend that just happens to be his ex-wife. Instead, he reserves a table at a highly-rated, and very expensive, restaurant in Chinatown, a place called *majordomo*, with a lowercase *m*.

On Saturday, when he rings Teresa's doorbell, Rico is as nervous as a schoolboy picking up his prom date. Teresa answers, looking stunning as usual. Rico thinks what a mismatch they are as a couple. Teresa is now all upscale L.A. while Rico still has a touch of the old barrio in him. Despite his misgivings back in the day, she has adjusted better than he has to the upscale California lifestyle.

But what really impresses Rico about Teresa is how she can look so cool, so sophisticated, and still be so sweet and trusting underneath, the same nice girl he fell in love with back in Mexico City.

Rico has another thought as they near Chinatown. Teresa and Carlos may have been a very handsome couple when they dated, one perfectly suited to the Los Angeles nightlife, but, in Rico's mind, he and Teresa, as mismatched as they may seem on the surface, are a much more authentic couple.

They have deep Mexican roots, yes, but, also, shared contemporary American values. Both are genuinely good people, even if she recently dated a pompous ass and Rico now lies for a living.

Fortunately, when they arrive at the restaurant, Rico's choice doesn't disappoint. It has the kind of upscale warehouse look that's so popular with young couples these days. Noisy, yes, but also alive with chatter, chumminess, and charm. A happening place populated with partiers on the move and on the make.

Ignoring the distractions around them, it takes no time at all for Rico and Teresa to begin the playful repartee that they both enjoyed when they were kids. Rico says he chose the place because it reminds him of Teresa, to which she replies, "Loud and pretentious?"

"Exactly."

They both laugh and Rico orders the drinks. Eventually, after some more verbal sparring and shared laughter, the waiter returns for dinner selections. Teresa decides on the marinated black cod while Rico goes with the grilled strip loin, two meals very different from what they ate in the old days.

How naive and poor they had been then and, yet, surprisingly confident about their future. They had no money but few needs. They lived on their love and their dreams, which never included anything as extravagant as eating in a place like this. Finding some way to live in the United States had been their shared goal early in life, but it seemed so unattainable at the time. Yet, here they are, thirty years later, living, and hopefully sharing, an even better version of the American Dream.

Rico brings up his old gang and Teresa goes through what she thought of each of them, both now and then, something she would never have done back in the day. The astuteness of her observations surprises him but, also, he's amazed that Teresa has kept in touch with some of his friends, the majority of which never really made it out of the barrio.

Teresa mentions that she ran into an old friend of Rico's right here in Los Angeles. "You remember 'Santa' Sanchez, don't you?"

"Of course. The only member of our gang that actually went to jail," Rico responds.

"Well, it obviously didn't hurt his career much. He owns a bunch of car dealerships and seems to be doing amazingly well. Lives right here in L.A."

"Where did you see him?"

"Carlos invited him to a dinner party a while back. They had some kind of business dealings and Carlos wanted to pay back a favor," Teresa says. "'Santa' didn't recognize me but I knew him right away. He hasn't changed much. Still that same kind of snarky look on his face."

"I probably had the same look way back then. We thought we were so tough. He and I were pretty close back in the day. He used to hang around my house, sweet-talking my mom. She loved him right up until he was arrested," Rico says. "Say, if you can get his number from Carlos, I would love to call him and catch up."

"I'm not in a position to get anything from Carlos. We didn't exactly part on good terms. Remember?" she answers.

Then, their conversation goes from the old gang to their shared school experiences and how bored Rico had been by it all back then. How the street held more allure for him than anything in a book. How real experiences trumped fictitious ones back then.

Rico's parents thought he was lazy but Teresa would have never married him if she thought that. To her, he was just bored and ambitious, a deadly combination for a boy that age. The only cure was to grow out of it, which, fortunately, he did.

They talk about the divorce, how deeply it hurt her, and how easily he seemed to move on from it. Teresa confesses that she always expected Rico to come back to her, even when he remarried. For years, when the phone rang, or the doorbell, she always thought first of Rico. She even avoided dating for a while, worried that he would find out and stay in America, rather than coming back to her.

Rico is surprised and embarrassed that Teresa had thought about him so much through those first few years when, in truth, he had pretty much moved on with his life. How could he have thrown away a love like that so cavalierly?

Finally, they venture tentatively into a discussion about Carlos, how Teresa met him, what attracted her to him in the first place, and why she eventually soured on him.

Rico hopes to learn whether Teresa knows anything about the Batista cartel but there's no appropriate way to broach the subject. They'll have time for that later in their relationship, anyway, Rico thinks. That is, if they have a relationship. He certainly hopes so.

That night, back in bed alone, Rico tosses and turns, trying to figure out what's going on in his head and his heart. He just can't wrap his mind around these new emotions and feelings; so unlike anything he's experienced before, and yet, in some ways, so familiar.

He likes what he's feeling but he's scared of it, too. And, then, to top it off, there is the Carlos issue to consider. Like Edgar, that man scares him.

Finally, Rico drifts off to sleep wondering what the next few days of cruising, partying and spying will bring. *Clarity perhaps?* He doubts it.

Chapter 22

What a life. Rico lies back in his deck chair and surveys the pale blue sky, blemished only by a few wispy clouds here and there. The sun is bright and warm to the face; but the sea breeze has a bit of a bite to it. He pulls his jacket off the back of his chair and puts it over his shoulders, cutting the chill considerably.

He's lounging on the main deck of an 82-foot, two-masted yacht, under sail to Puerto Vallarta, with a crew of four, and only two passengers, Caroline Pendley and him.

Where is Caroline, by the way, he wonders? He hasn't seen her in hours.

The crew is busy with the sails. Every so often, a boom swings across the deck and the boat sways lazily from one side to the other, in order to catch a fresh wind. The crew scrambles across the deck in response, their quick, athletic moves in sharp contrast to the fluidity of the boat slicing through the water. All is at peace with the world.

Rico enjoys watching the crew do their thing but he has some work to do himself. He needs to think about the operation just ahead, and what he can do to make it a success. His first thought is that Mike has come up with another of his cockamamie ideas and Rico is right in the middle of it; once again bearing the brunt of Mike's idiocy.

It's at times like this that he longs for the good old days before Mike showed up, uninvited, on his doorstep; back when the closest he got to a bloodthirsty drug-pusher was reading about him in the newspaper.

His crazy assignment this time is to pretend he's the adopted ne'er-do-well son of a very rich software executive and Caroline is his cousin. They are to act cordial but cold to each other; appropriate, given their age difference. They are to be just two spoiled rich partiers out for a good time, sharing a boat they don't own, hoping they don't cramp each other's style.

Once the boat docks, both will go their own ways, to separate bars, thereby, doubling the odds that one of Shine's agents will hit on one of them. What happens after that is anybody's guess.

Rico has been told that, if a young, beautiful, girl meets him in a bar, comes on to him, brags about her access to drugs, and wants to see his boat, she's probably working for the cartel. Rico could have figured that out on his own.

His job then is simple. He's to get her out to the boat, listen to her proposition, get the drugs in play, then, get out of the way. Somebody else will be there to deal with the messy stuff after that.

Rico can take comfort in the fact that he'll be well-supported on this operation. Mike wants to make sure that this new Batista sales arm is nipped in the bud, and he doesn't want all of the responsibility for that to rest on the shoulders of an amateur like Rico.

So, not only is Caroline here, but two drug agents are serving as part of the crew and, when Rico, and his drug pusher friend, whoever she might be, arrive back on the boat, the agents will already be there, ready for action. The boat has been wired for both video and sound. So, all Rico has to do is set up the target. Then, make sure there are good pictures of the transaction. And the professionals will take it from there.

In essence, Rico is just the lure that attracts the fish. But, given his record with women, he wonders how the hell he got that assignment. It's a far cry from his first assignment, which was to impersonate a property manager, something he has done every day of his adult life, to this, attracting and romancing a young woman. Not exactly his wheelhouse.

In fact, thinking back, Rico cannot remember a single time in his life when a young woman at a bar approached him, asked him to take her somewhere, and, coaxed him to romance her. He is embarrassingly unprepared for this assignment.

Caroline, on the other hand? Something like this, a guy hitting on her, must happen to her almost every night. So, the odds are high that Rico will be a spectator on this one, just watching Caroline work her magic.

Rico wonders again where Caroline is. She isn't on the back deck and she isn't in the cabin. Rico calls out her name and, suddenly, her blonde head pops up from the second deck, just above the door to the cabin, where she has been sunning out of the wind.

"What is it," Caroline says. "Is something wrong?"

She's wearing a bright pink bikini and is in one of the few places on the boat where the chilly breeze, and/or prying eyes, can't find her.

"What in the world are you doing?" Rico asks.

"Getting a tan, something you should be doing as well," Caroline replies. "Not many spoiled rich people hang out in Puerto Vallarta, sporting pasty white skin."

"Well, given my heritage, I don't think that will be my problem. I need to talk to you. Got a minute."

"Sure, come on up."

Rico climbs awkwardly up the ladder and steps out onto the roof of the cabin. A sudden swell rocks the boat, making him reach out for one of the many hooks used for, well, who knows what. Once he gets his sea legs back under him, he looks around the deck, seeing no one for a minute.

Then, there she is, very close to the cabin roof, tucked in a nook where she is shielded but can still get some sun. Rico is blown away by the vision before him, Caroline, now lying on her back, eyes closed, seemingly ignoring him and all of the other males on the boat.

He knew before this, of course, that she had a classic, almost perfect, Scandinavian face, even though she always tried to disguise it. But he had no idea that she had such a lush and lovely body as well. Here, sporting just two small pieces of pink fabric, Caroline is absolutely stunning, especially when contrasted with the memory of the portly middle-aged woman she played on their last caper back in Mexico City.

What a chameleon she is, Rico thinks. He can play a lot of roles, too but, somewhere in there, he's always Rico, always an ordinary guy. Maybe that's what makes him so valuable to Mike. But, in her own way, Caroline is even more valuable. She can be ordinary and extraordinary, depending on the circumstances.

It takes Rico several minutes to remember why he climbed up onto the top deck. Caroline just waits patiently, her eyes closed, probably aware of the effect she's having on him. It isn't the first time a guy forgot what he was going to say around her. Rico's sure of that.

Finally, Rico finds his tongue, "I'm beginning to wonder about my role in this operation."

"Welcome to the party," she responds. Rico ignores the comment.

"How do you see this thing playing out?" he says.

"Frankly, I don't think you'll play much of a role at all," Caroline answers. "If there is some young drug dealer in Puerto Vallarta who's looking to get hooked up, I will find him, or her, long before you do. We're in my area of expertise now. You just watch and learn."

Rico doesn't doubt the wisdom of her words but he's still worried. If he's in a bar and gets approached, how does he avoid drinking too much, or taking drugs he can't handle, or succumbing to the charms of the drug dealer, especially if she's particularly seductive? Can he stay in control and still be believable? That's the balancing act that worries him.

Caroline senses his discomfort and guesses what he is thinking. She sits up, looks him in the eyes and says, "Whatever it takes. That's what you have to do."

She pauses, "Listen, if you get our target back to the boat and talking, you have done your job. If you arrive back on the boat drunk or wasted or even have sex on the boat, and the target talks, you get a gold star. Just get the job done, anyway you can. That's what we do."

Rico is a little discomforted by the cavalier nature of her answer, He's far from a prude but there's something a bit tawdry in how this might play out. Spilling coffee on Edgar is one thing. Having sex with, and tricking a drug dealer who's out to trick him, that's another thing; especially now that he and Teresa are kind of dating.

In fact, he realizes, that is the entire reason he feels uncomfortable. If he had received this assignment a few weeks ago, he would have been all in, no matter what. Now it feels a little too much like cheating.

Eventually, Rico decides to heed Caroline's advice. He'll do whatever it takes.

They tie up at Vallarta Marina, right in the heart of Puerto Vallarta Jalisco. Their berth is just steps away from the hottest hotels, bars and nightlife in this trendy resort town. Rico's assignment just became a lot easier. If things go right, he can reach the boat in minutes, no matter what bar he's in, with very little time for the target to become suspicious and/or change her mind.

There's a Mexican drug agent named Martinez waiting for them on the pier. As soon as the boat is moored, Martinez boards and goes down into the cabin where Rico, Caroline, and the two crew agents meet him.

He spreads out some photos on the small drop-down table and begins his briefing. He's been following the prime targets for weeks, he says, and he shows the agents photos of their faces. The images are little grainy but they will certainly help when Rico and Caroline hit the bars looking to hook up.

Martinez then says, "I now know their routine by heart. Tonight, you could try to connect with them if you want, but I recommend against it. If they hold true to their schedule, nobody will be in this area tonight and you'll have to go too far to find them. Tomorrow night, however, at least two of them, probably more, will be hanging out in bars right on the pier and I suggest you make your move then."

"What do we do tonight?" Rico asks. Caroline rolls her eyes but doesn't interrupt the conversation.

"Just set the stage," Martinez says. "You and Caroline could have dinner and look as bored as cousins from two different generations would normally be. Later, separate for an hour or two, to see and be seen, then, turn in early. Get some rest and be ready for the main event the next night."

"The important thing," Caroline chimes in, "is that we get to know some waiters and bartenders tonight, spread our story as best we can, and leave a little blood in the water for the sharks to follow. Right?"

So, that is what they do; Rico, surprisingly, a little better than Caroline.

He plays the role of a spoiled playboy perfectly, bragging about his father's money and famous people he knows. He drops names like Saint Tropez and Amalfi, just like the world traveler he's not. He plays his role with very broad strokes, like an amateur actor reading for his first role.

Caroline, on the other hand, is a bit more reserved, kind of flirty and coy. She lets Rico be the star of the show but she knows full well that, as usual, most eyes are on her. And they will be tomorrow night as well.

Later, after they split up, she flirts with the young, attractive bartenders at several restaurants, even inviting one back to the boat before "remembering that her drunk cousin will be there."

There's little doubt that the two rich snots from L.A. will be remembered the following night; which is the point, after all.

Back on board, they compare notes and decide how to approach things the following evening. They'll certainly have an advantage since they aren't planning to hit the scene until close to eleven, fully rested and stone-cold sober. Their targets, on the other hand, should be well oiled by that time, on alcohol, drugs, or both. Advantage Rico and Caroline.

The following day, Caroline and Rico sleep in as best they can, enjoy a late brunch at an overpriced hotel restaurant and tour the city. Neither of them has been here before but they aren't surprised to see the same high-end shops and brands tourists see everywhere these days. Globalization may be a good thing for the economy but it sure has taken away the individuality of resort towns like Puerto Vallarta.

Rico is especially taken aback. There's virtually no hint of the Mexican charm and culture he remembered from visiting Mexican villages in his youth. Granted, they didn't go into the most authentic sections of town, because they are also the most dangerous.

Unfortunately, Rico thinks, *Mexico has been irrevocably changed by the drug wars that have made everybody fearful, especially the tourists that are such an important part of the Mexican economy. Maybe putting the Batista cartel out of business will help some. But not if another gang steps in and replaces it.*

At 11:00 pm that night, the two agents enter one of the bars frequented by Shine's main lady pusher. She's easy to spot, at a table just off the small dance floor; dressed to kill in a red dress with a plunging neckline that invites looks if not more.

She has long, black hair, a cute face, and is engaged in a lively conversation with a guy that she seems to know quite well. Her hands are in the air, flying around, punctuating every point she tries to make. Her Latin heritage is visibly on display, and she looks drunk.

Per their plan, Caroline goes immediately to the ladies' room while Rico walks unsteadily up to the bar and, a bit too loudly perhaps, orders a margarita. The bartender is not the one Rico talked to the night before but it hardly matters. By the time his drink arrives, Rico has company.

"Hi. I'm Margarita, named after your drink. But I pack more punch," the dark-haired beauty says, leaning over slightly to give Rico a full view of her smile and her cleavage.

"I bet you do," he says, slurring slightly, "Like Mohammed Ali."

"I hope not. I hope I look better than him."

"Well, he was beautiful. At least, that's what he told us."

Margarita smiles broadly, as if Rico's trite repartee is highly entertaining. She's obviously a professional, touching his arm at just the right time, leaning into him as she waves her earlier companion off with the other hand. She talks to Rico in hushed tones, as if they are already lovers.

She listens attentively, her brown eyes never leaving his, as Rico tells his cover story. She seems enthralled but, still, Rico gets the feeling that she already knows who he is, or more correctly, who he's supposed to be.

Out of the corner of his eye, Rico sees Caroline leaving, on her way to another bar where they think the male drug pusher might be. Their two-pronged operation is fully underway and so far, so good.

Around midnight, after paying the bill, Rico escorts Margarita back to the boat. They both stumble a bit on the pier, he because he's acting, she presumably because the drinks have taken their toll.

Nothing has been said about drugs yet but, as Margarita drinks, and Rico sips, she gets more loquacious, hinting that she knows all the right people in town and he's lucky to have run into her, and things like that.

Once aboard, Margarita gets a little more direct, saying that if he ever needed, or wanted, anything, she could get it for him. As if to emphasize the point, she shrugs the top of her dress off, exposing her breasts, and pats the place beside her on the couch.

Rico is thrown off a bit by the sight of her perfect tits, probably crafted by a high-end Mexican breast surgeon. Then, he regains his composure and, ever conscious of the hidden camera, slides in cautiously beside her, and says, "What about drugs?"

"You've come to the right place, amigo. What do you have in mind?"

They start discussing, then, negotiating, all as she sits there, unashamedly half-clothed. He peels off a big wad of American dollars and counts out what she wants. All of a sudden, she's all business. No slurring or any sign of drunkenness or anything like that. Obviously, she's a professional.

She repositions the top of her dress, wiggles back into it, and grabs his hand. "Come with me," she says.

"Do we have to leave? I was just getting cozy. Does your dealer deliver?"

"I'm the dealer. I have some stashed on a boat one pier over. We'll be back in no time," Margarita says.

In the meantime, the two agents watching the scene on screens below deck call Caroline to tell her that she should abort because, surprisingly, it looks like their boy, Rico, has gotten the job done.

Caroline immediately objects, "I think I have Shine himself here. I want to bring him to the boat for the bust. Call me the minute Rico returns." The agent on the boat reluctantly agrees, probably only because Caroline outranks him. Still, if they can get Shine, it will be a much bigger score than his underling, Margarita.

Unfortunately, Shine suspects a sting operation the moment he sees Margarita in the cabin, a packet of "blue moonshine" on the table, and Rico leaning back to give the camera an unobstructed view.

Shine pulls a small handgun from his waistband and directs Caroline to sit on the couch with Margarita. Then, he points the gun at Rico.

"Who the hell are you, *senor*?"

"Ronaldo," Rico begins but Shine interrupts. "Not your cover story. Your real story. Are you Federales?"

Suddenly, there is a clatter coming from the ladder. Some small, unidentified metal object slides across the deck toward them. Shine looks at it briefly, trying to see if it's a smoke bomb or something, and Rico takes advantage of the guy's momentary lapse to lunge at his gun.

At the same time, an agent, coming out of the lavatory, attacks Shine from the back, grabbing both of his arms. Shine's pistol explodes, the bullet grazing Rico's foot before lodging in the hardwood floor.

The other agent, the one who threw the metal object, comes hurtling down the cabin ladder, gun in hand. A brief scuffle ensues but Shine is no match for the three men. They get him splayed on the floor, knee in his back, and frisk him for more weapons, finding none.

Rico picks up Shine's pistol and hands it to one of the agents. Then, he looks over at the couch, where Caroline has the female drug dealer,

Margarita, in a headlock. The top of her dress is, once again, around her waist, and she's whimpering like a scared puppy.

It's a frightful scene, all those muscled, perspiring bodies in that incredibly small space and Rico, taking it in, has the thought, *So this is what a big-time drug bust looks like?*

Then, he notices that his foot is bleeding. It starts to throb, then really stings, and he drops to the floor in pain.

Chapter 23

Meanwhile, back at DEA headquarters in Los Angeles, Mike is preparing for a little operation of his own. He's decided to bring in Edgar Vegas.

With all of his agents scattered hither, thither, and yon, Mike knows he will have to do the grunt work on the arrest and interrogation himself. Todd Williams can help him but Mike will have to fill the role of lead arresting officer, something he hasn't done in quite some time.

Ever since the bag switch in Mexico City yielded so little actionable intel, Mike has known that he was going to have to bring Edgar in for questioning. It's time to stop tip-toeing around the edges of their investigation, hoping for Carlos or Pablo to say something to Rico. Edgar is the only one who actually knows where the courier bag came from, who gave it to him, and, therefore, who's running the cartel. They simply must break the guy.

Rico will be upset, of course. He will view it as some kind of failing on his part and, in a way, he's right. Weeks after being assigned to establish a relationship with Edgar, Rico still hasn't produced any actionable intel that Mike can use. And Mike has learned through the years that, in this line of work, patience is definitely not a virtue.

So, partially to put off the confrontation over Edgar that Mike is sure will occur, he sent Rico to Puerto Vallarta on a kind of pleasure junket. Caroline didn't need Rico. She was perfectly capable of pulling off the caper without him and, in fact, the odds of success might have even been better. But it got Rico out of the way so that Mike could move on Edgar, unencumbered. Which he does.

Fortunately, Todd and Mike are able to take Edgar Vegas in without incident. He immediately consents to answering their questions and doesn't ask for a lawyer.

Of course, he has no idea what they're going to ask him so he is on his best behavior, which in Edgar's case, means a scowl without saying much. The love fest doesn't last very long, however. Once seated at a small table in one of the interrogation rooms of the DEA offices, Edgar quickly becomes uncooperative.

Any answers he gives are one or two words without elaboration. Often, he declines to answer at all and, at one point, Mike just sits there looking at Edgar for a while, a tactic that's normally disconcerting to suspects, but one that Edgar finds humorous. He just smirks back. No discomfort. No anger. No nervousness.

For the entire first half-hour, Mike asks questions, slowly, with a small manilla folder on the table between them.

"Have you been to Mexico recently?"

"Yes."

"On business?"

"Yes."

"What is your business?"

"I own a machine shop."

"Why would a machine shop owner go to Mexico on business?"

"A customer requested it."

"What customer?"

"Confidential."

"What kind of work did he want you to do?"

Silence. Every line of questioning ends the same way. A few answers followed by a dull stare.

Finally, Mike opens the folder. Inside are black and white photos of people quite familiar to Edgar. His mother. His brother. His ex-wife. His nephew. Each photo Mike flicks onto the table with a disdain that speaks volumes.

Edgar looks up, visibly shaken for the first time. But, to his credit, he says nothing.

"Do you know these people?" Mike asks. Silence.

"Do you know that they are all in the drug business in Mexico?" Silence.

"So, here's the deal. We're about to arrest these people. Only you can prevent that." More silence.

"Actually, only your correct answers can prevent that," Mike says, his eyes fixed on Edgar's. Nobody blinks. Then, for the first time, Edgar looks away.

"What do you want?" He says back over his shoulder.

"What've you got?" Mike replies.

"Listen," Edgar looks Mike straight in the eyes again, "Your scare tactics are not going to work. First of all, I'm not saying anything just to keep my family out of jail. They're headed in that direction anyway. No skin off my nose. But, immunity? U.S. citizenship? New identity? Those are worth something to me."

"Depends on the value of your information," Mike says.

"Depends on the package you offer, for both them and me?" Edgar continues.

"Thought you didn't care about them."

Edgar looks away again and Mike knows he has the makings of some kind of agreement. Hopefully, Edgar has information that's worth the price Mike will have to pay. Because it won't come cheap.

When Rico gets back to L.A. from Puerto Vallarta, he's so excited to report on the success of their operation that he calls Mike right away. Of course, Mike already knows most of the details from talking to Caroline, but he listens patiently as Rico describes events that, although frightening to the normal person, are pretty common-place to Mike at this stage of his career. Eventually, however, he has to break into Rico's vivid account of the arrest to tell him about Edgar Vegas.

"We turned Edgar," Mike interrupts.

"Holy shit," Rico answers, "Why did you do that?"

Mike isn't surprised to hear Rico ask "why" not "how." It shows how much more Rico is concerned about protecting his asset, and his ass, than he is about shutting down the Batista cartel.

"It was time. We had hoped to get somebody higher up the food chain to turn but we didn't," Mike says, "so Mr. Vegas is it."

"You know I could have gotten you what you wanted without giving up anything," Rico counters. "My relationship with Edgar was developing nicely."

"I don't think you have a relationship with Edgar," Mike responds. "I don't think anybody has a relationship with Mr. Vegas. But that's water under the dam right now. Once the papers are signed, Edgar will tell us what we want to know. If you have any thoughts about what we should ask him, just let me know."

Rico's very disappointed with the supposedly good news. He knows, of course, that he failed to get much out of Edgar. And Mike bringing Edgar in only underscores that point. But he wishes Mike had told him the clock was ticking, or, more appropriately, that it was about to go off in his face.

Furthermore, Rico realizes, if Edgar Vegas is now a source, not a suspect, then, Rico isn't much use to Mike. Edgar was his only assignment and it's clear now that he fucked it up. That's obviously not good news, career-wise.

While lost in his self-deprecating thoughts, Rico vaguely hears Mike say something about a meeting scheduled for the next day and how he'd like Rico to be there. At least Mike isn't going to fire him just yet.

At 9:00 the next morning, everybody present is asked to report on their various operations. Caroline covers the events in Puerto Vallarta, calmly and succinctly. Rico is surprised that her report is received so matter-of-factly until he hears the other reports. He was not the only agent injured, for example. A raid on a drug-smuggling boat had turned violent. One of the smugglers was killed and an agent shot in the arm. Just another day in the drug wars.

Mike doesn't ask about the agent who was injured or even how badly Rico was hurt. Instead, he asks about how necessary it was to kill the smuggler. "A dead source is no source," he says, rather coldly. Once again, Mike doesn't let his emotions get in the way of accomplishing the mission.

All in all, despite the lack of information on who's running things, the intel from Edgar's courier bag has yielded quick results. Over 1 million kilos of drugs were confiscated. One new cartel selling arm was eliminated. Several new players in the Batista supply chain were identified and one is already under surveillance. All at a price of only two slightly-injured agents.

Rico is proud to be one of them, and he wears his heavily-bandaged foot as a kind of badge of honor, like a Purple Heart in the military. He's passed one important hurdle at least. He's shed blood for Mike and the agency.

After the meeting, Mike takes Rico aside. He asks if there is any way Rico can get closer to Teresa, to see if she knows anything more about Carlos and his possible involvement with the Batista gang. Rico is a little taken aback.

"Do you know something I don't know?" he asks.

"No. Just fishing," is the reply.

"How about I start to date her? Would that be close enough for you?" Rico asks half-facetiously.

"Works for me," Mike replies, turning toward the center of the room.

"I'll get right on it," Rico says to a departing Mike.

Chapter 24

It's been more than a week now since Rico last worked out and, although his injured foot will obviously be an issue, he feels that thirty minutes on the stationary bike will be helpful; especially if Mike sends him out on another operation soon.

With Edgar now talking, though, that probably won't happen anytime soon, but it's best to be prepared and in shape. So, Rico times his visit for late morning, when he's sure Edgar won't be there. No reason for drama.

Rico is pedaling along, blissfully happy that his foot doesn't hurt as much as he expected, when lo and behold, Edgar shows up and approaches him. He must have been waiting for a long time, somewhere out of sight, on the off chance that Rico would show up at some point.

"Hello, asshole," the big man begins, "Enjoying your workout?"

Rico says nothing. He knows that, at this point, any word coming out of his mouth could be life-threatening. Edgar's face is crimson-red, his veins bulging, and his arms tense, ready for action.

"I just learned my family is at risk," Edgar blurts out. "And, therefore, you're at risk. I finally figured out that you must be a federal agent or something other than what you told me. But, honestly, whatever you are, you're not very good at it. Thinking back, that whole circus at the Mexico City airport was really amateur hour, you know."

Rico is silent. He knows protesting will just make things worse.

"Not as chatty as normal, huh, Rico," Edgar continues. "Well, as you know, I'm a man of few words. So, listen carefully. If my family is harmed, your family will be harmed as well. An eye for an eye. Is that clear?"

"I don't have any family to speak," Rico finds his voice, although it comes out unnaturally high.

"How about your brother, Roberto? Or your nephew, Manuel, in Mexico? Or your ex-wife," Edgar counters. "I could go on but you get it. I can hurt them, or you, and I won't hesitate to do it. So, Mr. Undercover Man, have a nice day."

Edgar turns and strides away, past the front desk, and out the door, without looking back. He seems even angrier going out than he was when he entered, probably because he wasn't able to kick the crap out of somebody.

Rico remains frozen in place on his bike, legs not moving, in a state of shock, for a considerable amount of time. He's sweating profusely and shivering uncontrollably, all at the same time. *At least*, he thinks, *I didn't wet my pants. That would have really been amateur hour.*

As soon as Rico calms down enough to walk, albeit somewhat unsteadily and with a limp, he goes to the locker room, finds his cell phone and calls his brother.

"Roberto, It's Rico. How are things?" he says, trying to sound nonchalant. His unusually high pitch probably gives him away, though., and Roberto has a sixth sense about when Rico's in trouble, anyway.

"What's up, bro?" He asks, "You OK?"

"You might be in danger." Rico answers.

"Why's that?" Roberto asks.

"Because I messed with the wrong guy."

"Does this have anything to do with what went down at the cabin last summer?"

Rico is surprised by the question. Roberto had never given any indication that he knew about that. Still Rico decides to play dumb. "What are you talking about?" he asks.

"Well, that time you asked me about our cabin, neighbors heard gunshots and sirens and all kinds of commotion," Roberto says. "But, by the time I got up there, a few days later, everything was fine, as if nothing had happened. And there was nothing about it on the news or in any papers. I even googled it. Nada."

"Why didn't you say anything about it to me?" Rico asks.

"I figured that, if you wanted me to know, you would tell me, but you never did. So, I decided to wait until you were ready. Are you?"

"Well, Roberto, it's a long story that you deserve to hear," Rico says. "But not now. Just be careful. Keep your alarm on. And let me know if anything suspicious happens."

"If I'm in danger," Roberto says, "you must've really pissed somebody off. Right? How can I help if I don't know what we're facing together? So *Mi hermanito*, the time for secrecy is over. What gives?"

"I can't tell you over the phone."

"Then maybe I should come there, hear the truth, and, help you figure out what to do," Roberto says.

"Not a good idea. I'm sure this thing will blow over quickly. But, in the meantime, don't tempt the fates. Keep your security system on, and your dogs close at hand, OK?"

"OK, Rico. I guess you know best. By the way, how's Teresa?"

Rico is startled. "Why do you ask about her?"

"She called me a while back," Roberto replies, "trying to reach you. I assume she finally talked to you. Is she involved?"

"Yes, in a way," Rico says cautiously, wondering what Roberto might know. Surely, he doesn't know Rico is seeing her again.

"Well, she has to be in danger, too. Right?"

"You have no idea," Rico answers.

There's silence. Then, Roberto says, "I'm on my way." And hangs up.

Immediately, Rico calls back but there's no answer. Oh well. He probably couldn't have dissuaded Roberto anyway. Calling his brother was a big mistake, because, unlike Rico, Roberto isn't one to hunker down and wait. He's always been the superhero, flying in, cape flying, to save the day.

Realizing there's nothing more he can do from the locker room of a gym, Rico gathers his things up and drives directly to DEA headquarters. The closer he gets, the angrier he gets. It isn't clear how his cover with Edgar was blown but he suspects Mike was right in the middle of it. Fortunately, Mike is there, in his office, so Rico has a target for his rage.

"What the hell did you tell Edgar about me?" he says.

"Nothing. Interrogations are about getting information, not giving it," Mike responds. "Why?"

"I just had a very angry Edgar in my face, threatening me and my family," Rico says. "He thinks I had something to do with him being picked up."

"I wonder why he thinks that?" Mike says sarcastically, realizing a minute too late that this isn't the time to be funny. "I'm sorry. I understand why you would be concerned. Edgar is a scary dude."

"I think he got the idea from you," Rico says, ignoring Mike's apology. "I think you wouldn't hesitate to throw me under the bus if it served your purpose."

"No, I wouldn't do that, Rico. I'm not in the habit of burning my agents."

Rico went on, "Well, he said that, if his family is in danger, so is mine."

Mike replies, "I think he just put two and two together on his own. But I can tell you this. He's cooperating. His intel so far has been credible. So, his family is safe, and yours is as well. If anything changes, I'll let you know."

Rico leaves the office feeling a little bit better. He doesn't like the idea that Edgar knows he's an agent. But, eventually, Edgar will disappear into the hinterlands of the witness protection program. His family will go on with their lives. And all will be well. Another happy ending.

The fact that Edgar knows Teresa, however, bothers Rico the most. He'll soon have to come clean with her if their relationship is going to amount to anything. Rico certainly doesn't want Teresa to hear from somebody else that he's an undercover agent. That'll kill his newly-rekindled romance even before it has an opportunity to blossom.

Roberto arrives that evening, all primed for a fight. Rico sits him down and, over beers, tells him the whole story. Everything from Mike approaching him in the beginning, through his raids, up to his date with Teresa. They talk about Edgar and what kind of threat he might represent. Roberto is comforted by the fact that Edgar will be in some kind of witness protection program going forward and, if that's the case, it's unlikely he would want to punish Rico.

Eventually, Roberto finds himself actually reassuring Rico, "We have to assume that this guy Mike knows what he's doing, Rico. Edgar isn't stupid enough to jeopardize his freedom and his deal, just to seek revenge on you, or me, or anybody else, for that matter."

Then, they continue talking about other things, well into the wee hours of the morning. Roberto tells Rico, for instance, that the same thirst for adventure that got him into this situation, has been a concern of Roberto's since they were kids.

The difference this time, Roberto says, is that there's no gang or peer pressure involved and Rico is trying to do something good for society; rather than the other way around. That makes the risks more acceptable to Roberto. In fact, he respects Rico more than he ever has.

They revisit some of Rico's escapades back in the day and Roberto says that he always believed Rico's heart was in the right place, and he supported him as much as he could. He just felt that Rico was unduly influenced by his compadres, especially "Santa" Sanchez.

"That boy was never any good," Roberto remembers. "Things would've been very different for you back then if there was no 'Santa.'"

"They turned out all right, though, for me and 'Santa.'"

Roberto is surprised, "For you, maybe. But 'Santa'? I doubt it. He's probably in some Mexican jail as we speak."

"I just learned from Teresa that he's alive and well in L.A. He owns some car dealerships and is a respected member of society."

"I doubt that he's a respected anything," Roberto counters. "And, believe me, I wouldn't buy a car from that guy."

The hours talking to Roberto are a wonderful tonic for Rico. Just confiding in somebody he trusts lifts Rico's spirits considerably and he looks forward to the time when he can tell Teresa about his secret life as well. Nothing weighs more heavily on him than that little lie. Especially since he really wants her back in his life now.

The next morning, after many assurances of how he'll support his brother whenever he is needed, Roberto goes back home. And Rico is left alone with his still very real, undiminished, fears.

Chapter 25

Things are definitely more complicated for Rico now that he's invited Teresa back into his life. Before that, when she was just an ex-wife, Teresa wasn't a love interest of his nor a subject of his investigation. Things were cool.

Now, only a few days later, she's become both. To balance these two things, he decides he needs to be very honest about his feelings for Teresa and basically lie about everything else. Once she's cleared, however, and he's sure she will be, Rico can come clean, beg her forgiveness, and ask her to remarry him. Not the best plan in the world but, so far, he hasn't been able to come up with a better one.

To complicate things further, Pablo has once again invited both Teresa and Rico over for dinner. The guy obviously fancies himself some kind of matchmaker, and an evening that, under normal circumstances, would be fun and relaxing, now carries a lot of risk for Rico.

Mike sees it as an opportunity, of course. Mike sees everything as an opportunity. For Rico, however, as a guy worried about blowing his cover on one hand or his romance on the other, it's fraught with peril.

One of Rico's strengths has always been his open and honest approach to everything. But, how does he square that simple view of himself with the Rico who, while spending the whole evening with people he likes, will essentially be lying from the moment he arrives until he departs?

Rico picks up Teresa on his way to Pablo's house for dinner and, after explaining how he injured his foot (lawn mower accident), and how much he is looking forward to Alicia's cooking, he uses the rest of the time in the car to learn if Teresa is somehow complicit in this unexpected dinner invitation.

One part of him hopes she is; because that would show an interest. On the other hand, if she's close enough to the Cerritos to set up a dinner party, maybe she's working with them on other things as well. And, this evening could be more than just a pleasant diversion.

Teresa acts innocent enough, until, finally, in a weak moment, she admits that she might have told Alicia they were dating, and that getting together with them for dinner would be nice. Bingo. That makes everything much clearer, and less sinister. Just two women doing what women do.

As for Pablo, he probably considers this dinner simply a victory lap for the role he played in bringing them back together. He will smile, and hug and gloat all at the same time. It could turn out to be a very cloying evening.

Rico is proven right immediately when Pablo greets them at the door with a big smile, "There they are. The two love birds."

Alicia comes up right after Pablo, arms stretched wide, a big smile on her face as well, and gives each of them a hug. The mood is quite loving and convivial. "Come in. Come in," she says. "Dinner's in the oven. Would you like a drink?"

As usual, they are greeted by tantalizing aromas drifting into the hallway from the kitchen, making them immediately hungry. Pablo leads them into the living room, gets them seated, and then, he backs up to the ornate side bar where an already-iced shaker of martinis is waiting. All the while he keeps talking. If Rico had wanted to go easy on his drinking tonight that's no longer an option.

Pablo pulls two chilled martini glasses out of his bar refrigerator, plops double olives into them, and fills them with vodka from the shaker. "Chablis?" he asks Teresa. Meanwhile, Alicia leaves to tend to dinner.

"How's our business doing, partner?" Pablo asks. Rico has to admit that it isn't going that great. Two old-line customers have given notice and their most recent acquisitions are underperforming. Therefore, cash flow is down and it's fortunate that they have no debt to service, or they might be triggering covenants all over the place. Any bank worth its salt would be all over them at this point.

Pablo waves it all off. "All businesses have cycles," he says. "We'll talk more after dinner, perhaps over cigars, but, for now, on to more important things. Exactly where does your budding romance stand?"

"Pablo," Alicia yells from the kitchen door, where she's standing in a flowered dress topped by an apron. "You're so rude."

Rico is glad for the interruption, thinking Alicia has saved them all from an embarrassing conversation. But then, with a sly grin, Alicia continues, "Wait for me. I want to hear."

When, after dinner preparations are finished, Alicia joins them, Rico answers very diplomatically, "One dinner date does not a romance make. Teresa and I are just feeling our way, getting to know each other again. These things take time, Pablo." He smiles over at Teresa for support, but, gets none.

"Bullshit," Pablo interrupts Rico's well-rehearsed remarks. "You've already been married once. What do you need to know? I've seen the way you look at each other. Yours is a perfect match. Always has been. You should get on with it."

Rico sips his martini, grins at Pablo, then, looks again at Teresa who seems much more amused than embarrassed. Through the warm, alcohol-infused glow he's feeling, Rico wonders if she agrees with Pablo. Certainly he does but, at this point, Rico has to proceed cautiously, with both Pablo and Teresa. *Who knows if they're working together on a plan for matrimony...or something else?*

"Look," he finally responds, turning back toward Pablo, "I agree that, because we've been married before, it's different. But, in some ways, that should make us much more cautious. Besides, I think it would be highly inappropriate for me to say things to Teresa right now, in front of you, that I haven't said to her alone. I'm sure you agree."

"Okay. But, in my mind, we're like family," Pablo reluctantly responds. "Everything should be out in the open, especially since we can all see what's going on, except maybe you, Rico."

"Sometimes," he continues, "Things are just meant to be. You weren't ready for the commitment and risk all those years ago. But now you are. The love was there but the circumstances were not. At least, that's how I see it."

Then he concludes, "Take your time. We all have lots of that. Right?" He chuckles. With that, Alicia invites them into the dining room for dinner.

The dinner conversation is much less contentious. They talk about Trump, North Korea, and China; all safer subjects for Rico than the one they had discussed before dinner.

Then, near the end of dinner, Pablo gives it one more shot: "Here's what I'll do. I'll hold a party for you at the end of this month. You can invite anybody you want. I'll do the same. Then, if you happen to get engaged, we'll announce it as an engagement party and go from there. If not, we'll all just drink in silence, lamenting what might have been, and talk about what a boring time we had. No pressure, though."

Rico laughs. So does Teresa. But Pablo doesn't. He's very serious about the party.

After dinner, as promised, Pablo brings out the cigars and the two men talk about their business. Rico says he plans to call his old customers next week to check their temperature on things and he encourages Pablo to do the same. They need to find out if there's some common reason they're losing business. They agree to do some digging and, for a few days, at least, focus their attention on fixing the business.

On the way back home, Rico asks Teresa if she was uncomfortable with the conversation about their relationship. She's evasive in her answer.

Finally, Rico decides to tell her that he loves her, something he'd been hesitant to say before. And, also, that he agrees with Pablo that they are a perfect match. But, he says, they just started dating again, and they should remember, and sort through, the reasons they broke up, before taking things too far.

"Ok," she says, looking back toward her window. "Why don't you do that. I resolved those issues years ago." Obviously, she doesn't have as much to sort through as he does.

When Rico gets home, he calls Mike to tell him that, not only has he started to date Teresa, but Pablo is already planning an engagement party and is pushing the relationship beyond comfortable levels.

"It's an untenable situation," Rico tells Mike.

"I don't think so," Mike replies. "In fact, it might work to our favor."

How in the world can that be? Rico thinks.

Mike goes on, "I guess it's time to let you in on a few things. First, as you already know, Edgar has been talking. It turns out he got the courier bag from Carlos, not Pablo. He knows Carlos is part of the Batista cartel, probably just in the money laundering end, though. Probably not the leader of the cartel."

Rico isn't surprised. He had suspicioned as much.

"Second, Edgar does know Teresa a little. To him, she's just one of Carlos' many flings and Edgar doubts she's in on anything. Carlos has the reputation of being a ladies' man, a very smooth talker, but he's also tight-lipped about his drug gang activities. In fact, he goes out of his way to appear to be just a wealthy businessman. So, I don't believe Teresa is involved."

Mike continues, "And third, Edgar doesn't know Pablo at all and I believe him. Of course, that could just mean Pablo has been very careful, using only a small and protective inner circle to carry out his wishes. But, if so, that would be a first in the drug business. Normally, the leader likes to be visible, vicious, and violent."

Rico listens carefully, and then asks, "How good is the intel that made you think the leader of the Batista cartel is actually in the U.S.?"

"Pretty good. Why?"

"Well, you remember I was down there for a brief meeting," Rico replies. "If you are looking for sociopaths that could inspire the kind of things the Batista cartel is known for, those guys fit the bill a hell of a lot better than either Pablo or Carlos."

"Okay. I'll revisit our thinking on that. In the meantime, though, if you are of such a mind, I would suggest you go ahead with the engagement party idea. I'm sure Carlos will be there, and some of his friends. Maybe we can use the party to expand our list of suspects."

Rico's surprised, "Are you suggesting that I act like I'm going to marry Teresa just to give you a surveillance opportunity?"

"Of course not," Mike counters. "I'm suggesting you actually marry Teresa and give us two surveillance opportunities. Is that too much to ask?"

Chapter 26

Rico wakes up to the sound of loud knocking on his door. He glances at the clock. It's 5:30 a.m. "All right. All right. I'm coming," he yells.

He finds his robe right away but not his slippers. Finally, he just pads barefoot through the living room, onto the bare stones of the front hall, and then to the door, where he pauses before looking through the peephole.

Outside are two brawny cops in riot gear and a slim, young man hidden behind them wearing an oversized vest emblazoned with DEA in large white letters. Rico doesn't recognize any of them.

The door sticks briefly as Rico tries to open it, adding to the drama of the moment. One of the officers unholsters his pistol, obviously on the ready, as Rico finally jerks the door open.

Rico is unnerved by the size and serious demeanor of the three officers standing there but he takes comfort in the fact that they're probably just as nervous as he is. Still, they know why they're here and he doesn't. So, advantage cops.

"Good morning," says one of the police officers as if it is just a friendly courtesy call. "May we come in?"

"Of course. How can I help you, officers?"

There's no reply until they cross the hall and reach the living room. Then the biggest police officer, the one who seems to be the most senior, asks Rico if he's the Mr. Lopez who owns a warehouse on Carson Boulevard.

When Rico says yes, he goes on, "Well, we have it on good authority that there may be drugs in that facility," the lead police officer says. "Do you have any idea how drugs might have gotten into your warehouse?"

"No, sir," Rico answers meekly. All the while his mind is whirring. Mike is in charge of all DEA drug activities in Southern California and surely any raid would fall under his jurisdiction. *Is this one of Mike's games again?* These policemen don't seem to be playing a game, however. *Maybe the head office is running an independent investigation*, Rico guesses, *and they forgot to coordinate it with Mike's office. If that's the case, Mike will be able to clear everything up in due time.* Rico's best bet is to stay in character, reveal nothing about his undercover role, and do anything the officers request.

The lead officer continues, "Because we believe the information to be credible, the head of the DEA task force has decided to search that warehouse, and all of your warehouses. A search warrant covering that operation will be arriving soon and, although it isn't required, we would appreciate it if you would sign it."

"Of course," Rico responds. Then, he asks if he can go upstairs to shower and get dressed for the day.

The DEA agent speaks up for the first time, "As soon as you sign the warrant, you can certainly do that. But, for now, we would prefer you stay here with us."

"Am I under arrest?"

"No, Mr. Lopez, of course not," the agent says. "You aren't under arrest or even in custody. We consider you a cooperating witness with all the rights and privileges such a witness would have. If you want to call somebody, you're free to do that. If you want to refuse to answer our questions, you can do that as well. We'd like your help but you aren't compelled to give it. Do you understand?"

"Yes, but what information can I possibly provide?" Rico says. "I know nothing about any drugs. The pallets in my warehouses don't belong to me. I'm sure you realize that we don't search shipments that come in and out. We just store them."

"Of course, we understand that, Mr. Lopez. However, whether you're involved or not, we will need your help in figuring out which customers are involved, and what their tactics might be. If it turns out drugs are stashed in all of your warehouses that could take some time. The more you help us, the quicker this thing will be over. Still, I expect that the searches alone will take most of the day."

"In the meantime," the agent goes on, "Can we get the names and contact information of all of your customers?"

Rico knows, of course, that the drugs are probably not in his warehouses. So, he can hardly just stand idly by and let this happen without warning Pablo.

"Can I call my partner?" he asks.

"You have a partner?" The DEA Agent asks, "Our records don't show that."

"His ownership position is in a trust so you might not have seen it," Rico replies, "but he has the same authority I do. He needs to be informed. I'm sure he won't get in the way of what you're doing."

"Okay. We'd like full authorization for what we are doing anyway, if possible. Who's your partner?"

"Pablo Cerritos," Rico answers.

The DEA agent arches his eyebrow and exchanges a somewhat startled look with one of the cops. Obviously, they know the name. *That can't be good*, Rico thinks.

"You know, Mr. Lopez," one of the policemen says after a few seconds of silence, "maybe it would be best if you could come down to the station house with us, after all. You can sign the search warrant and call Mr. Cerritos from there."

Rico sees no reason to resist at this point. He's sure Mike will clear things up soon but, in the meantime, Rico should try to be the ideal suspect, or witness, or whatever the hell he is. So, he says, a little facetiously, "OK. May I get dressed first?"

"Please do."

Once at the station house, the feigned police friendliness disappears. The two officers that bring Rico in are all business. They log him in, get him to sign the search warrant and, then, leave him unattended in the waiting room. Rico isn't sure whether he's allowed to make a call but there's nobody around to ask, so he doesn't push it. The DEA agent isn't around either so Rico assumes he's somewhere searching warehouses with the rest of the team.

Rico knows it'll probably be a long wait so he stretches his legs out and makes himself as comfortable as possible. However, within minutes, a plainclothes officer comes over, introduces himself to Rico, asks a few basic questions, and then, leads Rico into a semi-private office with a telephone, and not much else.

The officer says that Rico can use the phone if he likes, or get a soda from the fridge. Nothing about the actions of anybody in the station house suggests that Rico is a suspect at this point, but who knows?

Rico looks around at his surroundings, surprised by how small and tight everything is. From police shows he's seen on TV, he expected a much larger venue, with a wasp's nest of activity swirling around here or there.

But, there's only the bored clerk at the front desk and a uniformed cop at an old metal desk in the back of the room, filling out paperwork. The guy who brought Rico to the back office never returns and nobody else seems the least bit interested in him. *I could probably walk out of here and no one would notice*, Rico thinks.

But, instead, he decides to make a few calls. The first to Pablo. There's no answer and it goes straight to voice mail. After leaving a message about the raid and where he is, Rico hangs up and calls Mike. No luck there either.

Not able to think of anybody else he should involve at this point, Rico goes back into the waiting room, spreads out again on the couch, and tries to sleep, comforted by the fact that he's sure he's in no real danger. *These guys don't know yet that I'm actually on their side*, Rico naively thinks, *and when they do, I'll probably get an apology.*

An unfamiliar policeman wakes Rico up from a surprisingly sound sleep to confirm who he is, and to tell him that the raids are going slower than expected, but they still want him to stick around so that they can update him when they're finished. Rico assures him that he will and goes immediately back to sleep, hoping for pleasant dreams.

It must have worked because, about an hour later, when he opens his eyes, there's a beautiful woman sitting on the couch with him. As his eyes focus, he sees it's none other than his ex-wife and current girlfriend, Teresa Wilson. She glances over at him, sees he is awake, and leans over to hug him.

"Hey, sleepy head, you don't seem too concerned about all this," she says, waving her open hands around to take in the whole room.

"What're you doing here?"

"Pablo sent me. He was tied-up with something and thought I might provide some comfort until he can break loose to join you," Teresa explains. "I told the guy at the desk that I was your wife. I hope you don't mind."

"I don't," Rico answers, "and that guy probably doesn't care much either. He's very, how should I say it, incurious." Then he goes on, "The security here is a joke. I don't see bars on the windows, or anywhere for that matter. And nobody is watching me. I'm not complaining, mind you. Just observing."

"I know. I expected to see you in a prison outfit, locked in a cell, with a bunch of drunks; and here you are, living the life of Riley," Teresa agrees.

"Well, for the record, I would rather live the life of Rico, thank you very much. This isn't exactly my cup of tea. Hopefully, I can get out of here relatively soon."

A few minutes later, Rico sees the clerk motioning him up to the front desk, where he's told that the raids are finished and somebody should be arriving soon to update him.

Rico's relieved. Maybe, he thinks, they just might get this thing over quickly enough for him to grab an *In-N-Out* burger on the way home. He thinks about asking Teresa to join him there, as kind of a date, but quickly decides it would be best for him get home as quickly as he can, and plot his next move. Romance can wait.

Then, surprisingly, he sees Caroline enter the station. *What the hell is she doing here?*

She walks confidently over to the front desk, and engages the clerk. For the first time, the guy gets animated and shows a small spark of interest. No personality, just interest.

They carry on an animated conversation, with Caroline gesturing toward Rico several times.

For Rico, with Teresa sitting right beside him, the situation just got more complicated. If he seems to know Caroline that would make Teresa suspicious. She would naturally wonder why he would be friendly with somebody who just told the officer on duty she's a DEA agent.

And, if Caroline greets him warmly, his cover is blown for sure. How will he talk his way out of this one? Fortunately, though, Caroline is a real professional. She sizes everything up quickly, and approaches him as she would a stranger.

"Mr. Lopez," she says, extending her hand. "I'm Caroline Pendley with the Drug Enforcement Agency. I apologize for any inconvenience we may have caused you. However, I need to inform you that we found drugs, a considerable amount of drugs, in fact, in several of your warehouses this morning."

"I already assumed that, Miss Pendley, or I would have been released hours ago," Rico says, with as much feigned indignation as he can muster. Then he continues, "And that's why I signed the search warrants earlier. I've been cooperating fully and will continue to do so. But, please understand that I had nothing to do with the drugs you found. I'm just as upset as you are about it. Obviously, some of my customers lied about what they were storing with us and the quicker you lock them up, the better."

Caroline smiles sympathetically, and replies, "The head of the search team will be here soon to go over the details of the raid."

Then, she looks at Teresa, "But, in the meantime, Mrs. Lopez, I suggest you go back home. We need to talk to your husband for an hour or two, then, we will bring him back to you in time for dinner. I promise."

Teresa looks at Rico, who nods. Then, she says nothing, just kisses him and leaves the station house.

Caroline waits until she's sure Teresa is out of earshot before speaking.

"Listen, Rico," she says, "this raid is a total screw-up. I wasn't aware of it and I'm sure Mike wasn't either. I don't really know what they found but I know the agents who did the search have no clue as to who you really are. And, for the time being, I suggest we keep it that way. Is that clear?"

Rico nods. He's a little concerned about getting caught in the middle of some kind of agency turf war but he trusts Caroline and decides to follow her lead. He's very thankful, in fact, that she's here to steer him in the right direction. Mike wouldn't have had her gentle touch.

"I need to go outside now and finesse things," Caroline says, "But I'll be back momentarily. Oh, by the way. I like your wife," Caroline flips over her shoulder as she heads to the door to meet the search team that's just arriving.

Chapter 27

The task force, all twelve strong, files through the police station door and fills up the small waiting area in front of Rico, milling around and chatting. They hardly notice him.

Caroline is front and center, introducing herself to each member of the search team. Then, she leads them down a long hallway to a conference room situated at the back of the building. Rico stays seated, waiting to be called.

About fifteen minutes later, one of the agents comes back to escort Rico into the conference room. He introduces himself as Bill and seems friendly enough, although he brushes off the questions Rico asks.

"Just wait a minute. You'll see," he responds.

When they enter the room, only the lead agent greets Rico, rising and introducing himself as Tom Staunton. The rest of them remain seated around a relatively small, unpolished wooden table that barely accommodates the whole group. Caroline is sitting near the wall on a desk chair she must have brought in from a nearby office.

After the introduction, Tom Staunton sits down at the head of the table, and he motions for Rico to sit at the foot. There's a brief period when it seems nobody's willing to speak. Feet are shuffling under the table. The officers look everywhere but at Rico.

Finally, Tom breaks the silence. "Mr. Lopez, around this table are the members of the team that you authorized to enter and examine your warehouses. They're all here in case you ask questions I can't answer. I can assure you that, aside from the removal of the illegal drugs, we left each of the warehouses as we found it. Right, guys?"

There are a few nods. Most seem pretty disinterested in the proceedings.

Tom goes on, speaking to Rico directly, "First, I thank you for authorizing these searches. That speaks to your innocence and it's the only reason we're treating you the way we are. If we suspicion anything going forward, however, circumstances can change quickly. But you know that."

Rico nods and says nothing.

"Second, we intend give you a summary report on what we found during our searches. You can comment or not as you see fit. And finally, we'll ask you questions that will, hopefully, help us identify who's responsible for the drugs we found hidden in your warehouses. Is that clear?"

Rico nods again.

"Okay, here's the situation. We found about 1/2 ton of meth and heroin, in fifteen different shipments stored at three of your facilities. We estimate the street price to be in excess of $20 million. According to the labels on the packages, the affected shipments came from six importers, which we would like you to help us identify and locate. Here are the names, markings, and code numbers from the labels."

He hands Rico a sheet of paper which lists letters and numbers indecipherable by anybody but Rico. He looks over the list and notices immediately that one shipment is from Pablo's own company, Global Transport, Inc. Also, he sees immediately that all of the customers involved were customers of Pablo's before the merger.

On its surface, it's pretty damning evidence that Pablo is somehow involved. Obviously, Rico will have to proceed carefully.

"I know who these customers are and will gladly give you their contact information when I get home," Rico says.

"Well, unfortunately, we need the information right away. So, let's wrap this thing up as quickly as we can so you can get us what we need. Do you have any questions, Mr. Lopez?"

"Only the obvious ones," Rico responds. "Am I being charged with anything? Am I free to conduct my business going forward? What can I tell my customers about the raid?"

Tom Staunton reassures Rico for the umpteenth time that he isn't under arrest or really even a suspect at this point. From their standpoint, Staunton says, Rico can go on with business as usual. There's no reason to say anything to his customers unless they ask. Then, if they do, he needs to be careful about what he says. "How much we found and what customers are involved; those things are off-limits. In general, don't give out any more information than necessary."

Finally, after all of Rico's questions are answered, the lead agent asks one final question, "Do you know where we can reach your partner, Pablo Cerritos? Obviously, we have a number of questions for him as well."

Rico says he doesn't really know where Pablo is at the moment, then offers up his partner's cell phone number and nothing else.

Finally, Staunton tells one of the agents to take Rico home. For the first time, Caroline speaks up, "I can do that. It's on my way. I'll get the contact information and return it to you right away. We don't need to inconvenience Mr. Lopez any more than we already have."

The agent nods and Caroline escorts Rico out of the room, saying nothing until they're safely out of earshot. Then, Caroline takes charge.

"Here's what we're going to do. First, I'll take you home to get the contact information. Then, Mike will meet us back at headquarters. He's anxious to hear your version of what happened before plotting any strategy going forward. Obviously, this raid changes things. If necessary, we may need to get you extricated from your assignment, both legally and physically, so that you're in a better position to defend yourself."

Rico is a little taken aback. He had expected more assurances that everything was OK and that he didn't have to worry. Surely, Mike will have his back on all this but nobody has told Rico that directly.

After her initial speech, Caroline is quiet on the way home, giving Rico time to weigh his options. Can he just quit and wash his hands of this mess? Hardly. There's too much at risk now. Pablo may already know about his involvement and, even if not, there's the sticky situation of his ownership position. If the partnership is to be unwound in a way advantageous to Rico, he needs Mike's help.

It seems that the more Rico tries to free himself from the agency, the tighter the bonds become, and the only thing clear to him right now is that his comfortable, ordinary life is solidly in his rear-view mirror.

A number of questions remain unanswered. Why in the world would a team outside Mike's control jump into his operation? Does some higher-up think that Mike is moving too slowly? Or is it all just a mix-up as Caroline seems to insinuate?

By the time Caroline and Rico reach Mike's office, Rico has built up a head of steam. He's both angry, and inquisitive. However, as usual, Mike is ready for anything Rico might ask.

"Hey, Rico, how ya doin?" Mike asks.

"Well, I was awakened by cops, taken to the station house, and accused of being part of a drug gang."

"Aside from that."

"There's no aside from that."

"Sure there is," Mike counters. "You're not in jail. You still have your business. You still have me. Life is good."

"Please, Mike, enough," Rico says, "How in God's name could you let such a colossal fuck-up happen?"

"Maybe I wanted it to happen."

"Explain please." Rico is finished with Mike's cat-and-mouse game.

"I didn't say I authorized it, because I didn't, but look on the positive side. We sure know a few things now that we didn't know yesterday," Mike says, pausing to let Rico wonder what they might be.

"As an example, Mr. Cerritos is somehow involved. Right? It isn't exactly a surprise that the drugs are in shipments from his customers, and not yours. Or that he's nowhere to be found. Or that he has been doing next to nothing to help you. No, Mr. Lopez, your beef about this raid should be with the guy who caused it, Mr. Cerritos, not me. That's what any innocent and concerned person would do. He'd ask his partner to explain himself."

Rico considers the logic of what Mike is saying, but there's one major flaw in it. Rico's boss is actually Mike, not Pablo; and if Mike knew there was a raid planned on Rico's business, he should have warned him. A good boss might have even included Rico in the planning but obviously, with Mike, that's way too much to ask. It's impossible to trust Pablo, as Rico understands all too well, but it's equally hard to trust Mike, a guy who should be in his corner.

Still, upon reflection, what Mike seems to be telling him is that, in his undercover role, Rico needs to redirect his anger toward Pablo. He should be less concerned about what went down, and more concerned about what was found. He needs to do what would be natural. Confront Pablo. Make him explain. His explanation, in fact, might even be the trigger event that makes Pablo come clean, and, perhaps, even implicate himself.

"You should wear a wire next time you talk to Pablo," Mike says. He then turns to Caroline, "Make sure he gets outfitted with appropriate equipment and trained how to use it."

"What about his phone?"

"His home phone is already bugged and, as you know, we can listen into his cell phone conversations anytime we want."

Rico is shocked, "Thanks for letting me know that."

"I am letting you know."

"Sometimes," Rico says, "I get the impression you don't totally trust me. Are we partners trying to bring down a cartel? Or am I just a resource to be exploited?"

"I'll get back to you on that."

Mike goes back to the paperwork on his desk, effectively dismissing the two of them without saying a word. Out in the hallway, Rico confronts Caroline, "How can you put up with that man?"

"Because he's the best agent we have," Caroline replies, "passionate about what we're doing. Smart about how to do it. Always looking for an edge. If his people skills aren't to your liking, well, that's just too bad. We aren't a corporation with some kind of human resource or compliance department to make sure we're politically correct all the time. And instead of customers we deal with criminals. Big difference."

"There's such a thing as professional courtesy," Rico argues.

"Not in our business," she answers.

Chapter 28

Once he's safely back in his house, and alone, Rico takes stock of the situation. He's under pressure on a number of fronts.

Mike wants Rico to confront Pablo Cerritos and make him explain why his shipments are so contaminated with drugs. Through some skill but, mostly, luck, Rico has positioned himself as a confidant of Pablo. Mike believes it's time to take advantage of that.

Edgar is another pressure point. He's talking to the Feds but that doesn't mean he's now on Rico's team. In fact, somehow Edgar has figured out that Rico played a role in outing him, and he isn't happy about it. It's only a matter of time before his suspicions about Rico reach the higher-ups in the Batista Cartel, probably including Pablo.

Carlos Silva is obviously a ranking member of the cartel as well and, to Rico, he may be the most dangerous of all. Rico never liked Carlos and he's pretty sure the feeling is mutual. Now, to add to that discomfort. Rico is trying to rekindle his romance with Teresa, just weeks after she broke up with Carlos, a move that most undercover agents would be hesitant to make in this situation.

So, when Rico lays his head down to sleep at night, hoping for sweet dreams about Teresa, it's not hers or Pablo's or Edgar's face he sees. It's the handsome, smiling, and malevolent face of Carlos Silva.

May as well get on with it, Rico thinks. *The best antidote for worry is action.* So, the first thing he does is call Pablo but, again, there's no answer. It's unlike Pablo to be so unavailable but, under the circumstances, Rico isn't totally surprised.

Then, he calls Teresa, who answers immediately, "Rico, I've been so worried about you. Is everything OK."

"It could be better."

"What do you mean?"

"Well, in their search, the Feds found drugs in a few of our warehouses. Quite a lot of drugs, in fact. I know nothing about them and I doubt Pablo does either, but I haven't been able to reach him. Do you know where he is?"

"I can reach him, I think," she replies. "Do you want him to call you?"

"Better that we meet at his office. The drug agents may be talking to a few of our customers already, and we need to plot a strategy for how we react. He knows these guys better than I do."

"Okay. How about later this afternoon. That OK?"

"Sure."

"Anything else I can do for you?"

Rico silently mulls his options. Finally, he says, "Yes, have dinner with me tonight."

"Okay," she answers quickly. "I'll find a place near Pablo's office. You can meet me when you're done with your talk."

Rico knows he's playing with fire. The smart move would be to cool it with Teresa, at least until there is more clarity on her relationship with Carlos, and on who Pablo really is. But Rico's heart isn't listening to logic. It never has.

When Rico arrives at Pablo's office, he's carrying the latest bugging device sewn into the lining of his sports coat. Mike has authorized two fully-armed agents to be standing by in a mini-van, in case something goes wrong.

But, once again, in terms of what he'll say or do, Rico is on his own. All Mike asks is that he push hard enough to provoke a reaction from Pablo; but not so hard that it jeopardizes the relationship or the operation. A delicate balance, to say the least.

As is his custom, Pablo greets Rico warmly but he seems more serious than normal. "Come," he says, taking Rico by the arm and guiding him into his office, "let me hear about the raid and what you think we should do now."

Rico's job is to get Pablo to talk, but it won't be easy. When it suits his purpose, Pablo is very skilled at not saying much and, conversely, coaxing the other guy to divulge more than he should. Rico, on the other hand, tends to be a "talk first, think later" kind of conversationalist, which puts him at a distinct disadvantage in a situation like this.

"It was pretty scary. I was awakened by cops who told me they had a tip there were drugs in one of our warehouses. I was taken down to the station house while the narcs searched our other warehouses," Rico starts. "When I found out the extent of the problem, I really got frightened. Three warehouses. 1/2 ton. Both heroin and meth. I overheard one of the agents call our business drug-infested. Not something a legitimate business owner wants to hear."

Pablo just nods, adding nothing.

"I have to ask you this. Did you know this was going on?" Rico asks, gazing directly into Pablo's eyes.

"No, I didn't. I'm as surprised as you are." Pablo answers, without averting his eyes.

Rico doesn't say anything further right away, hoping to encourage Pablo to say something more. It works. Finally, Pablo continues, "Well, you hear things, of course. You can't be in my business without hearing stories of cartels salting shipments with drugs here and there. But I've always been careful about background checks; I do sporadic drug testing of my people, and I occasionally check shipments. There was never anything that raised an alarm before."

He goes on, "The storage part of the business hasn't concerned me, frankly. It's just a necessary adjunct to the business of moving goods around. I've worried much more about drugs hidden in product on the move. In the past, that's what the narcs seemed to worry about, too. Have you ever been raided before?"

"No. Can't say that I have," Rico replies truthfully.

It sounds like Pablo is innocent but, of course, the guy has always seemed that way. He's calm, polished and persuasive. Rico needs to push him more, get him out of his comfort zone. So, he gets more aggressive, "But that isn't the point. These shipments came from your customers, not mine. Yet, I'm the one who was awakened, taken to the police station, questioned, and am now on some kind of list of possible drug smugglers. Pablo, I have to know. Did you get me involved in something that could bring me, and my business, and my reputation, down?"

"No. Of course not," Pablo responds. "Remember, this is my business, too. Why would I want this? Who needs it?"

There are a lot of reasons, Rico thinks, but he decides not to push that point. Instead, he says, "Pablo, I've been in this business a long time with never the hint of something like this. Now, almost immediately after we get together, I'm in a police station trying to explain something that's truly unexplainable. I would have never let this happen on my watch."

"It was on your watch."

"Hardly."

"You were the one who decided not to inventory the goods before accepting title, not me," Pablo says, his face reddening. "Don't try to lay the blame for this on me, Rico. You're as much to blame."

"Well, I feel blindsided," Rico complains.

"So do I. We're in this together, pal. Now, let's stop pointing fingers and talk about what we're going to do going forward, as a team," Pablo responds.

So, with the confrontation temporarily over, the two partners sit down and begin to work. They decide who will call which customers, and when. They develop a common script to work from and a list of potential Q and A's that can help in answering the expected onslaught of accusations and questions.

It's impressive to Rico how engaged Pablo is in solving a problem that he professes not to have caused. He acts the way any concerned business owner would act. *The guy seems so earnest and honest; he could be a politician*, Rico thinks. *Or maybe a cartel boss.*

On the way to the restaurant to meet Teresa, Rico calls Mike and delivers the disappointing news, that he tried to generate some anger or fireworks, but Pablo was having none of it. Mike is not very empathetic, probably because his mind is already engaged, plotting his next move, which makes Rico a little anxious, wondering what it might be and how he'll be involved. When Mike thinks, Rico gets in trouble.

Teresa is waiting in the lobby of the restaurant, radiant as ever. She kisses Rico, and his day immediately improves. No matter how crazy Rico's life is, Teresa can make him feel comfortable, normal, and good, just by being there; a quality he never noticed when they were young.

He's lived much of his life without her and now he can't imagine how or why. The last few weeks, often late at night, Rico tries to understand the guy he was back then; the one that not only let her get away but actually walked away from her. All those years missed. He's not going to let that happen again.

She takes his hand and leads him to their table, where the drinks are already waiting. She takes a sip of her white wine, then looks him in the eye and says, "So, what do you think? Was Pablo involved?"

"He says not and I tend to believe him."

"You think the shipments were compromised before they reached your warehouse?"

"I do. There's no way somebody could get in and out of our warehouses without help from Pablo or me. I know I didn't help. It sounds like Pablo didn't either."

"So, you suspicion your customers?"

"Well, one of them is actually Global, Pablo's own import/export company. So, if he's not involved, somebody in his organization is."

She takes another sip and says, "Kind of hard to believe, isn't it? If an employee is secretly hiding drugs in shipments, why would he store the shipment in a warehouse owned by his boss?"

Rico ponders the question, then, answers, "Good question. I don't know. How well do you know Pablo?"

"Not much better than you do. I met him through Carlos and we had dinner with him and his wife a few times, before you came along. That's it."

"How well do you know Carlos?"

"That's a little more difficult to answer. I thought I knew him. As you remember, he frequented the restaurant where I work, and he was very nice to me right from the start. A real gentleman. Sent me flowers. Sort of wooed me in an old-world way. I thought he was charming and sweet and very down-to-earth until…"

Teresa pauses, takes another sip of wine.

"Well," she continues, "until he wasn't. As soon as he felt he had me hooked, where I depended on him for a big part of my life, he changed completely. It was actually shocking how suddenly his personality hardened up. He started to treat me like I was his servant. Nothing I did or wore or said was right. He was verbally abusive, never physically, thank God, and, then, over time, he just lost interest. When I broke up with him, I got the feeling he welcomed it."

"Did you ever sense he was into drugs?" Rico asks.

"Never for a second. He drank occasionally but that was it. I don't feel his sudden shift in behavior was because of alcohol or drugs. I just think he enjoyed the chase a lot more than the catch. There are men like that, you know."

"I meant," Rico clarifies, "was he dealing drugs or laundering money or distributing or anything like that?"

"Lord, I don't think so," Teresa answers. "He certainly wasn't dealing. I would have seen that. He did hang with a pretty shady bunch at times and, often, wouldn't introduce me to any of them. But I never saw anything very suspicious. Do you think he might have been involved in the drugs found in your warehouses?"

"Actually, I do," Rico says. "One of the involved customers, *Savory Foods*, is partially owned by Carlos. He has an unusual arrangement with Pablo where all of Savory's shipments are kept under separate lock and key within our warehouses. We don't do that for anybody else. But, if their shipments contain drugs, and Carlos knows it, the arrangement begins to make sense."

The food arrives and Teresa is unusually quiet while she eats, obviously going over possibilities in her head.

Finally, she says, "I'm curious. Why are you asking me all these questions about Carlos and Pablo? It's as if you have some compulsive need to find out everything you can about them?"

The moment of truth.

Rico looks up at her and gazes into her big, naive, brown eyes. It's time to come clean. He can't continue to mislead her without jeopardizing any future relationship they might have.

"Yes. I do have a compulsive reason. It's my job."

Teresa doesn't understand at first but Rico's look speaks volumes. His meaning begins to dawn on her. She asks, "You're spying on them?"

Rico just slowly moves his head up and down. Teresa is shocked. "What are you telling me? First that Pablo might be a drug dealer. Then, that Carlos probably is. Then, worst of all, you, who I totally trusted, are some kind of what? For who?"

"The Feds," he answers.

Then, he tries to comfort her, "Everything you know about me. What I did. What I do. Who I am. Those things are all true. It's just that I'm something else as well. I didn't really want to be. But it happened."

Teresa starts to cry. She tries to do it without bothering other diners at first but her sobs draw the attention of everybody in the room. Rico leaves his credit card on the table and escorts her through the lobby and out into the parking lot. She starts to fold into his arms and, then, recoils, stepping away, with her arms out, as if to ward off some evil spirit.

"I hope you can understand," Rico starts. "I had no intention of being here, with somebody I love more than anything else in the world, confessing a lie that I've told you for far too long. But here we are. Let me try to explain."

And they sit there on the curb, as people walk by them to enter the restaurant, as the waiter brings out the check for Rico to sign, as Teresa's tears dry up, and, above all, as Rico lays out the whole story, chapter by chapter, until, finally Teresa leans into him, and kisses him passionately.

Then, she says, "Rico. I'm sorry about what I said before. What you're doing is wonderful. You're saving lives and protecting children. You're ridding the world of bad guys. You're making a difference. And I love you for it."

Chapter 29

"You did what?" Mike screams into the phone. "What an idiot. She's on our list of possible gang members and you tell her everything about our operation?"

"I had to," Rico replies. "In a way, you authorized it, maybe even ordered it."

"How do you figure?"

"You told me to marry her," Rico answers. "Surely you didn't think I would marry her with this kind of a secret between us?"

"Damn right I did. That's what agents do, Rico," Mike fumes, "or did you miss that in your training? We don't tell our girlfriends, our wives, our mothers, our kids, our best friends, our golfing buddies. Nobody. Otherwise, how in hell could we make any operation work? We would have a hundred people showing up with popcorn to watch every bust."

"Don't be so dramatic, Mike," Rico says. "Look at it this way. What if I was just recruiting her to be an agent, like you recruited me? She has better access and information than either of us. I think it was a brilliant move, like you do, from time to time."

"I'm the damned station chief. You're a part-time agent who doesn't know shit and should do only what he's told," Mike pauses. "There's a difference. Am I clear?"

"Yes. Painfully so. So, what do you want me to do now?"

"I feel like yelling a little bit more first."

"Have at it."

Mike looks at Rico and says, "You aren't scared of me, are you?"

Rico replies, "All you can do is fire me and, right now, that would be a blessing."

"OK. Here's what I want you to do. Take one of these badges and give it to Teresa. Deputize her. Debrief her. Get names and addresses. Ask her to keep her eyes and ears open. Then, feed all the information you gather to Caroline. Now, get out of here."

"There's one other thing, Mike," Rico says. "I want a badge, too." Mike just rolls his eyes.

That night, Rico drives over to Teresa's house and delivers the badge. She's thrilled, of course. And when she asks about her possible assignments and her possible pay, Rico finesses both questions by saying, "Mike is working on that."

Then, Rico has her write down all of the names and the contact information for every friend or acquaintance or goon that she's met through either Carlos or Pablo. She takes to the task eagerly, and her recall of names is spectacular. Fairly quickly, there are twenty names on the list, most with contact information. It's obvious that Teresa has the makings of a really good agent, probably better than he's been.

In fact, Rico is starting to wonder if he's really cut out for this line of work at all. He's losing his confidence. Every time he thinks he knows what is coming, there's a twist that he hasn't anticipated; like Mike telling him to continue recruiting Teresa. Rico wasn't even half-serious when he suggested that, but Mike jumped on it immediately and now Rico has Teresa knee-deep in an operation that could go south any minute.

The only good thing for Rico is that, now, he can propose to Teresa without concern, something he had been wanting to do almost from the moment she re-entered his life. Teresa finally has all the facts necessary to make an informed decision. And, best of all, if she accepts, he will have a trusted partner and soulmate by his side, something he really needs right now.

His resolve to go ahead with his plan is tested later that afternoon when, out of the blue, Maggie Smith calls.

"Rico, how are you?" she starts with, "I've missed you."

"Fine," he answers, followed by silence. The absence of "I've missed you, too," isn't lost on Maggie.

"So much has happened since the last time we talked. I got a new job. Went to Europe for a month. Broke up with two boyfriends. And, through it all, I kept thinking of you. How about I come over so we can catch up?"

"When?" Rico asks without thinking.

"I can stop by the pizza place, pick up a pepperoni and onions, and be there inside of an hour. It'll be just like old times. You got a bottle of red wine around?"

"That won't work, Maggie," he says, "I'm getting married."

"When?"

"I don't know the exact date. I haven't asked her yet," Rico says.

Maggie is silent for a few seconds. Then she says, "You're not even engaged?"

"Nope, but…"

"I'll skip the pizza and be there in fifteen minutes." Then, she hangs up.

When the doorbell rings about twenty minutes later, Rico doesn't know what to do. Remembering how provocatively Maggie can dress, he doesn't even trust himself to open the door. However, just telling her through the door to go away isn't such a great idea either.

So, he opens the door just a little bit, slowly and carefully, but not carefully enough. Maggie pushes her way in, throws her arms around his neck, and plants a wet kiss on his lips. Her tongue snakes its way through his teeth and starts to do its magic on his tongue.

He's immediately aroused, a fact that doesn't escape Maggie's notice. Her hand finds his bulge and encourages an erection that Rico has no control over whatsoever, betraying the "No, Maggie's" that he's trying to say, albeit with her tongue still in his mouth.

They stumble their way into the bedroom, throwing clothes aside as they go. Rico notices as the clothes came off that Maggie is wearing jeans and a modest white shirt with a frilly trim across the bodice. So, he can't really blame his behavior on how provocatively she's dressed.

Later, as they lay naked on top of the sheets, Rico tries to make the point that Maggie has seduced him.

"I was saying 'no' the whole time," he says.

"It didn't feel like 'no,'" she replies.

"You took advantage of me," Rico argues, "kind of like Cosby took advantage of all of those women."

"How so?"

"I think you slipped me a Viagra with your tongue," he says.

Maggie laughs, then says, "Viagra doesn't work that fast."

"I have a doctor friend who'll testify it does."

"Okay. Now I'm worried," she replies, touching his limp penis. "It'll be your doctor's word against mind." He doesn't respond to her caressing right away. But, soon, despite their recent lovemaking, he does begin to harden again. His willpower is no match for her hands, especially with her body turning over toward him once again.

"I'll listen this time to see if you say no," Maggie says. She waits a second or two. Rico says nothing, thereby, destroying his rape case completely. And, again, they make love.

Chapter 30

Much later, hours after Maggie has left, Rico lies awake, trying to make sense of what just happened. He wants to marry Teresa. Of that, he's sure. He doesn't love Maggie. He's just as sure of that. So, he asks himself, what did he just do and what does it mean?

As daylight steals its way under the window shade of his bedroom, Rico still has no answers. To make matters worse, as guilt-ridden as he is, Rico has to pick up Teresa first thing this morning and bring her to the DEA offices to meet with Caroline.

So, as much as he would like to avoid seeing his ex-wife until he sorts everything out, Rico will not be afforded that opportunity. He feels as guilty as he would if they were married. But, in fact, they're not married. They're not even engaged. They're just barely dating, a fact that should make Rico feel better but doesn't.

In order to marry Teresa, he needs to be absolutely sure that he's not attracted to another woman. Right? But, how can he make that case now, when any capable lawyer could prove beyond a reasonable doubt that Rico was definitely attracted to Maggie; not once, but twice.

"Good morning, darling," Teresa says as she slips into the front passenger seat of Rico's Tesla and leans over to plant a chaste kiss on his cheek. So sweet. So trusting. Making Rico feel even worse, if that's possible.

Adding to his feeling of guilt is the way Teresa looks. She's gorgeous and elegant and poised, dressed in a beige, summer weight knit dress that clings to her figure in a way that only suggests the soft lines underneath. In fact, Teresa is striking in a way that Maggie, despite her calendar girl figure, can never match.

True, Maggie's in-your-face, look-at-me persona can attack a guy's senses. She's sexy hot right out of the box, and follows that up with a cool, witty personality, that, for most guys, really closes the deal.

But, Teresa, who looks so cool on the outside, has a caring and honest, soul underneath, a trusting sweetness that makes a guy want to shield her from the cruelties of the world. That's what Rico loves most about Teresa, and why he wants to marry and protect her from, well, people like him.

Caroline greets the two of them warmly and takes them back into her office where they can talk in confidence. She gives them a fresh copy of the names that Teresa sent her the day before, annotated with notes showing what the agency knows about each.

Then, they go through each name, one at a time, reading their bios and pooling their knowledge as best they can. Several of the identified people work for Pablo in his import/export business so those draw particular attention. In the end, eight are picked to be targets because they're most likely to be cartel members.

Edgar Vegas, of course, is on Teresa's first list but Caroline chooses not to discuss him at all. Rico assumes why but wonders just the same where Edgar might be at this point. *Is he fully relocated? In prison?* There's nothing in the notes behind his name that gives Rico a clue, or comforts him. Rico remembers clearly the confrontation in the gym when Edgar threatened him, and his family.

It was certainly unnerving at the time and, still, at night, when he isn't picturing Teresa's beautifully-sculpted face, he sees Edgar's grotesque one, always scowling, flushed with anger. In his dreams, the blue stone in Edgar's right earlobe stands out next to his beefy, ruddy, face, just as it did the first time Rico met him.

Edgar is capable of anything, no matter how hideous or deadly, and the only thing standing between Rico and the wrath of Edgar is Mike's reassurance that he needn't worry. Given Mike's track record that isn't exactly comforting.

"Rico," Caroline says loudly, jolting him back into the present, "Anything more you care to add?"

"No," he answers, recovering quickly. "I'm curious, though. How are you going to get the resources to follow eight suspects at once? Mike had trouble getting any when we wanted to follow Edgar," Rico asks.

"I'd like to attribute it to my powers of persuasion but the truth is that the Batista cartel has recently become the number one target of the DEA. As a result, several more agents have been reassigned, and some even relocated, to help us. Mike believes that we don't have much time to gather information before we have to bring the cartel leaders in, ready or not. So, we're going balls to the wall."

"One other thing," she adds. "I need you to run the surveillance effort. There will be about twelve agents following eight suspects. All of their information will come to you for processing. Who and how many agents follow any one suspect will be up to you, depending on the intel you're receiving. I suspect it will be a highly fluid situation over the next few days and you need to be available 24/7 to make decisions."

"Why me?"

"Even with the reinforcements, we're short-handed, especially with only a few agents who have hands-on experience with this cartel. You're unique in the knowledge base you have and there isn't time to bring anybody else, even more experienced agents, up to speed. You're our only viable alternative at the moment,"

"Can Teresa help?" Rico queries.

Caroline takes a minute to think about it. She's not entirely convinced that Teresa is an innocent bystander who just happened to date one of the cartel's leaders. Still, it isn't realistic to assume that Rico will keep something from her at this point. So, she takes a calculated risk and says yes.

"One other thing. I want all the files on Edgar Vegas."

"That I can't do," she responds, "not because I don't want to but because Mike has kept them all to himself. I don't have access."

So, right in front of Caroline and Teresa, Rico pulls out his cell phone and calls Mike, who answers on the first ring.

"What is this bullshit about Edgar Vegas going off the radar? I want to know where he is; what he's doing; and how big a threat he is to me and my family. I deserve that."

"I don't care what you want," Mike replies, "Edgar is in protective custody now and nobody is allowed to know where he is. Not me, Not Caroline. And certainly not a rookie agent who is currently involved with the ex-girlfriend of a targeted cartel leader. You need to calm down and do what you're told."

Although Rico doubts that Mike could easily replace him at this stage, there's a certain logic to keeping witness protection people, and their whereabouts, secret. *He'll just have to trust the guy one more time*, he thinks, which, given Mike's record, isn't that easy to do.

"Okay, boss," he says, then, hangs up. Caroline has a smug look on her face that Rico doesn't appreciate but, in the interest of keeping their relationship cordial, he says nothing further.

"Okay," Caroline says, "with that nonsense behind us, let's get back to work. I've commandeered a small room next to our Batista war room that will serve as command central for your operation, which, by the way, we think of as primarily a mapping exercise, nothing more. You're to keep track of the agents in the field, and redirect them only if necessary."

"I got it," Rico replies.

Caroline continues, "The room will be just for your operation. Right now, it contains only a table with eight chairs, two flip charts, and both paper and electronic maps of the city. Three of the agents on your team are eagerly waiting there for assignments. And the other agents assigned to you will be available by conference call as needed. I'll be in my office if you need anything else. Good luck."

When Rico and Teresa enter the conference room, the three very young and eager male agents stand up, almost at attention. They are a little too attentive and enthusiastic for Rico's taste. *Probably their first operation*, he surmises.

Once reseated, their eyes rest on Rico for a second or two, then, linger longer on Teresa who must be twice the age of any of them. Rico makes a mental note to have Teresa dress differently in the future. Maybe she should wear jeans and a ball cap; although he doubts anything would keep these testosterone-driven young men from doing what their types have done for centuries. Frankly, Rico realizes, as beautiful as Teresa looks today, he doesn't blame them at all.

Once the other agents arrive, and the work is underway, however, Rico is surprised at how professional everybody becomes. Even the flirtatious boys.

Rico starts by giving them an overview of the Batista cartel; things like who runs it in Mexico, who may run it in the U.S., how big it is, and what recent raids have yielded in terms of product. A spirited conversation ensues and Rico is able to answer most of their questions with ease.

Then, once the contact information is distributed, and assignments made, the agents go their separate ways with orders to check in every hour. Their check in times are staggered to prevent overlap and either Rico or Teresa will be required to be on the radio every five minutes or so throughout the day and most of the night.

The first call-in isn't scheduled for two hours so Rico spends that time setting up the room. He and Teresa post pictures of the suspects being tailed. Each agent is carrying a GPS reporting device which will show up as a blip on an illuminated map that covers one whole wall. They look like stars as they pop up one-by-one, indicating each agent, or team, as they arrive at their station and activate their radios. The stars will move as the agents move, giving Rico and Teresa a visual representation of exactly where their team members are at all times.

Halfway through setting things up, a young girl knocks on the door and enters. She introduces herself as Carla Hagen and her appearance is in marked contrast to Caroline or Teresa. She's small, slight, and bespectacled, with dull, brown hair falling randomly around her face and eyes.

Carla says that she's been assigned to help with the administrative details of the operation. And, because she has considerable experience with managing things, and they don't, she proves valuable right away.

The war room team has about fifteen minutes to admire and test their set-up work before the first call comes in, and, then, things start to happen at a very rapid pace. Since field agents have the right to call in whenever they think they've learned something important, the radio crackles constantly. Rico's vision of having careful and informative conversations every five minutes or so goes by the wayside pretty quickly.

Agents are trying to talk over each other as they report activity that might or might not be important. Everything is much more reactive than Rico expected. He's reminded of the Mike Tyson quote that "everybody has a plan until you punch them in the face." His team is getting punched in the face repeatedly, as calls are coming too fast for them to handle.

One of the unanticipated and complicating factors is that many of the targets will meet up at times during the day, bringing two or more surveillance teams together, an event both teams feel compelled to report on in copious detail, and then, to ask for reassignment.

Still, patterns start to emerge. There are hot spots which most of the targets visit at one time or another. Rico decides to pull somebody off his individual surveillance to check out those hot spots, most of which are bars or restaurants.

There are people not being watched who meet up with people being watched. So, Rico has to switch assignments around, on the fly, in order to cover everybody that needs to be. His target list is growing by the hour, and his agent coverage is thinning.

It's interesting to note that not one of the targets meets with either Carlos or Pablo. Either those two are not the leaders Mike believes they are or the targets being followed are not as high up in the organization as originally assumed.

Caroline stops in a few times during the day to check on progress. She seems quite pleased although, for the life of him, Rico can't understand why. They aren't any closer to identifying the cartel leaders and it seems to him that lots of people meeting together, mostly in restaurants or clubs, hardly constitutes some kind of actionable intel.

Teresa turns out to be an incredible asset, however, who does what she is told, without question, but also finds ways to add value. Her follow-up questions to the field agents are spot-on and much of the re-sorting of assignments is at her suggestion.

Rico is impressed and surprised. He had assumed that, because Teresa, over several months of dating, never tumbled to the fact that Carlos was a drug lord, she was not very observant. But, it's clear to him now how wrong he was.

As each of the targets settle in for the night, the agents following them are given a few hours' sleep themselves, mostly at nearby motels. So, eventually, the phone calls slow down and, then, around midnight, stop entirely.

Rico and Teresa take advantage of the downtime to go back home, where they pack small suitcases, gather up necessary personal care items, and, then, return to the war room, better equipped to sleep on cots Carla has scrounged up from somewhere.

Rico notices that Teresa has actually changed into ragged jeans and a sweatshirt, as he had wished she would earlier. No ball cap, though. Rico doubts whether she even owns one.

Rico lies down on his cot, fully-clothed, but has trouble sleeping. He turns over, his back to Teresa, and tries to keep her face in his mind as he slowly falls asleep. But, as is usually the case these days, Edgar's face, with those hooded eyes and brooding features, crowds out everything else. It's going to be another sleepless night for Rico.

Chapter 31

Rico must have slept a little because he is awakened at 5:15 am by the crackling of the radio. One of the field agents is reporting that his target seems to be on the way to LAX for an early flight. Rico takes down the information; then, wakes Carla, who's sleeping in a small dorm room down the hall.

"How do I find out what flight somebody is on?" Rico asks her.

She gets up, goes down the hall to the computer room, and keys in the name of the target. Within minutes, she finds out the target is on the 7:05 United flight to Mexico City.

Bingo, thinks Rico. This may be the little tidbit of information that will make their massive stakeout worthwhile.

He calls Caroline who, surprisingly, hardly reacts at all, but says she'll be there in twenty minutes. *She wouldn't be coming in*, Rico guesses, *if this was a normal occurrence.* So, after deliberating for a couple of minutes, he decides to call Mike.

"Yes," Mike answers in a drowsy voice.

"We have one of our targets heading to LAX to board a flight to Mexico City," Rico blurts out. "Maybe we should…"

"Did you call Caroline?"

"Yes."

"She'll handle it," Mike says. Then, the line goes dead. Mike is probably back asleep a second or two after he cradles the receiver. *No worries in the world, that guy*, Rico thinks.

By the time Caroline arrives at the office, the target has reached the airport. She takes over control of the operation and tells the assigned field agent to make sure the target gets on the plane and, then, report back to the office for reassignment.

It turns out the target is a guy named Daniel Perez, a part-time construction worker who lives in Anaheim. He's been known to frequent a restaurant where other suspected cartel members dine but, according to the wait staff, has never joined them at their table. Still, he seems suspicious. He eats alone, never drinks, and carries a briefcase, even when he goes to the men's room. He might just be a lonely insurance salesman but, more likely, he's a courier for the Batista cartel.

Caroline contacts DEA agents in Mexico City to let them know Mr. Perez is on his way to them. She tells them to pick him up and interrogate him, but not to arrest him just yet.

The agents in Mexico aren't pleased. They were hoping that he was one of the cartel's leaders and that, finally, a round-up was in the works. We can't keep delaying our operation, they protest. Something is bound to leak. Caroline promises to discuss it with Mike, assuring them that it won't be much longer.

She's barely off the phone when other field agents start checking in with reports. A surprising number of their targets are on the move and look like they're headed to the airport as well. Carla uses her contacts to check them all out and, yes, three are confirmed on flights into Mexico, all with different destinations.

"It looks like something big is going down, or worse, the rats are fleeing the ship," Caroline says. "Rico, call Mike and get him down here."

When Mike finally arrives, he can feel the angst. There are now four targets on planes to Mexico and each will have to be picked up and interrogated by somebody. The fact that the targets are going to three different cities greatly complicates things, especially since two of the cities have no DEA presence. So, agents need to get on the road ASAP.

Arrangements will have to be made with local authorities to meet the targets when they deplane, take them into custody, and hold them until an agent can get there. Paperwork has to be prepared and submitted to authorities for approval. Carla has now been joined by three other clerks, all of whom are working feverishly on plane reservations, or interrogation requests, or ground transportation, all in support of what is turning into a major operation.

Rico and Teresa just step aside and watch the hubbub in amazement. Their part of the operation has been suspended and the field agents who were part of it are now on their way back to headquarters, ready for reassignment.

Mike and Caroline are in the war room, at the center of everything, making decisions quickly, trying to match up their assets with targets. Some of the agents have unique skills that make them more valuable back at headquarters. So, they are quickly recalled. Others stay with their targets. Everybody has an assignment. Except Rico and Teresa. They just stand there, observing the chaos admiringly.

At times, Mike looks like a conductor, his arms waving back and forth, as if he's leading a very large orchestra toward some climactic crescendo that will pull the audience to its feet.

At other times, he appears to be in a wrestling match, grabbing arms, pushing bodies around, all seemingly without purpose. And, at other times, he's like a half-mad professor, jumping up onto a chair to scribble something on a whiteboard; an assignment, perhaps, or a name, or a code name.

The guy is clearly in his element, driven by excitement or adrenaline, or both. People respond to his words and gestures without hesitation. For reasons that are hard for Rico to understand, all of the agents' trust that Mike's directives, no matter how bizarre, will turn out for the best.

Rico is fascinated by the innate genius of the man. This was obviously what he was born to do, and everybody in the room knows it. They may not be sure what Mike is thinking much of the time but they know it's more nuanced than what they would be thinking. His mind is always a few steps ahead of everybody else's.

Above all, everybody in the room is convinced he will outthink the bad guys and, therefore, they do exactly what they are told, without exception. They believe that Mike gives them the best chance to win and, in this business, winning is everything.

At one point, with activity levels at their most chaotic, Mike looks over at Rico and smiles, as if to say, *see, what did I tell you, is this fun or what?* Then, his face darkens and he's off pursuing another random thought that has just popped into his head.

The plan is starting to come into focus. The first thing they need to determine is if something is happening in Mexico that will require additional resources there. Caroline is the point person on that, constantly in touch with assets on the ground in Mexico City, Tijuana, and elsewhere. So far, there's no indication that something big, and coordinated, is underway.

Caroline is also the one managing the interviews in Mexico that will start taking place in less than two hours now. Agents have submitted questions and she's sorting them into applicable piles, to be passed on to the interrogating officers.

The interviews will start pleasantly enough, as if the passengers are just selected at random to answer simple travel questions. But, depending on their answers and what the agents find in the target's carryon bags, the questions will get more pointed and specific. The first objective is to simply keep them in custody until the higher-up's sort out what plan of action they want to take.

Rico is very surprised that Mike has allowed Teresa to stay. Although he, himself, is now sure that she's not tied into the cartel, in any way; he knows that Mike and Caroline may not be so convinced.

In fact, it would not surprise him at all if Mike is staging this whole thing for Teresa's benefit. Maybe he wants the cartel to think that the agency is going in one direction when, in fact, they're going in another. That would be a typical Mike move.

"You want a Coke or something?" Rico says to Teresa, who responds that she would. The cafeteria is remarkably quiet. Teresa and Rico are the only ones in the building who have time for a break.

"Can you believe this?" Rico starts.

"I can't. Just a few hours ago we were the only ones in this place," she says, "And now, there are dozens of agents and clerks, everywhere, running around, doing all sorts of things that, I think, only Mike understands fully."

Rico adds, "Just think about the four guys who got on planes this morning, perhaps only to visit relatives. They are laying back in their seats, enjoying their coffee, reading their newspapers, with no inkling of the shit storm that's coming their way."

"Not that I have any sympathy for them," Rico continues. "If they're Batista Cartel foot soldiers, and evidence suggests they are, no shit storm is big enough for these guys. The drugs they are sneaking into our country are killing people, young kids mostly. Anything we can do to stop it, we should do."

"I agree with that," Teresa says. "But, do you think we're really having an impact? Drug-producing countries like Mexico and Colombia will find markets for their products no matter what we do. If it isn't this gang, it'll be another one. There are hundreds of kids in Mexico right now who want to grow up to be just like the four guys we're going after today. Right? Somebody will step right in and fill the necessary roles. The drugs will keep flowing."

Rico shakes his head, "Not if we cut the head off the snake. Especially a snake as big as this one. If we can eliminate the leaders, shut down the factories, eliminate the flow of cash, we can put a serious dent in their production. If pushers can't get product, there will be fewer pushers. And fewer kids will die."

"I'm not so sure. Where there are kids that want it, there will be people providing the product. Law of supply and demand."

"The people who provide the product are called pushers for a reason," Rico counters. "They create the demand. They don't just meet it. These drugs are highly addictive and the pushers work to get kids addicted. Once they're addicted, the laws of supply and demand go out the window. As do the laws of common decency."

Teresa looks at Rico for a minute, then, she leans over and kisses him, saying, "You're so right. What we're doing is very important. I remember now why, way back in the good old days, I married you."

There's a throat-clearing sound from the doorway. Then, Mike says, "I hate to break this up but I have an offer for you that's a little time-sensitive. A lady friend and I were going to a convention in Vegas this weekend. It looks like we can't do it now, but you two certainly can and I don't need you around here anymore. In fact, you're kind of in the way. So, how about it? Want to party in Vegas?"

Rico and Teresa look at each other, big smiles on their faces.

"My plane tickets are for later today," Mike continues, "and I have a suite booked at the Cosmopolitan. I'd love for you to be my guests, a sort of 'thank you' for the help you've been giving us the past few days. What do you say?"

Their excited looks give him the answer he wants.

Chapter 32

The lights of Las Vegas twinkle beneath them as the plane circles on its final approach to McCarron Airport. Both Rico and Teresa have been here before, of course; but never together; and never under such unusual circumstances.

"Attendants, please make a final cabin check before landing. Welcome to Las Vegas."

Teresa squeezes Rico's hand as the plane descends. She feels like a young school girl doing something illicit, exciting, and very romantic. Part of the fun is that, only a few hours before, they were part of a major drug operation, sleep-deprived and scared, scrambling around trying to do a job that they were wholly unqualified to do.

Now, all that is behind them and ahead lies nothing but people and noise and leisure and play, everything that Vegas has to offer. Food. Games. Shows. You name it.

A few hours ago, Teresa could barely keep her head up because of the lack of sleep and now she's energized enough to catch a midnight show; if that is what Rico wants to do.

But, of course, that isn't what Rico wants to do. He already has their night planned out and it certainly doesn't include a show. A little gambling, maybe, a drink or two, capped off by, if all goes well, a lovemaking session back at the suite.

As soon as they're unpacked, Teresa and Rico take the elevator down to the lobby, wander into one of the large, tastefully-decorated casino rooms, and hit the blackjack tables.

The noise is unlike anything they've experienced before. Slot machine arms being pulled. Chips being counted. Roulette wheels being spun. It's loud and hushed, all at the same time. Every so often there's a bubble of excited voices coming from a table of craps or roulette.

Beyond velvet ropes, at tables in the back of the room, bored faces look at their two cards, expressionless while tossing a normal person's annual salary of chips into the middle of the table.

Neither Rico, nor Teresa are real gamblers. It has taken them too long to accumulate their money, one hour or one job at a time, to throw much of it onto a table where the odds are so stacked against them. Still, they brought just enough gambling money to try their luck, knowing full well that they'll lose it over time.

But, like most in Las Vegas, their goal is to make it last as long as they can. They're emotionally prepared for losses but, as their chips dwindle, as the dealer keeps turning 13s and 14s into 20s and 21s, they grow frustrated and eventually decide that they've had enough losing for one night.

So, they leave the black jack tables and start walking around, staring at all of the different people and wondering where they come from and what they might be like back home. Very different probably. *Vegas can turn people into something pretty unattractive*, Rico concludes. *Or, maybe that side of their personality is there all along. Vegas just surfaces it.*

Few of the people seem to be enjoying themselves. It's like they're so desperate for the high of winning that they can't really enjoy the process along the way. Also, to Rico, since winning is such a rare occurrence, it hardly seems worth all the angst and pain.

He thinks about how gambling addiction is like drug addiction, an attempt by people to run away from their real lives, if only for a few hours. In Rico's mind, they should be running toward life, not away from it. That's what brings real excitement and fulfillment, not the artificial kind found here under the bright neon lights of a superficial city.

And, then, far across the casino floor, Rico sees something that sends a shiver through his body. It's Edgar Vegas. He's sure of it. An oversized Hispanic. The same grumpy, hang dog look. The same slouch. The same shuffling walk. A big, conspicuous man trying to make himself invisible, as if that is at all possible.

Rico can't see the right ear of the man to see if the blue stud earring is there, which would positively identify Edgar.

"Do you remember Edgar Vegas?" he asks Teresa.

"Yes."

"Is that him?"

"Where?"

"By the elevators."

"I don't think so. Looks a little bit like him, though. What would he be doing here anyway?"

"Exactly my question. Let's go back to the room. I need to call Mike and find out."

When Rico looks back, the man is gone, probably into one of the many high-speed elevators, making it impossible to follow him, or even to know it was him for sure. One thing Rico knows though. Edgar, or whoever the man is, didn't see them. Which is a good thing.

When Rico gets back in the room, he calls Mike. As expected, there's no answer. The poor guy is probably still heavily immersed in the operation that Rico and Teresa so happily left behind to enjoy their unexpected little tryst. Rico leaves word for Mike to call and turns back toward Teresa.

"I'm hungry," Teresa says. "Can we grab a bite somewhere?"

"Why don't we do room service?" Rico says.

"I'd prefer to take a walk, see the strip, and get something light to eat before turning in. Is that OK?"

Rico is hesitant to go down to the lobby again so quickly after seeing the face that has haunted him for weeks. Another sleepless night is already assured and Rico doesn't want to risk something worse.

Sensing Rico's reluctance, Teresa says, "Please. I'll make it worth your while," an argument that Rico finds convincing.

Once outside, Rico is glad that Teresa insisted. The cool, clean desert air is refreshing and the walk clears some of the casino smoke out of his lungs. They pass several hotels, all glitzed up to attract people with more money than taste. The bigger, the gaudier, the better.

On the way back to their hotel, they find a coffee shop in the lobby of the *Vdara*, one of the few hotels on the strip without a casino, and order two sandwiches and beers. They smile at each other as they nibble and drink. Leave it to us, their shared look says, to find one of the only sane, understated, and ordinary places on the strip. It fits them and they love it.

"Can you believe this?" Teresa says. "Here we are, two survivors of a barrio in Mexico City, fresh from running a drug-busting operation, enjoying a little snack before we go back to our hotel suite and do whatever people who rent suites do."

"I think they sleep."

"We can do that, too."

Then, she leans over and kisses Rico. Not the sweet, tender kisses she had been giving him so far in their new relationship but a passionate kiss that hints at more to come. They both polish off the sandwiches and then walk the short distance, past the *Aria*, back to the Cosmopolitan at a pace much quicker than when they left.

The lovemaking turns out to be incredible. Rico thinks briefly about how hurried and rushed he'd been with Maggie. It's nothing like that with Teresa. Her clothes come off slowly, and seductively, revealing a body much more perfect than he had remembered, or even imagined. The girl he had shared sex with so many years ago is gone, and in her place is a woman who now knows exactly how to love him. How she learned so much is something Rico doesn't want to think about.

Afterwards, Teresa lies beside him, naked and unashamed, with the confidence of a woman who has been here before. Few words were spoken as they made love but her actions spoke eloquently.

Still naked himself, Rico turns away from her, reaches into the nightstand drawer, and retrieves the jewelry case he had put there when they arrived. He turns back toward her and presents it with a flourish.

"I'd get down on my knee but I'm afraid it would take years for you to erase that image," Rico says with a laugh. Then, "Teresa, will you marry me for the second time? This time, I promise to do it right, and keep doing it right, forever. Please say yes."

"Yes. Yes. Yes," Teresa says, putting on the ring with a diamond that's twice the size of her first one, and they fall together again, this time just to hug and kiss. Rico looks into Teresa's eyes and says, "We're in the wedding capital of the world if you want to tie the knot tomorrow."

"Do you remember our first wedding?" Teresa says.

"You mean in front of the clerk at the registration office in Mexico City."

"That's the one. Well, that's an example of what we aren't going to do this time," Teresa answers. "I want a real wedding. In a church. With friends and family. The more the merrier. The only thing that I want the same is the city, and the groom."

With that, she tosses the sheets back, slithers off the bed to retrieve the new, light blue nightgown that, a half-hour before, she had only worn for a few seconds. She drops it over her head. To Rico, with or without the nightgown, she's still a vision unlike any he has ever seen.

"Let's get some sleep," she says. "We have some planning to do, starting first thing in the morning."

But first thing in the morning, well before any planning could be done, Mike calls, waking them up.

"Don't have much time," he says, "you called?"

"Yes," Rico answers. "I wanted to ask you about Edgar again. I think I saw him last night, here in Vegas. Is that even possible?"

"Vegas in Vegas, that's cute," Mike replies. "No, I don't think that's possible. He's deep into the witness protection program and they aren't in the habit of hiding their witnesses in Las Vegas."

"Is that the witness protection program I escaped from?"

"The one I let you escape from. No, it isn't. This is the real deal and nobody knows where he is, even me."

"Can you find out if he could possibly be here?"

There's silence for a few seconds and, then, Mike says, "Why would I want to do that?"

Rico is fully awake now and he replies, "Did you forget that Edgar threatened me and my family?"

"Happens all the time," Mike snaps back. "I can't have agents running around chasing every threat that comes our way. That's all we would be doing."

"Well, when I say family, now I mean Teresa too."

"I thought you were divorced."

"Well, just like you told me to do, I asked her to marry me last night and she said yes. So, I consider her family now."

"Then, I consider her family too, Rico, and congratulations. You're a very lucky man that, after how you treated her all those years ago, she would even consider taking you back."

"Don't I know it."

"And, yes, that does change things. I'll see what I can find out."

"Thanks, Mike, and how's the operation going?"

"Looks like a bit of a false alarm," Mike answers. "One guy's talking but we haven't learned anything new from him. The others have clammed up pretty good. It may have just been a coincidence that they all headed home at the same time but, given that we brought them in for questioning, the clock on our operation is ticking anyway."

"Okay," Rico says. "Maybe we'll cut our weekend short and get back to L.A. today."

"Actually, I got nothing for you here right now," Mike replies. "Please, just stay there and enjoy yourselves. Look for Edgar. I doubt it's actually him but, if you confirm that it is, give me a call right away. We can't afford to have him just running around out in the open."

"Okay."

"And one other thing," Mike says. "Give Teresa my congratulations as well. She's getting one hell of a guy."

Chapter 33

The next day Rico wakes up a whole new man. He's once again engaged to his high-school sweetheart; the only girl he's ever really loved. And, instead of being afraid of Edgar, at Mike's urging, he's actually going to pursue the guy. That's what federal agents do, after all. *It's incredible*, Rico thinks, *how perspectives can change, literally overnight.*

An already awake Teresa turns over, reaches her arms high in the air, and, like a cat, arches her back up in a full-body stretch. Then, she brings her arms down around Rico's neck and kisses him, more lovingly than passionately.

"And, so, my fiancée," she yawns. "What shall we do today?"

"Let's start with breakfast in bed. Then, let's head down to the casino where you can gamble while I wander around looking for Mr. Vegas. Then, who knows? We'll play it by ear."

"By ear, really?"

"My mistake. I doubt our ears will be involved."

"Thank God."

When they reach the casino floor, the distinctive hum of hushed voices and clicking slot machines greets them immediately. Nothing has changed much since the night before. Even some of the faces look familiar.

Teresa slides into a comfortable chair at a blackjack table close to the lobby, with only two young men playing. Their facial expressions immediately switch from bored and disinterested to very interested. Rico notices, of course, mentally telling himself that he better get used to it. If you're marrying a head-turner you shouldn't be surprised when heads turn.

She wins a ten-dollar hand right away, then, turns back toward Rico and gives him a big smile, as if to say, *aren't I the lucky one?* But, looking into her beaming face, Rico knows who the lucky one really is.

He'd like to stay with her but he has work to do. Mike is relying on him to see if Edgar is actually here, in the casino, even though, given the size of the hotel, and the hordes of people moving through it, the odds of finding any one person are incredibly remote.

Then, suddenly, just as Rico has convinced himself that he'd been mistaken about seeing Edgar the day before, there he is. Fifty yards away, just across the casino floor, coming out of an elevator.

No mistaking him this time. Especially when their eyes lock and, after a second of disbelief, Edgar's face contorts into a malevolent look of hatred that leaves little doubt that he's recognized Rico.

The big man takes an aggressive step toward Rico but, then, thinking better of it, turns back toward the hotel exit. Suddenly, he breaks into a sprint, drawing a lot of attention, from the slot players near him, from the cocktail waitress he almost knocks over, from the pit boss looking down on the floor, who immediately calls hotel security. People don't run in a casino very often but, when they do, it normally means trouble.

Rico tries to act like a normal guest as he walks quickly back to the bank of elevators on his side of the casino floor, enters one, and pushes the number of his floor. As the door slowly closes, Rico lets out his breath, feeling a little bit safer. Still, when the doors open at his floor, he half-expects to see Edgar there waiting for him, like in a Hollywood horror film.

Fortunately, this is real life, not a scary movie, and Rico is very much alone in the hallway. Nonetheless, he runs the last thirty yards or so to his suite, to be safe, yes, but also to use up the nervous energy that's built up inside him.

After fumbling with the lock for a second, he gets his door open and, once inside, the door double-locked behind him; he heaves a sigh of relief and immediately calls Mike, who answers on the first ring.

"I saw him," Rico blurts out. "It was definitely Edgar. He's here."

"I figured that. The witness protection people got back to me this morning. They told me Edgar had disappeared," Mike answers. "Not exactly the smartest move on his part, going to Vegas, but, still, we're lucky you were there to see him. At least we know where to begin looking."

"There's a problem. This time he saw me too."

"Shit. That complicates things. Did you follow him?"

"No. He ran. So did I, by the way."

"Not good. You need to find him again and convince him to stay put. If the cartel learns where he is, he'll be in a lot of danger," Mike said. "I'll call our Las Vegas office to see if they can help you look for him."

"Mike. I would rather not confront Edgar and confirm to him that I'm working with you guys. That'll just infuriate him even more."

"For God's sake, Rico," Mike blurts out. "He already knows you're an agent. By now, probably everybody in the world knows you are an agent. But, unfortunately, you're the only agent I have near him at the moment. So, get off your ass and do as I say."

"Yes, sir."

"You're now officially in charge," Mike goes on. "If I can get support there quickly, I will. But, for now, you are it. Wait a minute. Where's Teresa?"

"Leave her out of this, Mike," Rico says, now worried that he just left her alone on the casino floor.

"No can do, partner. You just start searching for Edgar and I'll send pictures of Edgar to Teresa's phone so that she can circulate them around the hotel. The more eyes looking for Edgar the better. I doubt he's registered at the hotel under his real name but somebody should ask at the desk. Check the name 'Raul Castillo' as well. That's his new alias. Okay."

"What do we do if we find him?" Rico asks.

"Convince him to turn himself in. Arrest him if necessary," Mike answers. "Get a police officer to help you, at least until other agents arrive. Call me when you have him in custody."

Then he hangs up.

Fortunately, Teresa is still at the blackjack table where Rico left her, and she has a healthy stack of chips in front of her.

"Come on," he says to her. "We have work to do," eliciting the slightest little pout from Teresa, who obviously is on a winning streak.

But, despite the cooperation of security, and the help of a policeman who's on duty near the hotel, and the thorough search by three DEA agents, and a scouring of hotel records, there's no trace of Edgar Vegas anywhere.

He's vanished into the horde of partiers, gamblers, and sightseers that jam Las Vegas streets every day of the week. Of course, there's no worst place in the world to search for somebody than in this city of a million strangers, so Rico isn't really surprised. Disappointed, but not surprised.

He is, however, faced with the cold reality that there's still somebody out there who wants him dead.

Chapter 34

Once Rico and Teresa are back in L.A., still smarting from their failed Las Vegas operation, they carve out some time to focus on their wedding plans.

There's so much for them to do in a relatively short period of time.

They're fortunate to have found an available time and date for their wedding; three months out, at the *Intercontinental Presidente* in Mexico City.

Next, they have to pick out invitations and go to work on the guest list. The first cut includes a lot of family and friends still living in Mexico but, also, a few friends from L.A. There are federal agents, like Caroline, and suspected cartel members, like Carlos, on the initial list; something that'll have to be managed carefully as they get closer to the actual date.

When they tell Pablo about their engagement, he's overjoyed and takes legitimate credit for bringing them together. Moreover, Pablo insists on an engagement party at his house the following weekend. "The bigger, the better," he says.

Rico isn't so into it but Teresa is very excited. The party will give her the opportunity to invite some friends that she can't really invite to the wedding. Plus, she knows Pablo is a great host and the party should prove to be a lot of fun. Perhaps with fireworks. Or even gunshots. Or who knows what else?

Surprisingly, Mike is enthusiastic about the party as well. He won't be invited, of course, but he can put a wire on Rico, and maybe pick up something that could help him build his case. It's a rare opportunity for a wired Rico to meet a number of cartel members, some for the first time, and Mike feels certain that some useful intel will come out of those interactions.

Above all, the elusive U.S. leader of the cartel might be at the party, maybe even hosting it. With luck, Mike might finally find out for sure whether the leader is Pablo, Carlos, or somebody else.

It's truly amazing that they don't yet know who's running the Batista cartel. Normally, everybody knows who the leader of a cartel is right off the bat because he wants them to know. In this case, however, great pains have been taken to keep the top of the cartel organizational structure a total secret. Mike wonders why. This engagement party may be his last chance to figure that out.

To be safe, he asks Teresa to fill out the party guest list with all of the friends of Pablo and Carlos that she knows. He wants as many gang members there as possible.

Given the diverse mix of people attending, there's little doubt in Teresa's mind that something will happen at the party. But, instead of resenting or worrying about it, she's decided to embrace the uncertainty. Her wedding will be memorable, of course. She's known that for a while. Now her engagement party will be as well.

Rico, on the other hand, isn't as excited about the party, or anything else for that matter. He's feeling pressure on a number of fronts, which makes it harder to focus on the things he must. The drug raid, and the publicity surrounding it, has affected his business cash flow significantly; and that not only worries him, it could cause him to lose money this month, something that's never happened to Rico before.

Normally, under similar adverse business conditions, he would be a whirlwind of activity; making calls to old customers in an effort to win them back, and to potential customers offering discounted rents. He might even be meeting with current customers to tell them how much he values their loyalty. Hold their hands a little bit. But he has little time for that.

In addition, the requests from the team investigating his business is turning out to be more expensive and time-consuming than Rico could have ever imagined. There are endless information requests from the DEA, which is to be expected. But the real problem is on the legal front. It's astonishing how quickly the barracuda lawyers react when they see blood in the water. Several lawsuits have already been filed, forcing him to double his payments to his lawyers, contributing, of course, to his cash flow woes.

What's most time-consuming for him personally, however, are requests for information from the lawyers representing customers. He has to deal with all of them himself. It's ironic, Rico realizes, that his work as a drug agent is taking up time that he desperately needs to defend himself in the drug investigation the DEA has launched against him.

Fortunately, Pablo is sympathetic, not to Rico's work as an agent, of course, but to the business issues created by the raid. Rico meets with Pablo several times during the week and, eventually, asks him to advance a little cash to keep the business from triggering loan covenants. Pablo does so willingly, but not without extracting promises from Rico that the lost rental income will be replaced quickly; something that's a high priority for Rico anyway.

Teresa is busy, too, working at the restaurant and planning the wedding. So, for a few days at least, Rico is able to devote almost all of his waking hours to the business and investigation. He meets with his accountants several times; then, once with his business lawyer; but, mostly, he's at home, on the phone, drumming up business for his warehouses and following up on delinquent accounts.

On Thursday night, his doorbell rings and, without thinking, Rico just opens the door. There, pizza box and wine bottle in hand, stands Maggie, dressed casually in jeans and a modest blouse.

"Can I come in, stranger?" she asks.

"I would rather you didn't."

"I'll bet I can change your mind," she teases.

"Not this time," Rico counters, as he begins to close the door.

"Okay. Well, I'll just party out here on the porch," she deadpans, settling into the outdoor sofa and opening the pizza box, "Do you have a wine opener?"

"I'm getting married," Rico says to her.

"Do you have an opener?" Maggie repeats, holding the bottle up in the air.

"I want you to go away."

"I'll consider it after I get this bottle open. Oh, and two wine glasses."

The ever-polite Rico does as he is told. When he returns, she pours each of them a glass of wine and pats the seat of the sofa beside her. Rico remains standing, a small sign of resistance.

"I'm in love," Rico starts.

"Good for you."

"And I don't want to see you again," he continues.

Maggie has already finished her first glass of wine and pours herself another one. The slice of pizza she had pulled out for herself sits on top of the box, uneaten. She pats the seat again. And again, Rico ignores her.

"Let me do the talking for a minute," Maggie says. "I'm pleased that you've found somebody. I won't get in the way of that. But I've found somebody, too. And it's you."

She pats the sofa one more time and Rico actually takes a step backwards. The situation is becoming more uncomfortable by the minute. He hasn't touched his wine. Nor does he intend to.

Maggie goes on, "I tried to get you out of my life but it was impossible. The more I stayed away, the more I missed you. And I know for a fact that you missed me, too. We have something that few couples ever find; a connection, a spark that transcends everything. We can communicate without saying a word, with just a touch or gesture. We find the same things funny. And the same things grotesque. There's an honesty in our relationship that's hard to explain, but it's there. I know it. And so do you."

"I'm getting married in a few months," Rico repeats. "We had a good run, Maggie, but it's over. Go find yourself another man to obsess over. How's that for honesty?"

"I'll come to you anytime you want, married or not," Maggie says. "You just say the word. No promises. No questions asked. And nobody needs to know. My love is strong enough to share you."

"And my love for Teresa is strong enough not to share it. Goodbye, Maggie." With that, he sets his glass down, goes back into the house, noisily locks the door and turns off the porch light. Hopefully, Maggie gets the message.

Later, after trying unsuccessfully to get some paperwork done, Rico goes upstairs to his bedroom but, just as a precaution, before turning on the light, he goes back into the hall, looks out the window toward the front porch and, there she is, still on the sofa, in the dark, smoking a cigarette.

He briefly considers calling the police but he certainly doesn't need that complication right now. So, he gets undressed in the dark and tries to go to sleep, half expecting her naked body to slither into the bed beside him at any moment. But, thank God, it doesn't happen and, eventually, he falls asleep.

He awakens before daybreak and waits for several minutes until there's just enough light to see. Then, he gets up, and, once again, looks out the upstairs hall window at the porch. Thankfully, she's gone and so is her car. Maybe Maggie Smith has come to her senses. But he doubts it.

Chapter 35

Just when Rico thinks things can't not get any worse, he gets a call from one of his managers telling him the warehouse on Seneca is on fire. The fire department has been called but the manager doubts that they can save any of the building.

"Sorry, boss. I tried, but it was too widespread for me to do much with an extinguisher," he stammers. "Looks like somebody set the fire with an accelerant. When I arrived, the sections of the building not already on fire had been doused with gasoline or something. I'm sure everything is destroyed by now. I was probably lucky to get out."

"I'm on my way," Rico says.

When he arrives, the fire department is there, but there isn't much to save. As his manager said, although there are hot spots and embers burning everywhere, there's nothing left of the original structure. The smoke is intense. So is the heat. And most of the firemen are standing well back from the actual fire, waiting to clean up the aftermath.

Pablo is already there, also standing well away from what's left of the building and downwind to avoid the smoke, ashes, and embers.

"Can you believe it?" Pablo says to Rico. "What the hell else can go wrong?"

"Careful what you say," Rico counters. "We still have a lot of other buildings to worry about. Don't tempt the gods."

"You think somebody did this?"

"I do. The manager saw some flammable liquid splashed around and the fire spread too quickly to have come from a single source."

"How's our insurance situation?"

"Well," Rico answers, "there's good news and bad news on that front. The good news is the building is covered. Not sure about the stuff inside. But our customers probably have insurance on that. The bad news is I was working on consolidating your insurance and mine under one policy, to save us about $25,000 per year. I suppose that's gone now."

"We have to inform our customers," Pablo interjects.

"Well, your company was one of the companies affected, so consider yourself informed," Rico says. "I'll call the others right after I talk to the fire department."

Pablo blanches a little. "Global had stuff stored in there?" he points toward the charred remains of the warehouse, still smoldering.

"I really don't know yet what was actually lost in the fire. I'll let you know as soon as I can. But, as you know, the Feds confiscated any illegal drugs that were in the warehouse day before yesterday. So, if this was done by an arsonist to cover-up that situation, his timing is not good. Our manager must have an up-to-date inventory that lists everything else. I'll have him call you."

Rico's cell phone rings and he sees that it is Mike. He moves away from Pablo as he answers.

"Hello, Mike."

"Rico. They're telling me you had a fire in one of your warehouses. That true?"

"Yeah," Rico answers, "suspicious one too."

"Any suspects?"

"Well, one is standing about twenty feet from me now," Rico says but when he looks around, Pablo is nowhere to be see. "Pablo was on the scene when I arrived. He might have been here even before the fire engines. Who knows?"

Rico wonders where Pablo went and how he could possibly have disappeared so quickly. He must have covered at least a hundred yards of bare ground, dodging hoses as he went. Then, Rico remembers Pablo had been a soccer player when he was younger. And he ran with the Bulls in Pamplona.

"How would a fire benefit him?" Mike asks.

"Not sure. But it is one of his warehouses that was raided and it had Global goods in it. That's quite a coincidence," Rico answers.

"Still doesn't make sense. The drugs were taken in the raid and he wouldn't have stored any records or money there. Right?"

"Not sure, but I doubt it," Rico says, "Listen, Mike, I have to go talk to the fire department and inform both our customers and our insurance company. So, if you'll excuse me. I'm a little busy right now."

"Sure, buddy," Mike responds. "Keep me posted."

The fire lieutenant agrees to give Rico a few minutes; but he's obviously preoccupied. He confirms that they suspect arson and that arson experts are already on the premises gathering evidence.

"The fire burned too brightly and quickly to have started without the assistance of an accelerant," he says. "We haven't officially identified the source or sources but we will in time."

Then he asks if Rico's insurance company has arrived yet.

"I haven't notified them," Rico says.

"You don't need to notify them. In fact, that's probably them now," the lieutenant says, pointing to two well-dressed gentlemen stepping carefully around and over the hoses, trying to avoid standing water and burnt wood. They're carrying clipboards. The lieutenant excuses himself and goes back to his men who are putting out hot spots.

Rico decides not to identify himself to the claim officers just yet and, after searching unsuccessfully for Pablo, goes back to his car to make some calls. Most of the customers he reaches are sympathetic and supportive but Rico doesn't say anything about arson. No reason to start another fire, so to speak, at this point.

Meanwhile, Mike is doing his own investigating. Whatever material agents found in the raid were listed in the DEA data base and Mike pores over the list to see what might have been worth the trouble of a fire. It doesn't take him long to find out.

Their list shows boxes of paper ledgers and reports stored in the same bin as the drugs confiscated from Global. Those boxes were left behind in the raid. But, if it had not been for the fire, the agents could have come back and grabbed the paperwork at a later date. Not now.

That's too bad. If Mike had been in charge, the papers would have been the first thing he took. They are probably more valuable to the investigation than the drugs are. In fact, the papers may have contained intel that could have buried the Batista Cartel forever. But who knows now?

Naturally, Mike is still furious that he hadn't been consulted on the raid. The lack of cooperation and communication between federal and local law enforcement is legendary in the industry, and often chronicled in popular crime shows. But the same thing happens within agencies as well and, for obvious reasons, that's kept under wraps.

This raid was a complete fuck-up, Mike rants to himself. It was done by task force agents out of Washington, many of whom have probably never been in the field. *Arrogant pricks.* They hit Rico's warehouses and, then, it's on to the next target with little regard for the mess they leave behind, a mess that Mike, or somebody else, has to clean up.

Meanwhile, Rico is at home dealing with his own mess. For years, he had a nice little business. Revenue was steady. Problems were manageable. He had lots of free time to do what he wanted.

Now, since meeting Mike, and merging his business with Pablo's, Rico is always behind on everything. Unopened mail is all over his desk and his voice mail is at its limit. When Rico doesn't see Edgar in his dreams these days, he sees mountains of paperwork, which is almost as distressing.

The good news is that Rico is making considerably more money than he ever paid himself but is it worth it? Pablo, cartel boss or not, has turned out to be worthless at helping Rico run the business. And, so, Rico thinks, he might need to spend whatever extra income is coming in to hire clerical or accounting help. But, ironically, at the moment, he's too busy to even do that.

Another problem is Rico's lack of efficiency. He used to have a laser-like focus on his business and his clients. Not anymore. His mind keeps jumping to other things. The wedding. The drug investigation. The fire. Edgar. Carlos. Even his family, who may still be in danger.

And, then, there is Maggie. Several of the messages are from her and he erases them without listening to them. Maggie is one complication too many right now.

Chapter 36

The next morning, Rico receives another distressing phone call. Thankfully, he returned most of his phone messages the day before, and is half-way through his paperwork, so he takes the call.

On the line is Tom Staunton, the drug agent who had interrogated Rico at the police station after the raid. He wants to talk further about what they found, and what Rico knows about the customers involved. He suggests they meet at 10 am that very morning. Rico asks if he should bring something along to jog his memory.

"You won't need anything. Should only take an hour or so," agent Staunton answers.

"You want me to come to the DEA offices?" Rico asks.

"No. We'd prefer you meet us at the *Luxe Hotel* on Sunset, just off the 405, which is the headquarter hotel for our task force this week. We're using the Bridal Suite as command center for our task force."

How incredibly inappropriate, Rico thinks.

Unfortunately, because of unexpected traffic, Rico arrives a few minutes late for the meeting and the agents, Tom Staunton and Bill Wilson, are none too happy about it.

They shake hands with Rico briefly, offer him a seat, and then huddle up on the other side of the room to talk for a few minutes, ignoring Rico completely. Their act may have unnerved some in the past, but it just seems amateurish to Rico now.

"Mr. Lopez," Tom Staunton begins. "Do you know a Mr. Pablo Cerritos?"

"Of course. As I told you before, he's my business partner."

"And do you know Carlos Silva?" The haughty, prosecutorial tone is already getting under Rico's skin.

"Yes," Rico answers, then counters with, "And do you know Mike Andress?"

The two agents look at each other quizzically. They don't seem to recognize the name, or Rico's reason for asking. But, instead of pursuing the question, they decide to just push on with their interview.

"Please. For now, let us ask the questions," Staunton says to Rico. "Have you heard of the Batista cartel?"

"Yes, I have."

The other agent arches his eyebrow a bit but remains silent. With their sighs and occasional throat-clearing sounds, the two agents are acting like each answer is burying Rico even more. They're having some fun with this, Rico realizes. Perhaps they watched too many cop shows growing up.

"And Global Transport?"

"One of our customers, yes. But, before I answer any further questions, I need to call Mike Andress."

"Who's he? Your lawyer?"

"Hardly," Rico replies. "He's the DEA agent I work for here in Los Angeles."

The two agents look stunned and Rico takes advantage of their silence to stand up quickly, turn around, and go to the other side of the room; phone in hand.

He calls Mike and, in hushed tones, gives him a quick recap of where he is and what's happened so far. Rico expects Mike to ask to speak to one of the agents. But instead, Mike just tells him to stay put, say nothing of consequence, and keep them occupied for a half-hour or so. He's on his way.

"What the fuck?" Mike blurts out as he enters the room about twenty minutes later. "Who the hell do you think you are, questioning Mr. Lopez like this? He works for me and you should have cleared this interview with me before-hand Is that clear? So, what exactly is going on here?"

"Mr. Andress, we have reason to believe that Mr. Lopez has been working with the Batista cartel, behind your back I guess," Tom Staunton answers.

"Bullshit," Mike explodes. "Everything he's done over the past few months has been at my direction. I know exactly who Rico is and I trust him more than you two clowns. Now, I repeat. Who the hell are you and what are you doing?"

They show Mike their badges and, then, in an attempt to regain control of the meeting, they ask Mike to see his. Once satisfied, they turn back toward Rico, as if to ask for his identification.

"I'm an agent, too, just like you guys," Rico says to the two agents, one of whom responds angrily. "The hell you are. Where's your badge?"

"He's operating off the books," Mike interjects.

"I never heard of such a thing," Tom replies. "Either he's an agent or he isn't." Turning back toward Rico, he says, "I repeat, let me see your badge."

"Don't show it to him," Mike says to Rico. "Just go sit down in the lobby while I get my boss on the line to straighten these boys out."

"And who might that be?" Tom asks.

"Chuck Rosenberg, the acting head of the Drug Enforcement Agency," Mike responds. "Ever heard of him?"

There is an uncomfortable silence. The two agents stare back at Mike for a few seconds, then huddle and whisper, like they did earlier.

Finally, Staunton turns toward Rico and says, "Okay, Mr. Lopez, you can go home now. We don't need you anymore. Please stay in town, though, in case we need to question you further."

Rico answers, half-sarcastically, "Thank you. I will, sir," bows slightly, and leaves the room; confident Mike has the situation under control.

Staunton turns back toward Mike and says, "Now, you know who we are. Who are you exactly?"

"I'm the guy in charge of all the DEA activities in the Southern California region. You're out of your jurisdiction, by the way, and, more importantly, you're in the process of screwing up an investigation into the Batista Cartel that we've been conducting for months now."

"Mr. Andress, I understand your feelings but," the agent counters, "we were told that some agents in Southern California are a little too cozy with the Batista Cartel and we should raid first and ask permission later. I guess that's what we're doing,"

"Permission denied."

"A little too late for that now, isn't it?"

"Listen, guys. This may surprise you but your precious raids are not the most important thing happening here right now," Mike says impatiently. "We've had an ongoing investigation of the Batista Cartel underway for some time now. There are informants embedded in and around the cartel, gathering evidence. We're at a critical juncture of our investigation, and with luck, we will take the whole cartel down in a matter of weeks. That is, if you don't screw it all up for us."

"Is Rico an agent, like he says?" Staunton asks.

"Of course not. Does he look like an agent?"

No answer was needed or given.

Mike continues, "That's one of the reasons he's so useful. He's just an ordinary guy I recruited off the street, who, granted, I may have inadvertently led to believe was an agent. But I'll say this. Agent or not, he's an invaluable resource to us that has to be handled with kid gloves. Do you think you guys are capable of that?"

"Not our specialty."

"I can see that," Mike responds. "So I need your word that you won't bother him again, or me for that matter, until this operation is totally over?"

After exchanging looks, both Tom and Bill nod. So, Mike walks out of the suite, leaves the hotel and, on his way back to the office, calls Rico.

"Hey, buddy. Sorry about that," he says. "But we have a lot of cowboys in this agency, who like to come in with their guns blazing. Sometimes innocent bystanders get hurt."

"Am I an innocent bystander?" Rico asks.

"No, of course not. You're one of us and, right now, I consider you the most important guy on my team. So, just trust me, do your job, and, together, we will get those Batista bastards. Gotta go. See you Saturday."

Rico looks at the phone and contemplates why a guy who's so deceptive would keep asking for trust. But, then again, isn't that what con artists do?

Chapter 37

That night, Rico tosses and turns in bed trying to make the pieces fit. Mike undoubtedly knows things he's not telling Rico. But what?

Is Carlos a card-carrying member of the cartel? And, if so, why hasn't the guy been arrested? Another thought pops into Rico's head. *Mike has been pretty tight-lipped about what Edgar said to his interrogators. It must be good stuff to have offered protective custody. On the other hand, Mike doesn't seem to be any closer to identifying the leader of the cartel. Could it be Pablo?*

It's been a couple of days since Rico last talked to Pablo. In fact, it was at the fire when he behaved so strangely, disappearing quickly, without saying anything to anybody. Frankly, as much as Rico likes Pablo, the guy seems guiltier by the minute.

His shipments had illegal drugs hidden in them. Now a fire, possibly to destroy evidence before anybody can review it, and Pablo is on the scene immediately. *Pretty suspicious.*

And, with the cash crunch they've been experiencing, he's certainly dumping a lot more of his money into their partnership. *Where the hell is that coming from?*

Still, Pablo continues to treat Rico the way a good friend might. He's friendly, supportive, and caring. A good example is the party tomorrow night.

Who does that? Spends thousands of dollars to throw an engagement party for two people he's only just met. Then, invites a whole lot of people, most of whom don't even know the engaged couple, just to make the event more festive.

Rico has been watching Pablo closely, for months now, and, aside from being friendly with Carlos, there's been no hint of Pablo being involved with drugs, and certainly not running a cartel that distributes them. *Hell,* as Rico knows, *he can't even run a small property management company.*

Above all, except for a few temper flare-ups, Pablo has always been incredibly affable and social, the perfect gentleman. *What cartel leader behaves that way?*

Finally, after what seems like hours spent worrying, with little clarity, Rico falls into a fitful sleep, his morbid thoughts slowly giving way to thoughts about his wedding. Teresa flits in and out of his dreams, a kind of a warm presence that hints of a simpler life in the future, full of love, although, when conscious, Rico has no idea how he can possibly get from here to there.

The next morning, Rico wakes up later than normal, surprisingly well rested. It's the morning of his engagement party and there are some last-minute details to attend to before he gets ready. The party starts early, around five, but Teresa has asked him to be available around four.

Before that, he's to pick up some liquor and party trimmings, deliver them to Pablo's house, decide what to wear, and think about remarks he might make if somebody asks him to speak.

What is there to say about the most beautiful, wonderful girl in the world? he thinks. *The one he's already divorced once? And the one who may be the answer to his dreams, or perhaps a spy for a cartel? Or vice versa. Oh well, he'll come up with something.*

Then, after that, what are the right words to thank his good friend and host, who just might be the cartel leader they've been trying to identify for months now?

The more Rico thinks about it, the more he realizes this could turn out to be the most interesting party he's ever attended, not because of anything he might say but because it feels like things may be coming to a head very soon. And Rico is ready for some answers.

The doorbell rings, but by the time Rico gets to the door, there's nobody there. A small, nondescript package, addressed to "Teresa and Rico," with no return address, is sitting on his doormat.

Rico wonders who in the world would send something to the two of them at this address. He calls Teresa to find out if she's expecting something from one of her friends. She says no, but seems far less concerned about the package than he is.

"Probably just some guest who knows your address and not Pablo's or mine," she says.

"So, I'm confused. Are we getting presents tonight?" Rico asks.

"Of course, silly. Not as many as we'll probably get for the wedding but a few. In fact, I've received about a dozen at my house so far and I bet Pablo has more at his."

"When do we open them?"

"Right after the speeches, I suppose," Teresa says. "Pablo is handling the emceeing and your only responsibility will be to talk about how much you love me and how much you're looking forward to the wedding. Think you can handle that?"

"Not so fast. How much I what again? Let me write this down," Rico wisecracks.

"Well, anyway, just bring the package tonight and we'll open it with all of the others. Let me handle the ooh's, ah's, and thank you's; by the way, I doubt you'll know most of the people anyway."

"Are you worried about what I might say?" Rico asks.

"A little. Your sense of humor can be an acquired taste," she pauses briefly. "I love it, by the way. Just not in every situation, and tonight might be a good time to keep some of your most entertaining thoughts to yourself."

"Well-said," Rico deadpans.

"Oh, and by the way, your brother is coming tonight. He wanted to surprise you but I convinced him that wouldn't be a good idea," she says.

No matter how nonchalantly Teresa presents the news, however, Rico is surprised and more than a little concerned. Edgar is still running around loose and his threat to do something to Rico's family is still very real, at least as far as Rico knows. In fact, this party could be a perfect opportunity for Edgar to exact his revenge in a fairly dramatic way. But there's not much Rico can do at this point.

After hanging up, Rico takes a closer look at the package in his hand. It seems too small for a bomb and too large to contain some kind of dangerous chemical. He shakes it gently. Nothing rattles. Rico knows he's being overly cautious but, at the same time, he makes a mental note to check the other presents at the party, in case one of them looks suspicious as well.

Then, in a moment of almost shocking clarity, it occurs to Rico how much his life has changed since he made the fateful decision to help Mike. Normally, something like an engagement party would be joyous, a time to celebrate the important decision that he and Teresa made to spend the rest of our lives together.

But, instead, from Rico's point of view, this party promises to more closely resemble a military operation. He'll be wired. Half the guests will be carrying. The security around the venue, though, hopefully, invisible to the guests, will be very heavy and on high alert. And, as Rico and Teresa look at each other, all dewy-eyed with anticipation of their big day a few months down the road, all around them eyes will be darting from one guest to the other, alert to any movement that's out of the ordinary.

This party has it all. Dreams and cold reality; love and hate; living happily ever after and living to see another day. Rico has no idea what to expect tonight. But he isn't exactly looking forward to it.

Chapter 38

When Rico finally arrives at Pablo's house, it's already a hubbub of activity.

Chairs are still stacked up on the lawn, waiting to be taken inside. A tent has been erected in the back yard and is in the final stages of being decorated. Soon, it will house buffet tables of exotic and savory dishes, all provided by a Beverley Hills caterer.

A florist truck is in the driveway, with various colorful bouquets sitting around it, all of which will soon be moved inside the house or tent. Dozens of people Rico doesn't know are scurrying around, making everything just right for an event that, in spite of all the good intentions, could turn horribly wrong before the evening ends.

At this moment, however, everything is happy and hectic. More like at a wedding than an engagement party. In fact, Teresa will have to go some to make their wedding in Mexico live up to this party, and that's not a good thing for Rico's wallet.

Rico carries the liquor, wine, and soft drinks he just purchased into the kitchen, depositing all five cases on the counter where dozens of other cases are already in place. This party is obviously catered so why he needed to get any more drinks is beyond him. Perhaps, Teresa just wanted to keep him busy and out of the way.

Inside the house, sitting by the front door, is a modest collection of presents. Rico adds the one he brought from home, still in its shipping container, and glances through the others. Nothing looks suspicious.

What kind of gifts do you bring to an engagement party? he wonders. There are bottles of wine, and a few wrapped gifts that look like cooking utensils or trinkets for their house. The one he and Teresa will share some day, when all this is over.

It's still a half-hour before the party starts so, to get out of the way, Rico decides to take a walk around the block. Part of him just wants to commune with nature, relax, think about what he might say later. But, another part of him wonders if he'll be able to see any part of the surveillance team he knows is here. His wire is in place and he speaks into it as he walks.

"Oh, there you are," he says to a delivery van parked in a driveway halfway down the block. The van backs up, out of the driveway, and leaves. "Sorry, fellas. Didn't mean to scare you away?" Rico says into his wire.

A car comes by with four burly men in it. *Agents for sure*, Rico thinks. *Who else drives a medium-sized vehicle filled to the brim with muscles and testosterone, ready for battle?*

He's reminded of the old clown cars in the circus and wonders how it worked. *How could so many clowns get into such a small car? These guys are in a bigger car but the comparison with clowns seems apt,* Rico chuckles to himself.

Doubling back to Pablo's house, Rico sees nothing out of the ordinary. He's impressed. Either these guys really do know how to disappear right in front of your eyes or Mike has suspended the operation. If it's the latter, Rico sure wishes he'd been told. That way he could enjoy his own party without fear that he might not survive it.

As he walks up the driveway to Pablo's house, the first guests arrive, and give their car keys to the valets. *Probably, the kids parking the cars are agents,* Rico surmises, *but they look authentic enough. Long, shaggy hair and that insolent look California teenagers do better than anybody else in the world.*

When the first guests go into the house, Rico hears the strains of soft music greeting them. All strings it sounds like.

"Hey, Rico, come up here," Pablo bellows from the front door. "I want you to meet these folks."

And so it begins.

The first hour or so is all cocktails and *hors d'ouvres* and conversation. Rico goes from group to group; being introduced or introducing himself. Other than the few people he works with in his business, he knows nobody, but they all seem to know him.

Teresa is doing the same thing, wandering around, but she seems to know quite a few more than he does. Every so often, she looks over at Rico and nods or winks. Only twice does she join him, delivering a remark like, "These are my favorite people, Rico. You must remember me mentioning them. The Simpsons. The whole restaurant lights up when they come in." Or words to that effect.

Around 6:30 pm, Carlos Silva sashays in. He's not alone, of course. His entourage consists mostly of beautiful, young, mixed-race women and a few Hispanic men. The women are laughing at everything Carlos says and the men, not surprisingly, never crack a smile. Carlos is as immaculately-dressed as always, and he makes a bee-line for Rico. *Oh, oh*, Rico says to himself, thinking the worst.

But his fears are misplaced. Carlos could not be more charming and gracious, even telling Rico under his breath, what a lucky man he is and how stupid Carlos was to let Teresa go. This with three gussied up and gorgeous young ladies hanging on his arms belying his every word. Then, Carlos does something even more surprising. He thanks Rico for taking over Pablo's property management business.

"He was making a mess of it and really didn't know what to do about it," Carlos says. "He's a different man now that you have all the headaches."

"There are certainly a few of those lately," Rico responds. Carlos touches Rico's arm affectionately, and says, "Nothing you can't handle," Then, he moves away into what has become a fairly large crowd at this point.

By about 7 pm, everybody has been through the buffet in the back-yard tent and gathered back into the large, open indoor-outdoor room that doubles as both a living room and family room for the Cerritos. It amazes Rico how many people can sit or stand comfortably in a room that hadn't seemed that large the times just he and Teresa would join Pablo and Alicia for dinner.

Rico glances around the room and is impressed by the warmth and conviviality, especially with so many people he's never seen before. The only familiar face is that of his brother, Roberto. All of the affable strangers seem to be anticipating what comes next, probably because they know that Pablo can be entertaining and eloquent at times. And he doesn't disappoint.

There's a very loud clink of glass as Pablo tries to get everybody's attention. "Don't break it," somebody says, "We're listening."

Followed by a few titters. Everybody seems to be in a good mood.

Pablo starts in the usual fashion, thanking everybody for coming, acknowledging old friends and welcoming new ones. Then, he thanks his staff, the caterers, and his wife, Alicia, for all the work they did to make the dinner such a success.

"But this is not just an ordinary dinner party, is it?" he asks, then, answers himself. "No sir. It's much more important than that. We're here because of love, more love, and even more love to come. Our story begins in a barrio in Mexico City where two young, poor children decide to get married, for the right reasons. They love each other. They want to live together. Forever. But their timing is bad. Too young, perhaps. Too soon, perhaps. And, sadly, they split up."

There is an audible "aah," from Pablo's audience. He has them listening intently.

"But, then, thirty years later," he continues, "the hero of my story arrives and, lo and behold, it's me." Groans erupt throughout the room.

"I found these two wonderful, naive, awe-struck, and penniless people, separated and all alone, in the scary place that is Los Angeles; and like the king's men with Humpty Dumpty, I put them back together again." More groans.

"Okay, maybe a bad analogy, but, several months ago, I did invite them to my house for dinner. Alicia did serve them her incredible leg of lamb. They did get engaged."

"And," Pablo raises his glass, "we are here tonight to celebrate the reuniting of two wonderful people, and to wish them well in their Mexico City wedding and for the rest of their lives. All our best to Rico and Teresa."

The room erupts in cheers and well wishes. Rico looks around, finding it inconceivable that so many people he doesn't know could be so excited about an event that has nothing to do with them. But they certainly are, and his job right now is to make them feel that their joy and happiness isn't misplaced. He stands up.

"Pablo, you are indeed the king's man to my Humpty Dumpty," Rico starts. A few polite laughs follow. So far so good.

"And I want to thank you for your wonderfully kind remarks and for re-introducing me to the amazing Teresa Wilson, who was once, and will be once again, my wife, Teresa Lopez. These people here laughed at you, Pablo, when you called yourself the hero of this story but I see you that way, my friend. Cheers." He drinks a sip of wine as there is a smattering of applause. Then, he raises his hand and continues.

"But the heroine of this story will always be Teresa. To you, darling. I look forward to the wedding I was never able to give you. And to the life I was never able to give you. And to the love I will give you forever."

Rico raises his glass and, with everybody in the room joining him, takes a sip of wine. Then, the room explodes again in joyful noise and applause as Teresa comes up, kisses Rico passionately, and, amid a shower of tears, waves away the requests for her to speak.

Finally, just to quiet everybody down, she thanks Pablo for the party and his remarks, toasts the love of her life, Rico Lopez, and then announces that soon they will open a few of the gifts people were kind enough to give them. Anybody who wants to stick around for that is welcome to join them, she says. Then, she grabs Rico's hand and leads him away, toward the presents, most of the crowd following behind.

A few minutes later, after bringing the presents in from the foyer, Teresa and Rico sit on the couch and rather ceremoniously unwrap presents together.

The one that Rico brought from home is still in its shipping container so, as Teresa struggles with a particularly large and gaudy present, Rico pulls the small present out of its mailing package and silently reads the simple card on top.

Los labios no pueden repitir lo que Los oidos no pueden oir. "The lips can't repeat what the ears can't hear," he translates to himself, forgetting for a moment that there are agents listening to every word he says.

"What the hell does that mean?" Rico asks aloud, to himself but, also, to those on the wire who can hear him.

Then, on instinct, he decides to open the present himself, before Teresa even knows he's doing it.

Inside the wrapping paper is a jewelry box large enough to hold a bracelet or necklace. When he opens the box, and peels back the tissue paper, it takes a moment for him to comprehend what he is seeing.

There, nestled in the paper, is a blue stone stud, which is appropriate enough for a jewelry box, but it's attached to something horribly out of place; a bloody, crumpled ear that once belonged to Edgar Vegas. The message on the outside of the box is now frighteningly clear. Edgar will not be testifying anytime soon.

Teresa slowly realizes what she's seeing and screams, followed immediately by gasps and yells from those close to her. What had been a wonderfully warm and friendly evening, had suddenly turned into something quite different.

People step back, away from Rico, Teresa, and the package, thinking that will make them safe. But, of course, they're wrong.

When Rico looks up from the package, the first face he sees is that of Caroline, coming toward him quickly, as everybody else shrinks away. The agent grabs Teresa, shoves her toward the door, and then takes hold of Rico's arm. Very quickly and quietly, as everybody else is coming to grips with what they just saw, she hustles both of them through the kitchen, out the back door, and toward the pool house in back.

They pass armed agents everywhere, the back porch, the lawn and around the pool, all wearing riot jackets with *DEA* emblazoned across the back. Most are crouching, with their AK-47s, or similar riot guns, at the ready. Some are behind bullet-proof shields, moving slowly toward the back door.

Where in the world did all of these agents come from? Rico wonders. He thinks back to his little stroll before the party started. *Were there buses hidden somewhere he didn't see? Did they rent a house nearby and fill it with agents?* Rico is once again amazed by the logistical capabilities of the Feds, something he always undervalued until now.

As the three of them stumble into the cabana filled with pool equipment and lawn furniture, they hear gunfire break out behind them. Teresa stands up, looking out the one small window that faces the house. "Get down," Caroline yells, "You might get hit." And she draws her weapon.

"We need to get Roberto," Rico yells. Caroline talks into a small microphone, then, tells Rico that Roberto is safe in an upstairs bedroom.

Another shot rings out.

Rico grabs Teresa, shielding her with his body while Caroline ignores her own advice and looks out the window of the cabana, hoping to get some idea of what they might face when they leave. She knows from experience that much of the gunfire is just an overreaction to a few initial shots, probably fired by gang members. The immediate show of overpowering force is always a deterrent, that's for sure. And her guys had to do it, she knows. But it comes with a price. She wonders how many innocent guests will be killed or injured today in the crossfire triggered by the unexpected engagement gift. Obviously, if they could have raided the house on their own schedule, they might have avoided much of this bloodshed.

Just as suddenly as the gunfire starts, it dies down. There's a brief silence, punctuated occasionally with a few muffled cries or the banging of doors inside the house. Then, as guests come out of their hiding places, there is a cacophony of noises, yelling, screaming, crying. Agents are still shouting at people to get on the ground and stay out of sight. But no more gunfire is heard.

Caroline leaves the pool house for a minute, walks the perimeter of Pablo's yard, then comes back and tells Rico and Teresa to follow her. They scurry around the pool, across the lawn, and through a back gate that leads into the property behind Pablo's.

Within minutes, they are in the back seat of a black Mercedes sedan that was waiting for them on a back street. The car takes off, weaves its way through adjoining neighborhoods, and, finally, enters the freeway about a mile away from the gunfight scene.

"Where are we going," Rico asks.

"Some place safe and comfortable," Caroline answers. "Just relax. We have a couple of hours before we get there,"

"So, did you know about the gift?" Rico is too curious to relax.

"No," Caroline responds. "But, when we saw you add it into the pile of other presents, we were worried about what it might be. So, we were ready for the possibility of a surprise."

"Meaning what?" Rico keeps probing. Caroline sighs and answers, "Meaning we were going to get you and Teresa out of there at the first sign of trouble. That was my assignment, and I was already mingling with the guests just in case."

"One other question. Other than his ear, do you know where Edgar is?" Rico asked, a little too flippantly, perhaps, for the circumstances.

"Unfortunately, no. But, by now, we probably have at least a dozen cartel members in custody. One of them might tell us something that can help us."

"Do you think he's dead?" Rico asks.

"We're assuming he's not," Caroline responds. "Now, that's the last question I'll answer. As I said before, sit back, relax, and enjoy the ride."

Meanwhile, back at Pablo's house, the chaos is over but the confusion is not. Ambulances and EMTs are on the scene taking care of the injured. Police have arrived and secured the perimeter. Only authorized vehicles, emergency personnel, officers or agents can enter or leave the property, and interviews are underway to identify and interrogate guests that may be of interest.

Mike sets up a command central in the dining room, complete with everything necessary to prioritize and direct the work. He has five agents on hand, all trained to do the interrogations. Each is in a separate room upstairs, equipped with computers and printouts. Two are interviewing guests that, Mike feels, aren't part of the cartel, and the other three are doing preliminary work on suspected cartel members.

The objective at this point is simply to determine who should be retained and who can be released; a decision only Mike will make. No arrests will actually be made until suspects are transported to DEA headquarters or to jail. But, still, based on initial attitude and willingness to engage, judgements are being made about how to handle each suspect when the real interrogations start a few hours from now.

By 11 pm, all of the preliminary interviews are over and twenty-one suspects are still in some form of custody. Carlos is one of the first transferred to DEA headquarters and, despite his obstinance, the very first one to be questioned at length. Not surprisingly, he's arrogant, petulant, and stubborn, and insisting on a lawyer the whole time.

Two of his female companions are questioned soon after and they're more talkative. They tell the interrogating officer that Carlos has bragged to them about being high up in a cartel, but, other than the wads of cash he carries, they've seen no evidence of it.

In fact, they really don't believe he has the balls or wits necessary to lead anybody, especially hundreds of drug pushers. "They'd see right through his bullshit," as one girl put it.

The girls confess that they only run with Carlos because he foots the bills and, when he stops paying, they'll just move on to another patsy. Their story sounds authentic and, in the morning, after background checks are completed, they're released.

Carlos gives the agents nothing in his interview and, eventually, he's put in a cell by himself. The interrogations will start in earnest the next morning, probably with Carlos' lawyer present.

Meanwhile, back in the car with Caroline, Rico realizes that he and Teresa are probably headed toward the safe house on Lake Arrowhead; the one that Rico knows so well. So, he asks Caroline.

"Yes. good guess," she says.

"I would rather go to my family cabin. I'd feel much safer there, and I bet that's where Roberto goes, too," Rico explains.

"Not a good idea. Edgar knows about your brother, remember. Probably knows about the cabin as well. I'd advise you to do exactly as you're told."

"By you?"

"You see anybody else around?" Caroline is tired and cranky. "Well, other than sleeping beauty there in the back seat. You should be following her lead, by the way. Who knows how much sleep any of us will be getting in the coming days?"

"What about Pablo?"

"What about him?"

"Is he in custody?"

"I don't know. I've been with you the whole time, remember? Now, again, get some sleep." Which Rico finally does.

Chapter 39

The next morning, Rico awakens to the sound and smell of bacon sizzling on a grill. Caroline is already up and cooking breakfast.

Teresa is still asleep in the bunk bed beside him, oblivious to any sounds or smells. To Rico, she looks beautiful; even with no lipstick on to speak of, her hair in a tangled mess; and the clothes she wore to the party last night still on, and around, her in a crinkly mess.

There's a nightgown hanging in the closet but, the night before, Rico decided not to wake her just to change her into it. She was sleeping so soundly that Rico and Caroline half-walked and half-carried her straight to bed where she has been, virtually comatose, for six hours straight now.

Rico, on the other hand, did find fresh pajamas in one of the pine bureaus beside the bunk beds, and was able to put them on before crashing into the other bed. He hoped to go right to sleep, but no such luck, and when he finally did sleep, his dreams were unpleasant ones. The raw memory of such a seemingly joyous occasion, ended by the sudden explosion of violence; had him tossing and turning the whole rest of the night.

Rico has no idea where Caroline slept but she's already up early this morning, wearing a different set of clothes than she wore to the party, and busily preparing eggs. *A woman of many talents*, Rico thinks, including some unusual ones for a woman in her position. He's grown to respect and admire her in a way that hardly seemed possible when they first met.

The three of them are alone in the house and, other than the sounds of Caroline cooking and the trill of an occasional bird outside, the house is quiet, in marked contrast to the deadly din of the night before.

"What is our plan now?" Rico asks Caroline.

"Well, your plan is to stay here for a few days. Enjoy the lake but stay away from town," she answers. "You have everything you need to be comfortable, including a fully-stocked pantry and refrigerator. I have to go back into the office this morning, help with the interrogations, and plan our next steps."

215

"Was the raid a success?" Rico asks.

"Hard to tell. We'd have preferred to build evidence for a few more days but circumstances forced our hand a little," Caroline answers. "The real success will not be known until the trials are over."

"What about Mexico. How is the cartel down there reacting?"

"Not very well, I hear. Actually, we're picking up the Mexican leaders as I speak. Several have resisted, and we'll know more in a few hours," Caroline said. "Three of their manufacturing plants were raided last night as well. And several more factory raids are planned for today. We should cut production dramatically by day's end."

"Do you know yet who the main leader is in the U.S.?"

"Well, Pablo fled before we arrived. At the moment, we don't know where he is but all indications point to him as the guy orchestrating things up here. Whether he ran the whole operation or not won't be clear until we get some gang members to talk."

"Pablo got away?" Rico asks incredulously.

Caroline answers, "It looks like somebody tipped him off about the raid."

"Maybe he caused the raid."

"What do you mean?"

"He set up the party. He probably knew about the ear as well, right?" Rico asked. "He had to know that you guys wouldn't just let that slide by, especially with so many cartel members present at the party. I suspect he just slipped out before we started opening presents."

"Interesting thought," Caroline responds, "but I don't know why he'd want us to come down on his own drug ring. It doesn't make sense to me."

"It does if he could feel the noose tightening anyway," Rico counters. "Or maybe there was a coup within the ranks. He needed to do some cleansing,"

"Got some eggs for me?" Teresa asks as she enters, obviously unaware of the conversation she's interrupting.

"You bet," Caroline answers as she turns back toward the stove to prepare Teresa a plate. She's happy that Teresa has interrupted a discussion Caroline didn't want to have anyway. Rico is wrong in his conclusions but right in his line of thinking and Caroline isn't ready to provide clarification. Not yet.

"So, what the hell happened last night?" Teresa asks.

"Rico can update you. I have to leave. Places to go. People to see," Caroline says. "Can you guys clean up my mess?"

"You mean here or back at the office," Rico wisecracks. Caroline rolls her eyes, says her goodbyes, and walks out the door; leaving Rico and Teresa with more questions than answers.

After breakfast, Teresa turns on the 9 am news to see if they can learn more than they've been told by Caroline. As usual, that's the case.

The gunfight in Brentwood headlines every newscast, even nationally, with graphic photos and titillating information. Six people have been taken to hospitals. Quite a few, as-yet-unidentified, party-goers, including some suspected cartel leaders, have been taken into custody. The owner of the mansion, where it all happened, remains unidentified but neighbors describe him as a "very nice man who owns a few small businesses in town."

Rico understands neighbors might feel that way but, with Pablo's escape before all the hubbub, it's now abundantly clear to Rico, at least, that he must be the cartel boss they've been trying to identify all along. And, if that's truly the case, the adjectives people have used to describe him certainly don't apply. He has to be an evil man, greedy and uncaring, who's caused more death and destruction than some despotic leaders of small nations.

Rico thinks back to the dinner parties; to Alicia, the gracious hostess that has to be in on this subterfuge as well; to the stories Pablo told about his upbringing and travels. All of it just makes Rico angrier by the minute. Oh, and Pablo's engagement speech, about Humpty Dumpty, and how he put Rico and Teresa back together again. Shattered us is more like it. And hundreds of other people as well.

"So, how did you enjoy our engagement party?" Teresa says, trying to break Rico's somber mood.

"It had its moments."

"Do you think we're properly engaged," Teresa continues. "Or should I give you the ring back and we reshoot the whole scene. Take two, so to speak."

"As far as I'm concerned, we got engaged in Las Vegas. Nailed it on the first take," Rico smiles. "And we're getting married in Mexico City, just like we planned."

They kiss, then, gaze into each other's eyes for what seems like hours.

"The fiasco Pablo staged had nothing to do with us," Rico continues. "I didn't want to do it going in and I really want to forget it now. In fact, if we could, I would get married tomorrow and leave on a six-month honeymoon the next day; somewhere incredibly obscure, where no one can find us. Not Pablo. Not Carlos. And certainly not Mike."

"Wouldn't that be like surrendering?"

"What do you mean?"

"Well, Rico, in some ways, we're finally close to dismantling this drug cartel you have been going after for close to a year now. Do you really want to walk away right before your moment of triumph? Let the bad guys succeed in making us give up our wedding? And chase us into hiding?"

"You're right, of course," Rico responds. "I wasn't really serious anyway. Nothing would please me more than seeing Carlos behind bars. Pablo even more so. And Edgar, too, if he's still alive."

"So, what do we do?"

"We stay here today and tomorrow. Maybe get some sun. Take a boat out on the lake. Then, the following day, we drive to your house, pick up your belongings and we move in together at my place. It'll be safer for both of us."

"Sounds like a plan."

"Then," Rico goes on, "the following day, we call Mike and tell him we're ready to go back to work. By then, he should have a better idea of what needs to be done going forward. And our role in it."

"If any," Teresa says.

Chapter 40

On the drive back into L.A., Caroline has time to do a lot of thinking. She's not sure what she'll find at the office but she expects a shit show. There is so much to do after a raid like this; some of it very important, like interviewing detainees; some of it less so, like filling out paperwork, or finding ways to cover your ass, a major activity in the DEA these days.

The raid can be judged a success or failure, depending entirely on how somebody wants to view it. On the positive side, they did pick up a number of suspects. And, if they're lucky, the press coverage will be positive because of that. On the negative side, the raid was messy and, so far, inconclusive. Caroline doesn't know the exact numbers yet, but quite a few people were transported to area hospitals, and that's never a good thing. It means the story will be on the front page for some time.

The real success of the whole operation, however, will depend on how badly the Batista operations have been damaged, both here and in Mexico. Drug smuggling businesses, like other businesses, depend on cash flow. But, unlike other businesses, the cash will keep flowing for months after the leadership has been dismantled. The head may be cut off but the body can keep wriggling for a long time. And even grow a new head.

Unfortunately, the problem with trying to stop any drug trafficking is that if the demand doesn't go away, and the money keeps flowing in, does it really matter who's actually running things. The Batista Cartel is just a name after all. All it needs is another leader and another name. Same drugs. Same customers.

One thing is for sure, though. Mike will take a lot of heat for not letting his bosses know that a raid was imminent. Caroline wonders how he will play it. *Will he acknowledge the agency's role in making it happen or will he just go with what seems obvious, that the raid was a reaction to events on the ground? And, above all, can he convince his superiors that he had to step in at the point he did?* Those judgements will be made in time but, for now,

Caroline knows Mike is juggling a lot of balls, perhaps too many. Even he has his limits.

The raids in Mexico are still going on and Mike is coordinating those. He has to manage the interrogations in L.A. And, above all, he has to keep Washington in the loop, and, hopefully out of the way, all at the same time.

In the best of all worlds, Mike would have a lieutenant that, in a crisis, could pick up some of what he has to do. But, if there's one thing Caroline knows, it's that Mike doesn't have, nor does he want, such a person. She's the closest thing to a right-hand person he has and, most of the time, she has no clue what Mike is thinking, or doing.

As a leader, Mike is a bit of an enigma. He likes to free-wheel in his decision-making, but play it close to the vest in terms of explaining his decisions or letting anybody else in on his game plan.

So far, Caroline has been the perfect lieutenant for Mike. By nature, she does just what's asked of her, without questioning the reasons or the plan, and, because of that, she's highly effective in getting done whatever Mike wants her to do. That makes them a good team; until Mike gets overloaded, as he is now. Then, Caroline doesn't have the knowledge or experience to really help out. She wishes Mike would explain himself a little more, help her learn enough to help, but she recognizes that just isn't part of his makeup.

Caroline really likes Mike, respects his creative thinking, and understands that it's led to considerable success for their office, and for her personally.

But, despite her supportive demeanor, she is as ambitious as the next person. Like Mike, Caroline wants to run an office some day and, although she may not think the way Mike does, she chafes at the lack of opportunity Mike has given her. She might not be him but who can say that she won't be just as effective in her own way. This operation would have been a perfect time for Caroline to spread her wings some, without Mike's direct supervision, and see if she has what it takes.

But that isn't going to happen any time soon. She arrives at headquarters knowing that, although she needs to talk to Mike about her concerns at some point, now isn't the right time.

"Boss," Todd Williams says, poking his head into Mike's office. "Carlos Silva's lawyer has arrived. Do you want to be part of the interrogation?"

"You bet I do. Who's the lead investigator?"

"I am. I have Ricky Smith in the room with me," Todd answers.

"Let me play Ricky's role," Mike says. "Just introduce us by first names and, then, as the guy in charge, you set the table and maybe conduct the whole interview. I want to see their faces as you apply the pressure. But I don't want to be part of the conversation."

So, the two men enter the conference room, Todd in front of Mike, and they sit down across from Carlos and his lawyer. For the first time in his memory, Mike notes that the client is better-dressed than the lawyer. Of course, that doesn't mean much. According to surveillance reports, Carlos is always dressed better than anybody else in the room.

"Hi. I'm Todd. This is Mike. We'll be conducting the interview today."

"I'm Scott Pierce, Mr. Silva's lawyer. I'll be representing him through the arraignment. After that, depending on charges and evidence, another lawyer might be added, or replace me for the trial, if it gets that far, obviously."

The two agents nod and Todd begins with the preliminaries. Name, occupation, and so on. Carlos seems supremely confident as he answers many of the questions without even glancing at his lawyer. *The arrogance of the man might be his downfall*, Mike thinks, and hopes.

"So, Mr. Silva, do you know why we are talking to you today?" Todd asks amiably.

"Not a clue."

"We believe that you're part of a drug-smuggling operation that is bringing a number of different drugs into the United States from Mexico."

No response from Carlos.

"This operation has been labeled the Batista cartel by the press, if not by them, and has thousands of people working in it, producing, distributing, and selling drugs."

"That so?"

"There's also a money-laundering arm of the cartel that cleans millions of dollars of illegally obtained money through legitimate and semi-legitimate businesses."

Carlos sighs and looks at the ceiling, in an overly-dramatic sign of how bored he is. Once again, he doesn't speak.

"So, my first question for you, Mr. Silva, is whether you are in the sales, manufacturing, distribution, or money-laundering part of the business, or all four?"

Carlos' face seems to light up. "So, you don't know," he says, then, turns toward his lawyer. "That should be helpful for our case, right, counselor?"

Mike speaks up, "So you think we only ask questions that we don't know the answer to?" He turns toward Scott Pierce, "That should be helpful to our case, don't you think, counselor?"

"Why don't you tell me what you know and we'll go from there," Carlos replies with a smirk. "That'll save a lot of time."

"We know everything," Mike says. His role as the silent junior partner on the interrogation team has ended abruptly. Both Carlos and his lawyer look at Mike as if to ask, "Who the hell are you?" But, they don't.

Todd tries to get control again, "Mr. Silva, you pulled your firearm at the party and may have even fired it. Ballistics is testing it as we speak. Are those the actions of an innocent man?"

"They are the actions of a scared man. I had been fired upon. When I realized it was law enforcement, I put the gun down and surrendered peacefully."

"Who is Pablo Cerritos?" It is Mike again.

"A friend of mine. We were at his house, but maybe you didn't know that," Carlos answers. "We were celebrating the engagement of an old flame of mine, Teresa Wilson. Nice party, too, until you guys arrived. Have a search warrant, by the way?"

Mike is pleased that Carlos is so talkative, even if it is just to be a smart ass. Obviously, his lawyer has not yet counseled him to just shut up and answer "yes" or "no." Even better, he has said nothing to Carlos about pleading the Fifth. *They may get lucky yet*, Mike says to himself.

"We can prove that you are part of the Batista cartel," Mike says, "We have documents and witnesses. This is not about whether we get you or not. That's a foregone conclusion, it's about whether you help us get others."

"Why would I do that?"

"Okay. This interview is over," Scott Pierce says. "As you know all too well, my client is innocent until proven guilty. And we will not discuss deals until you prove to us that he has done something wrong."

"What would you like to see?"

"Let me be clearer," the lawyer adds, "my client has done nothing wrong so there is no reason to talk deals." Then, he rises rather theatrically, as if to leave, only Carlos is still handcuffed to the chair, making a dramatic exit all but impossible. He sits back down.

Nobody cracks a smile.

"Okay. No deal. I withdraw it," Mike says, "How pissed were you, Carlos, that somebody stole your girlfriend?"

"I have dozens of girlfriends."

"Pissed enough to draw your pistol and attempt to shoot her or her fiancée? What if I told you that you pulled your gun before any shots were fired and we have security camera footage to prove it."

"If I did that, and I am not saying I did, it was because I sensed trouble," Carlos answered. "And I was right, wasn't I?"

Mike is getting irritated and it shows in his body language and his questions. Carlos, on the other hand, is becoming more confident by the minute, and that's showing as well. So far, Carlos is winning the verbal give-and-take by a wide margin.

Todd is sure Mike has something up his sleeve so, despite his misgivings about how things are going, he remains silent. Also, Mike is his boss.

"Where is Edgar Vegas?" Mike spits the words out like bullets from a gun.

"Who?"

"Is he dead?" Mike is getting angrier by the minute.

"I'm sorry. Why would I know if somebody I never heard of is dead?"

Carlos is having a lot of fun with this exchange and his lawyer is allowing him to do it. Either Mr. Pierce is intimidated by Carlos himself or he feels the exchange is good for his client, which Rick is beginning to believe as well.

All of a sudden, Mike reaches across the table, grabs Carlos by the collar of his shirt, and pulls him as far across the table as he can. The handcuffs and chair come with him. Finally, nose to nose, he yells, "You killed him, didn't you, you piece of shit."

Todd grabs Mike from behind, causing him to loosen his grip, and allowing Carlos to tumble back to his side of the table, visibly shaken. Mike is still steaming, though, and he reaches out for Carlos again. Fortunately, despite his smaller stature, Todd is too strong for his boss and he forces Mike back into his chair and holds him there.

Mike looks like a little kid who is being punished. His lower lip is protruding in a pout, a look Todd finds particularly disconcerting on the face of a man always in such control of his emotions. But the little boy look disappears quickly and is replaced by a sardonic grin similar to the one that made Jack Nicholson so famous.

"What the hell was that all about?" Todd asks Mike when they are alone.

Mike, with eyes still shining, looks at the smaller man and asks, "I almost had the bastard, didn't I?"

Chapter 41

Rico has tried to call Mike for two days now, reaching voice mail every time. Finally, he leaves a message.

"Please, Mike, call me. Teresa and I are ready to go back to work. From what I read in the papers, you can use the help, that's for sure. And we want to contribute anyway we can. So just let us know."

After he hangs up, Rico checks his messages and sees one is from Maggie. Every few weeks she calls and normally he would just erase it. But something tells him to take this one.

"Hey, Rico. This is Maggie. I have great news. I'm engaged to. a wonderful guy I met at church; an ex-cop who loves me and makes me very happy. No need to worry about me anymore."

She starts to hang up then adds, "No need to call back." Then a pause and, "No, you will not be invited to the wedding." Click.

Rico chuckles and says to himself, "Neither will you sweetheart. Neither will you."

Then, Rico goes back into the kitchen where Teresa is seated at the table and says, "I left another message for Mike. This is so unlike him. No matter how busy things got at the office, he always returned my calls before."

"Shall we just go in tomorrow morning as if it's a normal workday," Teresa asks.

"Normal workday? I don't ever remember having one of those." Rico answers, "and I hate to put Mike in an uncomfortable position. With everything else on his plate, he shouldn't have to worry about us. But I suppose we need to do something other than just sitting here waiting for a call that probably won't come."

So, the next morning Rico and Teresa show up at the DEA office ostensibly ready to go back to work. The place is a hubbub of activity, with a dozen people waiting in the reception area, and lots of impromptu meetings taking place in the halls, in full view of anybody who might happen to be around. The security is non-existent.

The receptionist is nowhere to be seen, and all of the desks they can see are empty. Nobody looks familiar but, given the limited time Rico and Teresa have spent in the offices recently, that's probably not surprising. Still, they should see somebody they know.

They weave their way through the people, passageways, and cubicles until they reach Mike's office. Through the window, it looks dark and, when they try the door, it's locked. They knock, not really expecting a response, but hoping Mike is in there anyway. Maybe resting. But no such luck. There's no answer and the lights remain off.

Then, they go down the hall and enter the old Batista Cartel war room. It's unlocked and virtually empty, with only a few post-it sheets on the walls. One has the interview schedule of a few weeks before and there, featured prominently in red, is the name Carlos Silva. They don't see Pablo's name anywhere. That could be a good sign; or a bad one.

The receptionist finally catches up to them and asks if she can be of assistance. When they inquire about Mike Andress, she gets a quizzical look on her face.

"Who may I say is asking?" she says, to which Rico answers, "Agents Lopez and Wilson."

When she asks for identification, however, they realize they have nothing that proves they are, in fact, agents. The receptionist looks increasingly, and understandably, skeptical. Fortunately, just when she starts to get a little testy, Caroline comes around the corner.

"Oh, my God," she says. "What are you two doing here?"

"We thought it might be a good time to come in from the cold and go back to work, but we haven't been able to connect with Mike," Rico says. "Do you know where he is?"

"He's been transferred," Caroline says, without a hint of surprise or regret, "Some new job in D.C."

"You're kidding. Right in the middle of everything?"

"Well, We're not exactly in the middle. I expect most of the Batista work will be done in a matter of weeks now, and mopping up an operation isn't exactly Mike's forte anyway."

Caroline is trying to be dismissive but it isn't working, so she reluctantly invites Rico and Teresa into Mike's old office where she promises to answer all of their questions.

Once Caroline is settled in behind Mike's desk with Rico and Teresa perched on uncomfortable straight-backed upholstered chairs in front of her, she raises her arms to shoulder-level, opens her hands wide and says, "Okay. What do you want to know?"

"Has Mike been canned?" Rico starts.

"Not that I know about."

"Who has taken over for him?"

"No one yet. I'm acting head of the department."

"Congratulations," Rico says sincerely, but Caroline just rolls her eyes.

Rico is struck by how cold, efficient, and terse Caroline is. Such a contrast with Mike who, no matter how distracted he was, still made you feel important and part of the team. Despite her many skills, Caroline doesn't have that knack.

Rico wonders if she's angry, busy, or just trying to behave the way she thinks a boss should. No matter what it is, the mood in the room is decidedly unfriendly and both Rico and Teresa are put off by it. They exchange querulous looks, then, Rico continues, "Have you captured Pablo?"

Caroline shifts a little uneasily in her chair. "No." she answers. "We don't even have enough evidence to arrest him if we do. But we're still looking, both for evidence and for him."

"What about Edgar?"

"He's dead."

"You're sure?"

"We have his body now, as well as his ear," Caroline says callously, then softens her tone just a little bit. "So you don't have to worry about him anymore. Chapter closed."

"And Carlos?"

"Not dead. But you don't have to worry about him either."

Rico is running out of questions to ask about the case. He senses he's on shaky ground anyway, and Caroline is losing the very little patience she had to start with, so he shifts his line of inquiry.

"When can we come back to work?"

"I'm afraid that won't happen any time soon, if at all," Caroline answers, "Listen, Rico, your arrangement, whatever it was, was with Mike. You're not officially an employee of the U.S. government, and you're not agent with the Drug Enforcement Agency. We appreciate all you've done for us and I suppose that there could be occasions where we ask for your help in the future. But it will always be as an independent contractor. I'm truly sorry if that wasn't made clear to you before."

"But I went into a training program to be an agent. Ask Todd Williams. Or any of the guys I worked with."

"Look, Rico. I can assure you that everything you did for Mike was as an independent contractor. Your checks came out of a special fund set up just for that purpose. You were never on the books as an employee, believe me."

"And me?" Teresa finally enters into the conversation. "I have a badge."

"Yes, well, we'll need that back, Teresa," Caroline answers. "Mike overstepped his bounds there too. You aren't even on the books as an independent contractor. He may have been paying you out of his own pocket or out of some secret fund. I really don't know. Whatever the deal was, it's over now. I'm sorry. We really appreciate what you did for us and," turning toward Rico, "especially what you did, Rico. You are a very talented guy. We would not be where we are without your help."

"Can I talk to Mike?"

"That's up to him. You have his cell phone number. But, as for his office number in Washington, I don't have that. Frankly, I don't think he'll want to talk to you anytime soon, anyway. He's moved on and I recommend you do that as well. Focus on your wedding in a few weeks and, then, get on with enjoying your life together."

"Will you be at our wedding?" Teresa asks.

To which, Caroline answers, "I doubt it but I'll sure try. Somebody will be there to represent the department. I just don't know who yet."

"What about my property management business?" Rico asks.

"What about it?"

"I'm a business partner with Pablo because Mike asked me to be. Do we unwind that now? And how do we even go about doing that?"

"I'll have to get back to you on that," Caroline answers. "I have no idea how to handle those kinds of things but, for the time being, I guess you should keep running it as if Pablo is your partner."

Rico isn't sure how that might work but, as long as he's not buying or selling anything, he supposes it doesn't matter. He doesn't need Pablo's signature to conduct business as usual.

"Oh, and one other thing," Caroline says. "Don't tell anybody about your work with us. It's still highly confidential."

Later that afternoon, Rico and Teresa sit down, with two glasses of wine in front of them, and discuss the situation.

"Can you believe what a bitch she has become?" Teresa says. "I thought of her as a friend and you two have been through so much together. Why would she treat us this way?"

Rico ponders the question for a minute. In his mind, he goes over all of his interactions with Caroline, from when she deposited him at the safe house to the bag switch in Mexico City to the operation in Puerto Vallarta. She was always professional and efficient. Not exactly a close friend, no matter how much Rico tried to be, but certainly someone he trusted, especially when the chips were down.

"She's not a bitch," he answers Teresa's question. "She's trying to succeed in a world that's always been dominated by males with big egos. I think there's a soft side to Caroline that she hides incredibly well. I also think she's ambitious and the golden ring for her, running her own agency, is now within her reach, as long as she doesn't screw it up. She's bound and determined to grab that ring."

"I beg to differ," Teresa counters, "she was absolutely rude to us. There was no reason to be like that with us, especially with you, Rico. Would it have hurt her career to treat you decently? Here at the end? With nobody else around? I don't think so. She's a bitch in my mind."

"Consider this possibility," Rico continues to argue, "We have no idea what happened to Mike. He could be back in Washington receiving awards for all we know. But what if he's become persona non grata in the agency. What if his letting Pablo slip through his fingers was a career-ender for him? Wouldn't it make sense for Caroline to distance herself from him as quickly as possible?"

"Well, yes."

"And wouldn't that require her to distance herself from us as well? We're a glaring example of Mike's bizarre management style. If it works, he's a genius. But, if not, she needs to let people know her style would be more mainstream. No off-the-books agents, for instance."

"Ok, but why be so mean about it?"

"There was no nice way to tell us that Mike used us," Rico continues. "And I think she wanted to cut the relationship off as quickly as possible. It wouldn't help her to have us hanging around as a constant reminder of Mike and his failings. Even if she likes us, and I believe she does, by the way, a clean break was necessary."

"OK. Then, you're saying Mike is the bitch, so to speak."

"Mike is a more complicated case for me," Rico goes on. "I never understood what drove him or why he did what he did. He was the most dishonest, honest guy I have ever known. When he asked me to do things for him, I always felt it was with the purest of motives. But, to get me to do them, he felt he had to lie. The ends justified the means, or some such."

"And maybe he was right," Rico continued. "If he had just come to me and said I want you to risk your business and your life to work for me as a private contractor at a very low hourly rate, I would have laughed in his face. But that is what I ended up doing."

"Remember," Teresa says, "you said he might be getting awards or getting promoted as we speak. It looks like the Batista cartel is going down and isn't that the bottom line? In my mind, he's a hero."

"Well," Rico answers, "maybe he is. But I'm not sure it matters to him whether he's recognized or not, as long as the operation is a success. So, not to be immodest, but this thing would have had a very different ending if we had not been involved. Right? And neither of us would have been involved without Mike."

"So," Teresa concludes as she downs her second glass of wine, "Mike is either a bitch or a genius, depending on your point of view."

"I guess that about sums it up," Rico agrees.

Chapter 42

Rico and Teresa wake up early on their wedding day. It's a beautiful day in Mexico City and they share a kiss; perhaps the last before they seal the deal at the altar later that afternoon. Teresa hops out of bed, anxious to get at all the last-minute tasks that await her.

She has a wedding coordinator, of course, taking care of the nitty-gritty details of the wedding itself but Teresa wants to follow up on some things herself. The rehearsal went perfectly but who knows what will happen at the actual event, especially if Teresa gives it short shrift. She's determined to make her wedding perfect.

Teresa's major task, however, is getting everything ready for the reception which will be held at a golf club not far from the chapel. She and Rico are not members, of course, but that doesn't seem to matter to the club staff. They act as if the Lopez's are not only one of theirs, but, in a sense, royalty; at least for one day.

Rico is luxuriating in bed when he hears Teresa's voice from the bathroom, "Rico, get up. I have a list of things for you to do and you're already a half-hour behind."

A preview of things to come, Rico whispers to himself; but even that thought does little to diminish the excitement he feels; not necessarily for the wedding or reception, for that is Teresa's thing, but for everything that will follow.

It's amazing to him how much he's looking forward to spending the rest of his life with this woman, the same one he so cavalierly threw away over thirty years ago.

But that was a different time and a different Rico. Whether it was a different Teresa or not is open to debate but he sure loves the one that's about to become his wife. And he silently promises never to do to this one what he did to the last one.

Since their last conversation with Caroline, neither Rico nor Teresa has given much thought to Mike or Caroline or the agency or the cartel or anything to do with the life they had been living before. With the wedding, honeymoon, and a new life, in front of them, there's so much else to think about. But, above all, they're ready to close the book on the whole drug agent thing. The way it ended was a blessing for Rico and Teresa because it made it so much easier for them to get on with their lives.

The previous night, Rico went over the list of confirmed guests and was surprised to see Caroline's name on it. As far as he knows, nobody else from the agency is coming and it's unusual that she would make the trip by herself.

Still, it makes Rico feel better to see she's coming, not only because it's a nice thing to do. But maybe he can do a better job of repairing bridges with her than he did when they last met.

After seeing Caroline's name, Rico wonders if Mike is coming, too. He rechecks the list to see if the agent's name is on it. No such luck. Not that Rico expected him to show, anyway, especially given that the guy never returned any of their phone calls. But it would be nice to see him again and clear the air a bit, as well. Theirs was a strange relationship but Rico still considers Mike a good friend, and it would be too bad to have it end so unceremoniously.

The chapel is modest by most wedding standards. It holds only about 150 people and, with the cancellations running higher than expected, it's apparent to Rico that the actual attendance will be even lower.

To Mike's eye, the place is a bit over decorated but he's been told that's the norm for weddings held in Mexico these days. There are white ribbons and linens and colorful banners everywhere, at the ends of the pews, around the pulpit, and even going up the walls, all serving to highlight and/or complement the bright colors of the admittedly beautiful flowers and bouquets scattered about here and there.

Teresa has chosen both religious and romantic music for the ceremony, appropriate for a very traditional, American-style wedding anywhere. But, outside, after the ceremony, mariachis will be strolling around, adding to what, Teresa hopes, will be a very upbeat and festive occasion. They are in Mexico after all and, like Rico, she's very proud of her roots.

Rico takes one last look around, then, positions himself on the steps of the chapel, to greet guests as they arrive. His brother/best man, Roberto, does the same, accompanied by two ushers; one an old friend from the neighborhood and the other a nephew of Rico's living just outside Mexico City.

Most of the guests are friends of the family who never left Mexico or its capital city. Rico knows some well, but most are strangers to him, so he introduces himself with a big grin on his face and chit chats amicably, something Rico does very well.

He knows Teresa's family from the old days, of course, and also knows that a few still resent him for divorcing Teresa thirty years ago and a few others resent him for having made it in America, something they should have celebrated, especially since Teresa will be the beneficiary of his good fortune. But jealousy can be a powerful emotion at times.

Rico enters the church without seeing Caroline, which is fortunate. They haven't talked since the last time, in Mike's office, when Caroline essentially fired Teresa and Rico. He'd like to clear the air, *but after the wedding will be a much better time to do it*, he thinks. Rico has other reasons for going into the church now anyway. He needs a few moments alone, to steel himself for the ceremony that lies ahead.

Rico gave up his Catholic religion many years ago but he still feels bad whenever he enters a church, any church. He remembers the robes and rosaries and gold chalices as if it was yesterday and he's still intimidated by the pomp and circumstance that is so much a part of Catholicism.

Today, actually, a part of him feels as guilty as a little boy sneaking back into the church after a day of truancy, rather than an adult coming back after decades of spiritual inattention.

Maybe he can find a Catholic Church and do confessional after the ceremony, he thinks, although that would certainly be peculiar timing. And his confessional, if it covered all his sins, would probably last longer than the ceremony itself. Not such a good idea.

Suddenly, the organ music rises in intensity, signaling to the congregation that something is about to happen. Much quicker than Rico had anticipated, Roberto is entering the chapel and the coordinator is pushing him to follow. The show is beginning.

If he had been calm before, looking into the coordinator's pinched face, sweat beading on her forehead, as she aggressively pushes him into the aisle, would have taken it way. Rico was calmer facing drug thugs than he is facing the wrath of this woman.

He scans the room briefly, as he walks down the aisle, looking for Caroline's blonde hair, which should be easy to spot; but he doesn't see her, in fact, he has trouble seeing anybody. The faces are all running together, their features sort of merging into one big sympathetic smile.

He can almost hear everybody saying, "How wonderful you are to be doing this. Now, be a good boy, run along to your place, so we can see the bride."

By the time Rico reaches the altar, everybody has stopped looking at him and, after doing his practiced, military-like spin back toward the back of the room, he can see why.

There, at the top of the aisle, is the most beautiful vision Rico has ever seen. It's Teresa, of course. He's sure of that although she looks like somebody he hardly knows, a model in a glamour magazine. Teresa has never been so stunning, and that's saying something.

Her face is framed by just a hint of lace tumbling down around both of her cheeks. Her hair is pulled back and up, tucked inside the delicate cap and the dress is covered in a sheath of satin that perfectly accentuates her figure. There's no train, perhaps a concession to the fact that they've been married before. Or perhaps it's a nod to her sense of modesty.

Teresa is escorted by her father, a wonderfully friendly, and portly man of about seventy, who's enjoying his moment in the limelight almost as much as she is. He smiles and waves to friends, completely oblivious to the fact that nobody is really looking at him.

As Teresa gets closer, Rico is struck by how radiant she looks and how happy. He can't believe that he is in any way responsible for that look on such an exquisite face, one that he knows so well and, yet, at the moment, one that is totally new to him.

Then, her searching brown eyes find his and her smile becomes even bigger and broader. Her eyes are twinkling with tiny tears, he sees, and his eyes begin to well up as well. This ceremony is going to be tougher than he thought.

But it isn't. The congregation just melts into the background as Teresa and Rico clasp hands and look at each other, only at each other. Both have regained their composure, the tears have disappeared, and each one of them seems to draw confidence from the other as the minister prattles on about how wonderful they are, despite the fact he just met them the day before.

When they kiss and turn to walk back up the aisle, the congregation erupts in applause and the music explodes with what sounds like *Ain't No Mountain High Enough.*

Tears have come back into both Rico's and Teresa's eyes, making it hard to navigate the aisle. They stop and kiss again, letting the tears subside. Then, as Rico's eyes clear, he looks for Caroline but, instead, there standing at the back of the church, he sees two very familiar faces.

It's Mike Andress and Pablo Cerritos. Or, at least, he thinks it is.

The faces disappear for a second but, just as Rico and Teresa reach the top of the aisle, about to exit, the two men reappear suddenly, very close, with big grins on their faces and two thumbs held high in the air, in the universal sign of enthusiastic endorsement. There's no mistaking who they are this time.

Rico and Teresa exit into the small reception area, and are immediately cornered by the overzealous coordinator. She escorts them both to a back room where she has them wait until everybody else has left the church and gathered on the lawn. Then, they are to reappear to be escorted, under a shower of rose petals, to the 1949 Packard that will transport them back to the reception. At least, that's the plan.

As the coordinator exits, leaving the bride and groom alone in the tiny waiting room, Rico turns to Teresa immediately to tell her what he saw but she smothers his lips with a kiss. After a few seconds, he decides that, at the moment, what he saw isn't that important, and he finishes the kiss in the way any new husband should.

After a few seconds, he pulls back and says breathlessly, "I saw Mike. He's here."

"Wow," she responds. "I'm really pleased."

"And that isn't all. Pablo is with him."

"Pablo? But that doesn't make any sense…" she says.

As the ever-present wedding coordinator interrupts with, "We're ready for you now." So, they head down the steps of the chapel, dodging rice and well wishes, and Rico scours the small crowd, looking for the familiar faces he saw earlier.

But they aren't there. Mike and Pablo have escaped into the Mexico City streets, or bars, or who knows where; probably never to reappear in Rico's lifetime.

Caroline does emerge from the crowd, however. She gives Rico an appropriate peck on the cheek and then whispers into his ear, "Congratulations. I couldn't be happier for you."

Rico just beams, and tries to tell her what he saw.

But she interrupts, saying, "By the way, you asked about your partnership with Pablo. The Agency has decided to give you the whole business outright. Think of it as a little wedding present."

"A million-dollar wedding present?" Rico asks.

To which, she answers, "And a little 'thank you' gift as well. Enjoy your honeymoon and your life, partner."

Then, she kisses him.

Epilogue

It's been several months since the wedding, and brief honeymoon, of Teresa and Rico. But the glow still burns brightly. They're now officially living together, under one roof, which hasn't been the case for decades. It's a more comfortable roof than the tin one from the first house they rented; as is the relationship that now flourishes beneath it. Life is good.

Rico's been very busy trying to make his business profitable. Thanks to Caroline, and probably Mike, he now has the revenue to carve out a very comfortable living. But, first, he has to repair what the drug raid did to his business. It could have been more devastating, reputation-wise, but most of his customers and ex-customers have cut Rico some slack on that. It certainly helps that they all like him.

With the prospect of more income, Teresa doesn't really have to work but she wants to, and, thanks to some friends in the restaurant business, she's once again employed as a hostess at a prestigious dining club near their house. It's a perfect place to meet couples that could be friends of theirs over time. Hopefully, better ones than they had before.

It's Saturday. Teresa is getting ready for her shift at the restaurant and Rico is catching up on the local news in the Los Angeles Times when he comes across a news item buried on page two.

It seems that the Drug Enforcement Agency has arrested a prominent local businessman, Santiago Sanchez, on suspicion of running a drug ring that operates on both sides of the border. Since arriving from Mexico City in the eighties, Mr. Sanchez had built a string of car dealerships all across Southern California. The article concludes with these two sentences:

"The Director of the Los Angeles division of the DEA, Ms. Caroline Pendley, has no comment on the arrest of Mr. Sanchez or on the speculation from an unnamed source that he may have been the leader of the Batista Cartel. Their investigation is ongoing, she said."

Rico looks up from his paper, a wry smile on his face, and yells to his wife, "Teresa, you're not going to believe this one. Remember my friend, 'Santa'?"

CPSIA information can be obtained
at www.ICGtesting.com
Printed in the USA
LVHW081804091020
668432LV00016B/114

9 781647 509774